1€

D1435507

Joanna Trevor read English at the University of York and taught in various schools. She specialized in vocational and educational guidance before becoming a freelance writer. This is her fourth novel to be published.

MURDER IN THE
CATHEDRAL CLINIC

The Cathedral Clinic is an expensive alternative therapy centre within a peaceful setting. All the more shocking when head of the clinic, Sebastian Kingsley, is brutally murdered there. DCI Simon, himself a visitor at the clinic only the day before, returns to try to solve the case. With the murder victim being the nephew of the dean of the cathedral, Simon has to keep the investigation discreet, despite media interest. Then the victim is revealed to have been a control freak with a more complex personal life than at first appears. With a second violent death, Simon must pull together the threads to catch a killer.

Books by Joanna Trevor
Published by The House of Ulverscroft:

A GATHERING OF DUST
THE SAME CORRUPTION THERE

JOANNA TREVOR

MURDER IN THE CATHEDRAL CLINIC

Complete and Unabridged

ULVERSCROFT
Leicester

First published in Great Britain in 2005 by
Robert Hale Limited
London

First Large Print Edition
published 2005
by arrangement with
Robert Hale Limited
London

British Library CIP Data

Trevor, Joanna
    Murder in the Cathedral Clinic.—Large print ed.—
Ulverscroft large print series: mystery
1. Simon, Christopher (Fictitious character)—
Fiction 2. Clinics—England—Fiction 3. Detective
and mystery stories 4. Large type books
I. Title
823.9′14 [F]

ISBN 1–84617–100–8

Published by
F. A. Thorpe (Publishing)
Anstey, Leicestershire

Set by Words & Graphics Ltd.
Anstey, Leicestershire
Printed and bound in Great Britain by
T. J. International Ltd., Padstow, Cornwall

This book is printed on acid-free paper

*With love to Colette
(Not forgetting the polar bears)*

1

The Cathedral Clinic was within the cathedral precincts, an imposing eighteenth-century red-brick Georgian house built for some church dignitary in times when the clergy were housed in a manner that befitted the status of the Church of England. Health and fitness were the new religion, Detective Chief Inspector Christopher Simon acknowledged, but most purpose-built architecture for that burgeoning enterprise was sadly lacking in this degree of comeliness. He winced as a twinge of pain shot up his spine and down his leg from the action of raising his head to get a better view of the fine building.

The building was four storeys high, the top floor with dormer windows and a low parapet with carved stone gargoyles at each end. Two tall windows balanced each other on either side of the shiny black front door which was set under a plaster portico and reached by worn stone steps. Five windows on the next two floors completed the elegant simplicity of the façade. Sharply pointed *fleur-de-lis* cast-iron railings contained a semi-basement below and curved up the stone steps to the entrance. A row of clipped-globe box was set into planters just within the railings, their neat shapes still lightly dusted from the overnight frost.

The clinic fronted a narrow cobbled lane for pedestrian use only. Behind him more railings enclosed an ornate shrubbery which gave on to the Cathedral Green itself, still busy at this late time in the year with coachloads of tourists milling about the splendid ancient building. Simon lingered, staring up at the building, aware that cowardice in the face of the ordeal to come, as much as appreciation for fine architecture, was keeping him here at the foot of the flight of steps to the shining front door. Its discreet brass plaque set into the wall quietly identified it as one of the most expensive — and successful — alternative therapy clinics for many miles.

He had had to be persuaded, by Jessie his long-time partner, who knew something of the place, that someone here would know how to cure him of the crippling back pain he had suffered since an over-zealous session of clearing some of the brambles and saplings from the remaining uncleared areas of her garden. He had wanted to be finished with the job, that had been the problem, and so he had gone too fast and too furious. Having spent a full day stretched out on Jessie's living-room floor he had visited his GP who cheerfully told him that backs weren't his thing and anyway, didn't half the population suffer from back problems and here were some strong painkillers. He had endured two excruciating days at work, at times conducting conversations with his staff from a supine position, the undignified state in which Detective Superintendent Munro found him and demanded that he 'got himself sorted'.

She had scolded and echoed Jessie's recommendation of the Cathedral Clinic, and so here at last he was, with an appointment to see the resident chiropractor, Jonathan Hadden. He clutched the worn cast-iron railing, hauled himself up to the door and rang the bell. A click sounded and a voice encouraged him to enter.

'Mr Simon?' a soft voice enquired. A young woman with shoulder-length black hair regarded him expressionlessly from behind the reception desk.

Simon approached her slowly, managing a strained smile.

'To see Mr Hadden?' She did not return his smile. Her eyes, large and dark, looked up at him and he was struck by how full of sadness they seemed.

'Yes.'

'Take a seat. He won't be long. Can I get you something to drink? Herbal tea? Decaffeinated coffee?'

A large brandy? Simon wondered without any hope. 'No, thank you,' he said and limped to one of a group of hard and expensive-looking wooden chairs that comprised the waiting area. It seemed deathly quiet but as his hearing adjusted Simon began to discern subtle soft sounds of voices and movement, of vague musical emanations, unidentifiable but relaxing.

The telephone on the desk trilled and at the same moment a door opposite the reception desk opened and voices sounded loudly as a man and a woman emerged. Simon had noted that the name on the door was Jonathan Hadden's and he watched the man, his hand hovering behind her back but not touching her, ushering the woman gently to the desk. She was smiling up at him, a sight that reassured Simon. The two waited a moment while the receptionist finished the call, then Hadden murmured a few quiet words to them both before turning to Simon.

'Chris Simon?'

Simon agreed half-heartedly.

'How's Jessie? I haven't seen her for ages. Not since she stopped working here in fact.

4

It's a shame how we get too busy to keep up old friendships.'

Simon immediately warmed to him on seeing that, rather than the muscle-bound bruiser he had been fearing, Hadden was slightly, if wirily, built, and several inches shorter than his own six foot four.

'She's very well,' Simon responded. 'Busier than ever.'

'She would be now that she's got the professorship. Do give her my best wishes.'

Jessie, now professor of psychology at the university of Westwich, had at one time had a part-time psychotherapy practice at the Cathedral Clinic.

Hadden had begun ushering Simon towards his room.

'I will,' Simon said. 'She was the one who recommended you.'

Hadden smiled as he pushed open the door to his room.

'Let's hope I can help. It's your back that's the problem but you haven't been given an X-ray I understand?'

Simon reiterated the substance of his interview with his GP and expanded a little on his symptoms.

'And you've been getting headaches?'

Simon nodded as they paused inside the room.

'Could be a problem with one of the vertebrae. There's a good chance I may be able to put it right. Any previous back problems?' As he asked, Hadden looked Simon up and down.

'No,' Simon said, a little mendaciously, as if in denying the occasional earlier twinges he might stave off some more radical and painful therapeutic approach.

Hadden seated himself behind his desk and indicated that Simon should take the chair in front of him. It was comfortable, much more so than the ones in the reception area.

The room was simply furnished, the treatment couch standing in the middle and dominating the room. The single window looked out over the shrubbery to the green and the cathedral. There was an expensive-looking music centre to its left and a bookcase to its right with some chairs placed in front of it. Hadden's desk was in the rear of the room.

'Often, tall men such as yourself have developed some compensatory stoop, usually earlier in their lives, often when they are still at school. At what age did you reach your full height?' Hadden asked, pulling a sheet of paper towards him and writing Simon's name at the top.

'At fourteen,' Simon admitted.

'Tough,' Hadden smiled. He shifted some sheets of paper and began asking Simon questions about his previous medical history, which was brief, and about the 'event' that had led to the current problem. As Simon explained, Hadden gave a wry smile.

'So Jessie's finally managing to get to grips with her couple of acres,' he said.

'No, actually, it's mainly I who am 'managing it',' Simon said, unable in the circumstances to be noble about it. 'All the heavy stuff anyway.'

'Of course,' Hadden agreed solemnly. 'She must be very grateful to you.'

'Not as grateful as she ought to be,' Simon replied, smiling.

Hadden grinned back. He placed the notes he had been making to one side.

'Do you know anything of what chiropractic involves?' he asked.

'Only a little,' Simon admitted.

Hadden went into some detail about the intricacies of the spine and its attending pairs of nerves. 'The vertebrae are connected to the organs of the body and misalignment can cause a variety of symptoms.'

'Including back pain,' Simon said, not really wanting to know about any further repercussive effects of his injury.

'Indeed,' Hadden said sympathetically. 'I

think I'd better get on and take a look at you.' He gestured to a small changing-room to the right of his desk. 'Get your clothes off. You'll find a dressing-gown and towel in there.'

Simon did as he was told, the pain he endured simply taking off his clothes encouraging him that he was doing the right thing in entrusting his almost-naked body to a stranger.

Hadden indicated the couch as Simon emerged clutching the towel around his waist with his left hand and holding the dressing-gown close with his right. He climbed painfully on to the couch. Hadden lifted the dressing-gown from his shoulders and helped adjust the towel around Simon's hips.

Hadden's touch was subtle and gentle as his fingers ran along the length of Simon's spine. He felt hands move down each of his legs and his eyes began to close as he relaxed for the first time in days. His body felt heavy and he was ready to fall asleep after nights of only snatched sleep. The movements continued and time became immeasurable when suddenly a sharp jerk and even sharper pain brought him back with a loud expletive. He felt Hadden gently pat his back.

'Quite simple really. I think you'll find you'll be fine now.'

Simon gingerly lifted his head and began to move his body upwards and then into a sitting position. Apart from a slight sensation of soreness in the lower part of his back there was no pain at all.

He could not conceal his delight.

'You're a genius,' he said warmly to Hadden.

Hadden shrugged with a smile.

'I wish,' he said. 'As I thought, it was a simple misalignment and it helped that you sought help sooner rather than later.'

Simon slid from the couch to his feet, his towel forgotten. He tried twisting his neck from side to side and then bent to touch his toes. Bliss to find all traces of pain gone.

'Don't overdo things for a while,' said Hadden. 'Don't put any stresses and strains on your body.'

'You mean vigorous gardening is out?' Simon asked, cheered.

'It is. Apologies to Jessie. But you could do with some gentle exercise to strengthen the muscles in your back. I advise some warm salt baths for the time being until the soreness has gone. And swimming would be a helpful exercise. Do you swim regularly?'

Simon shook his head.

'In fact you don't do regular exercise at all, I would guess.'

'Jessie's garden's been demanding enough,' Simon protested.

'Gardening is excellent exercise if it's done wisely. But I would imagine that Jessie's been doing the gardening and you have been doing the hard labour, which is not quite the same thing. And you need to take more care of your posture. Like a lot of tall men, you're developing a compensatory stoop which will cause you problems later. You should try the Alexander technique. We do classes here weekly.'

'I'm sure you're right,' Simon said, unbeguiled.

'Jessie was very keen on yoga. Is she still practising it?' Hadden returned to his desk and jotted a few notes.

'She does, usually before her morning shower. She's encouraged me to join her many times.' Without success, Simon did not need to add.

'She'd be a good tutor. Have a think about it. We can rely on the energy and strength of youth for only a limited number of years. Then our negligent habits begin to show.'

'Depressing, isn't it?'

Hadden smiled. 'Lecture over. But I wouldn't have had you down as a macho type who was prejudiced against holistic therapies. On the other hand you are a senior policeman, aren't you? Perhaps the culture gets to you more than you think.' Hadden put down his pen. 'I'd guess you don't fit too easily with the rank and file.' His ready smile was sympathetic.

Simon remained silent.

'Sorry,' Hadden said, his open boyish face colouring slightly. 'None of my business.'

Such were Simon's feelings of benevolence to his saviour that he reassured him.

'No, just a bit too close to the truth perhaps.' He gestured to the changing-room. 'I'd better get dressed.'

When he emerged, himself again, Hadden was standing by the window at the front of the room looking out at the cathedral.

'You are in a very privileged position,' Simon remarked.

Hadden looked up at him with a quick frown, then his face cleared.

'Oh, you mean being here in the cathedral precinct?'

'And in such a lovely old building.'

Hadden nodded. 'All thanks to Sebastian's contacts. His uncle is dean of the cathedral.'

Simon remembered Jessie making some comment about it when she had been working here.

'That's Sebastian Kingsley, the homoeo-path?'

'That's right. He set up the clinic with me initially and very quickly afterwards with our other full-time staff. We're gradually expanding with other alternative therapists joining us on an *ad hoc* basis at the moment.'

'It's a large enough building, and a prestigious address.'

'Would you like to see over the place?' Hadden asked. He looked at his watch. 'I'm free for a while and I also have to go out to buy someone a present, so I'll quickly change my tunic.'

'Yes, I'd like that,' Simon agreed. He loved old buildings.

Hadden emerged from the cubicle moments later in a shirt and tie with sports jacket. The tie was incongruously bright, a psychedelic swirl of colours. Seeing Simon's gaze fixed on it Hadden said, with a degree of pride:

'My son Marcus chose it for me. Its main redeeming feature is its quality — an expensive silk.' He held the end of the tie out, examining it with a rueful smile. 'I'm seeing him later and I didn't want to forget to wear it.'

As they went into the hallway a man was standing with his back to them, speaking sharply to the young woman behind the desk.

'It just won't do, Franny. That's the second

time you've double-booked me in a week. You'd really better get your act together or you'll be out of here.'

Franny's pale complexion had flushed and she was blinking rapidly, as if staving off tears.

'What's the problem?' Hadden asked unnecessarily, moving quickly towards them.

The man turned to him. He was of an age with Hadden, in his mid thirties and strikingly good-looking in an almost feminine way, his lashes dark and thick around deep-set blue eyes, his full lips set bad-temperedly.

'I expect you heard well enough, Jonny. Franny has messed things up again and Mrs Fordham-Jones was not well pleased.'

'It's not true, Jonny,' Franny pleaded, getting to her feet. 'Mr Barlow was the correct appointment. Mrs Fordham-Jones was booked for next week at the same time of day. Look!' she said, turning the appointments diary so that both men could view it, then swivelled the computer screen towards them and pressed some keys.

'She kicked up a fuss, did she?' Hadden asked them both sympathetically. His acknowledgement that they had both been put in a difficult position seemed to calm them a little.

'Old bag barged in on me when I was with Barlow,' Kingsley complained.

'I couldn't stop her,' Franny said anxiously. 'I even followed her up the stairs but she shrugged me off.'

'Well, she insisted her appointment was today!'

'It wasn't!' Franny's voice rose. 'You can see she was booked in for next week!'

'Well that's not what it says in my appointment book!'

'Perhaps you should make sure you check with the computer,' Franny retorted.

Hadden looked up at the mandala above the reception desk.

'Peace, Joy, Love,' he quoted. 'Peace, my children, please.' He put out a hand to each of them giving them a wry smile.

The buzzer for the front door sounded and perhaps that more than Hadden's efforts restored the other two to calmness.

'That's probably my next appointment,' Kingsley said. 'Send her up in three minutes, Franny, if you can manage that.' He sprang up the stairs two at a time.

Franny sat down, visibly composing herself, and pressed the button to allow the visitor to enter. Two women came in, bringing a blast of chill air. One of them immediately crossed the hall to Hadden and Simon.

'It's perishing out there!' she exclaimed, her pink nose testament to the fact. 'I wouldn't be surprised if we get snow.'

'Ruth Maguire,' Hadden said, introducing Simon. 'Ruth is our medical herbalist. She's been with us for a while so she knows Jessie too.'

'So you're Jessie's man,' she said, giving a swift-eyed assessment. She was probably in her early forties, a small slim woman whose straight fine brown hair was escaping the hood she wore. She was pretty in an understated way, her nose and other features neat, her skin good, flushed from the cold air. Her voice was her most distinctive quality, low and a bit throaty. Perhaps that was due to the low temperature outside too.

She asked after Jessie and after a few more remarks to Jonathan on the subject of a meeting they were all to have the next day, went up the stairs to her own room.

'Sorry about all that,' Hadden said with a glance towards Franny who had dispatched the latest client to her appointment with Kingsley. 'Shall we go on?'

He led Simon across the entrance hall through a door to the right of the reception desk, where Franny had her head lowered to a book. The room was large, taking in the two tall windows fronting the lane, with high

15

corniced ceilings and an Adam fireplace.

'This is where we run courses on various things like yoga, meditation and the Alexander technique, should you care to join us,' Hadden said. 'We keep it simple to limit distractions.'

'Lovely proportions,' Simon murmured, feeling like a prospective purchaser.

Hadden's room on the opposite side of the hall had only one window, Simon remembered. 'There must be another room beyond yours, then,' he said.

'There's a small corridor behind my room, leading to Anil's room. He's our acupuncturist.'

Hadden led Simon out into the hall again and on to the room behind the room they had just been in. It was of similar size and design, looking out on to lawns and shrubbery, only the roofs of old nearby buildings showing above the trees at the boundary of the property.

Having checked with Franny who was in consultation or otherwise Hadden led Simon to the acupuncturist's room, similar to Hadden's own but with the addition of three golden Buddhas, then upstairs, avoiding the rooms currently occupied by therapists and their clients, to the staff meditation room on the top floor. This was a pleasant room with a clean atmosphere, crystals, soft cushions and candles. Back on the third floor Simon was ushered into the staff rest room, empty at the moment.

'We could have a cup of something, if you'd like?' Hadden suggested.

Simon cast a wary eye over the pots and packets waiting on a unit under the side window. The words 'decaffeinated' and 'herbal' failed to entice his untutored taste buds and suggested that it was time he was getting back to work.

Hadden nodded. 'We're having a sort of anniversary bash here soon to mark the five years since we've been open. Perhaps you and Jessie would like to come along?'

'I'm sure Jessie won't want to miss it,' Simon agreed, a little mendaciously. From what he could recall, Jessie's reasons for discontinuing her work here had had less to do with pressures of other commitments than the occasional histrionics such as Simon had observed earlier. Certainly she had expressed wariness over Sebastian Kingsley, the head of the clinic.

In the hallway below Hadden repeated some of his advice to Simon and let himself out of the front door, leaving Simon to approach Franny, wondering just how high the fee for his treatment was going to be and extracting his cheque-book.

She lifted a small white hand, waving it away so that he felt he had committed some vulgarity.

'We'll bill you, Mr Simon,' she said.

2

Frances Fulton closed the appointments book, switched off the computer and collected her coat from the cloakroom. She opened the front door and paused at the top of the steps, looking across the frost sparkling on the cathedral green to the cathedral, lit by floodlights that warmed the ancient stones every night of the year. It was only just past six and bitterly cold.

She entered Candlemaker Lane, the ancient thoroughfare joining the precinct with the West Gate, still shaken by the scene earlier with Sebastian Kingsley. She stamped her booted feet down on the slippery paving as much in residual anger as in an effort to keep her feet warm. It was not the first time he had held her up to ridicule in public: he seemed always to take a delight in belittling her if an opportunity arose.

Not, she was aware, that she was the only one he treated this way. He appeared to enjoy making people uneasy about their position at the clinic, implying that there were plenty more therapists to replace them in such a prestigious place. He usually picked on anyone he perceived as of lower status, like herself and the less highly qualified part-time practitioners, but the demand for aroma-therapists and reflexologists, colour-therapists and so on, was growing and he was being forced to adapt, to make plans for their greater accommodation within the clinic.

Of late he had begun to hint to her that her services could readily be dispensed with but despite his obnoxious behaviour she had no desire to leave just yet. She had worked at the clinic for over six months now and got on with other members of staff, who had never complained about her work.

The vacancy had come up soon after she had arrived back in Britain from Australia where she had taken a year out for travel. She had had to return earlier than planned when the news reached her that her mother had terminal cancer. It had been totally unex-pected and a horrible shock — and she had arrived too late. She was still raw from the loss and the clinic, where she had soon afterwards managed to get the job she wanted, was bound up in her memories and experience of that terrible time.

Neither had her father yet recovered from his wife's death. He had retired from his GP practice and still lived in the family home, an old and inconvenient Victorian house in a suburban 'village' to the east of the city. His grief and depression at the loss of his wife had forced his retirement and he lived a lonely existence, managing always to make her feel guilty when she visited him. He had wanted her to come and live with him after her mother's death but there was too much history between them. He had always disapproved of her lack of commitment to a career, frowning on the fact that she wanted to see something of the world before she settled down to either career or family or preferably both. On her part there was resentment that he had not tried to contact her sooner when her mother's cancer was diagnosed. He had pleaded that it was what her mother had wanted. *She didn't want to spoil this chance you were having to travel and have such a wonderful time, doing all the things she never was able to do herself. It made her happy, Frances, to think of you seeing all those places, doing all those things. She loved to get your postcards . . .*

Her mother had understood her need to get away from Westwich and the existence that she herself had had as the wife of a GP who was totally absorbed in his work, took few holidays and never wanted to go far when he did. But there *had* been things she, Franny, might have done, had she been here to influence matters. There was the whole business of her mother's treatment . . . She tossed her head in remembered frustration and grief. She would perhaps have been too late anyway, even had her father notified her when he should have. She should never have gone away. Sometimes it seemed she was being punished for the fact that she had gone seeking her own pleasures, taking her eye off the ball of the gritty realities of life like suffering and death.

Near the city centre gaudy Christmas illuminations lit the faces of late shoppers, their breath smoky in the frosty air. Frances turned from them into the narrow lane where she lived. Aisha, the woman Frances shared with, had bought the flat in a converted printer's warehouse and was looking for someone to help bear the financial burden soon after Frances had got the job at the clinic. Her father had pleaded for her to stay at home but there was still too much anger in her towards him. And besides, the sharing of their pain seemed only to double rather than halve it, as received wisdom suggested.

Frances trod heavily up the flights of steps to the second floor and let herself in. The lights were on, something fragrant was cooking and soothing music sidled around the pastel walls.

'Hello Franneee!' Aisha cooed musically from the kitchen. Frances felt a familiar twinge of pain at Aisha's use of the name Frances's mother had always called her by, but the name was in common usage at the clinic, distinctly patronizing on the lips of Sebastian Kingsley. Aisha was blessed with a name that did not lend itself to irritating amendments. She peered around the door, waving a spoon.

'And how is Anil today?' she asked with a feline smile.

Anil Patel, the acupuncturist at the clinic, was a slender and rather beautiful young man whom Aisha had met at one of the open days at the clinic when she had gone along with Frances. The fact that Anil had brought with him the young woman to whom he was formally betrothed, who had recently arrived from India, had not repressed Aisha's overt interest him.

'He should not marry her,' Aisha had declared to Franny as they walked home. 'Anil is like me, we were both born in Britain. She will not suit him. She is too passive, too much the polite, submissive little Indian wife.'

Franny hadn't known what to say. Aisha's self-confidence never ceased to astonish her with her own, very British, diffidence so much in contrast.

23

'But some men in certain cultures like their women to be submissive and obedient, Aisha. You would probably terrify him.'

Aisha had laughed. 'I don't think he was terrified of me, do you? In fact I think he was delighted with me. His little girlfriend was quite mortified!'

Her insouciance was infectious and Franny had laughed in return, thinking this one of Aisha's many passing fancies. But Aisha had shown more persistence in this case. She had joined one of Anil's meditation classes at the clinic and their friendship had developed as a result. Franny was beginning to fear for the consequences of her friend's absorption with the clinic's acupuncturist.

'So, is he well, my beautiful Anil?' Aisha enquired again. 'Did he ask after me today?'

'Yes he is well and no, your name did not pass his lips,' Franny answered repressively.

'Oh!' Aisha pouted. 'Well I expect you did not see him much then.' She turned back into the kitchen, Franny following to check what she was cooking tonight.

'Prawn byriani with broccoli and shitaki Gujerati style,' Aisha announced, lifting the lid from a pan and letting the scent waft upwards.

'Smells great,' Franny said. 'You're a star.'

'I know that,' Aisha agreed. 'And you are

not — at least where cooking is concerned and which is why you do the boring domestic tasks. The living-room has not been cleaned properly this week and you must do that before you get your supper.'

Franny groaned but got on with it. They had a fair exchange of tasks and Aisha did not leave her to do all the rest of the work. Aisha came and watched as she vacuumed the living-room and plumped up cushions, putting away Aisha's seemingly endless copies of Hello magazine and others of similar content.

'Any more trouble at the clinic today?' Aisha asked as the noise of the motor died away.

'What do you mean?' Franny asked quickly.

'You know, any little incidents that you haven't been telling me about? Like Anil's troubles with his needles and Mr Kingsley's homoeopathic pills? You are not a very good communicator you know Franny,' Aisha said disapprovingly.

The acupuncturist had arrived for work on Tuesday to find his sterile needles scattered on the floor, and in similar fashion Sebastian Kingsley had found several bottles of tablets emptied all over his room. It had delayed both practitioners in beginning their sessions that day.

'How do you know about it?' Franny asked, guessing what must be the answer.

'Anil told me, of course,' Aisha said simply with a feline smile. 'Are you ready to eat now?'

She was, and they were just piling their plates with food when the doorbell rang. Aisha went over to the intercom. Her response to whoever was at the other end was a peal of laughter:

'Come on up,' she said, pressing the door release.

Anil entered the room as she resumed her seat at the table.

'Hello Franny,' he said easily.

'Have you eaten?' Aisha asked him. 'Get a plate from the kitchen.'

He did so, pulling up a chair comfortably as if he did so every night. Aisha got up and collected a bottle of wine and some glasses from the kitchen. She chattered lightly to him as they ate, Franny looking on in silence, disturbed by the implications of this growing friendship.

'I hear Sebastian was unpleasant to you today, Franny,' Anil said abruptly, turning the attention on her. 'Something to do with double-booking clients, was it?'

'I didn't,' Franny said shortly. 'It was Mrs Whatsername's fault.'

Anil nodded, slowly chewing his food. He swallowed.

'Sebastian seems to be getting even more short-tempered these days.'

'Perhaps it is because of all the things that keep going wrong at the clinic,' Aisha said brightly.

'They don't help,' Anil agreed. 'Who on earth is doing these things? Last week all the cups and coffee and dried milk were scattered all over the rest-room, then we've had the mess made in Sebastian's room and mine. But what happened today was worse.'

'What was that?' Aisha asked quickly, her eyes on Franny.

'Some of my acupuncture needles were found in Hannah's relaxation chair. They actually injured a patient.'

'Not badly, I hope?' Aisha said, her eyes wide.

'Nothing too serious. The lady concerned was very good about it,' Anil said.

'You said nothing more had happened!' Aisha accused Franny.

'It's news to me,' Franny said. She picked up her glass and took a sip of wine.

'You haven't been immune, either,' Anil reminded Franny. 'Don't forget the computer was wiped with all the appointments on it a couple of weeks ago.'

'I'm not likely to forget.'

'It always seems to happen after we've had an evening course, have you noticed?' Anil remarked. 'Perhaps there is someone with some sort of grudge who stays behind afterwards.'

'I could understand a grudge against Kingsley himself,' Franny said.

'He's not exactly endearing himself to people these days,' Anil agreed.

'Can we change the subject now, please?' Aisha requested. 'Let's talk about something more interesting, like me!' She put her small pointed chin in her hand and turned her glowing brown eyes on Anil.

He gave her a shy smile.

'And how is Salena?' Franny asked. 'How long is it now to the wedding?' She began collecting the plates and dishes.

'Salena is very well,' Anil said formally, looking down at his hands and examining his perfectly manicured nails.

'And the wedding?' Franny persisted, pausing with the dishes in her hands and ignoring the annoyed snort that came from Aisha. 'There is still to be a wedding, isn't there?'

'Of course,' Anil said quietly. 'Why not?'

As she stacked the dishwasher Franny

could hear suppressed hissings and mutterings from Aisha. Music was suddenly turned on too loudly and as suddenly lowered. Franny hesitated then returned to the living-room to finish clearing the table. Aisha was lowering herself on to the sofa beside Anil who was looking up at her with that shy half-smile. Franny was struck anew by just how attractive he was and hoped that Aisha's interest in him was as superficial as her interest in men usually was.

They both ignored her as she picked up the rest of the dishes and went through to finish clearing up the kitchen. It didn't matter: she was planning to go out.

★   ★   ★

The traffic over the West Gate bridge had thinned but Jonathan Hadden was still running late to arrive at his former marital home three miles to the west of the city, on the far side of the flood plain. He put his foot down and overtook an elderly driver who was wavering over the central line, anxious not to give Jean any excuse for her ready anger that so easily could threaten his access to Marcus.

Tonight was an unusual chance to see his son on a Thursday evening rather than on the increasingly irregular weekends she had

29

allowed recently. She was going to see a film with her policeman boyfriend and had ordered Jonathan to be there by seven at the latest. It was already one minute past.

She was peering from behind heavy lace curtains when he pulled into the cul-de-sac. They had moved into the small housing development in the village of Madderley soon after they had married eight years ago. He had moved out four years later, when Marcus was three, and despite her comfortable life and apparently harmonious relationship with her traffic policeman, she still took pleasure in making him pay for his desertion of her.

'Late as usual,' she remarked acidly as she met him at the front door.

He followed her into the overfurnished living-room. The boyfriend also appeared to be late, which meant that her dissatisfaction would be meted out entirely on Jonathan.

'Sorry,' Jonathan said, appeasement habitual to him with his ex-wife. 'I had a late appointment and couldn't get away sooner.'

'How *is* the Cathedral Clinic these days?' she asked with mock interest. 'Still flourishing? Sebastian still expanding the range of therapies and increasing his income?'

Despite her sneers about his work and the clinic she seemed to make sure she kept abreast of any developments. Her hostility to the clinic was at one with her hostility to himself, Jonathan realized that. It was ironical that the two of them had met at a Mind, Body and Spirit fair. He had been manning a chiropractic stand and she had appeared to be fascinated by the atmosphere, the colour, the scents, the gemstones, the music. That she was easily threatened by anything outside her immediate experience had only become clear after they were married and her earlier apparent fascination with the world of alternative medicine had turned into well-honed bigotry.

'That awful dyke you've got at the clinic came in to the society today with her pretty little girlfriend,' Jean was saying. 'They are buying a big house together. Isn't that nice?'

She meant Anne Stillings, the nutritional therapist, a pleasant warm-hearted woman. Jonathan nodded non-commitally. 'Where's Marcus?' he asked, his anger strangling his words.

Instead of answering, she went to the drinks table and poured herself a sherry. After taking a sip, and pointedly not offering him one, she said vaguely:

'Oh, upstairs with his computer, I expect.'

'Do you mind if I go up and say hello?' he asked.

'But we don't get much chance to talk these days, Jonathan,' she said, pouting her carmine-red lips. 'I thought you might be glad to find me on my own for once.'

'Where *is* Terry?' he asked as neutrally as possible.

She sat down slowly, displaying a great deal of thigh. She was overdressed for a trip to the cinema.

'He telephoned to say he would be a little late. A policeman's lot and all that,' she said, taking a small sip from her glass.

'Dad! Is that you down there?' Marcus's high voice came from the top of the stairs.

Jonathan was immediately on his feet. He looked round the door and up at his son.

'Shall I come up?' he asked.

'Yeah!' Marcus said enthusiastically. 'Do you want a go on my Gameboy?'

Later there were voices from the hallway downstairs: Terry had evidently arrived but they were going to be late for the start of the film. Jonathan debated whether to join them before they left and decided it would be wise. Despite the number of times he had been babysitter, Jean always had some fussy new demand.

Terry, in his garish traffic-cop uniform, filled the hall, Jean clinging to his arm.

'We're not going out, after all,' Jean

announced with a malicious smile. 'So you won't be needed.'

'Can't I stay until his bedtime at least?' Jonathan asked, trying not to sound pleading.

Jean nodded carelessly and took Terry by the hand to lead him into the living-room.

'Come on, Dad,' Marcus, waiting for him on the landing, called. 'You're not going yet, are you?'

Jonathan went quickly up the stairs.

Much later, after bathing him and reading him his bedtime story, Jonathan sat beside his sleeping son, feeding on that image of lovely innocence. He feared for his son, feared the influence of his mother and the corruption of her shallow, furtive mind, and his heart ached with how much he missed having him in his daily life. Only the truly impossible nature of his relationship with his wife had made him leave; he had struggled to live with her as long as he had only because of the deep love he bore his son.

★ ★ ★

Anne Stillings left the clinic shortly before Frances Fulton that Thursday night and crossed the cathedral green to Martyr's Arch. She lived in Prior's Court, a short distance away. It was the development's proximity to the ancient cathedral and its environs that had guaranteed its quality and aesthetic credentials and Anne had been pleased to be able to buy a two-bedroomed apartment there after her divorce five years before.

Her mind was occupied with Sebastian Kingsley. He had looked through the door of her consultation room in the afternoon to speak to her about some minor administrative matter. Then he had entered the room further, wandering slowly between desk and window before coming to a dramatic halt and exclaiming:

'My God, Anne, I had no idea you had had a visit from the Cathedral Clinic gremlin, too!'

It was unfair. In her specialism of nutritional therapy she used more paperwork than probably any of the other therapists in the clinic — advisory notes for clients, research papers and endless information sheets on aspects of nutrition and nutritional supplements. It was true, perhaps, that she could do with more organization but her energies tended to go more in the direction of her clients than in presentation. And this did not impress Sebastian Kingsley, who was big on image as much as or more than on any professional content.

To add to the injury, he had looked her

over and suggested that she could do with smartening up a bit.

'Looking professional is every bit as important as being professional, you know, Anne,' he had said threateningly. 'There are plenty of very good people who would be glad to work at the Cathedral Clinic. We are regarded as the most professional alternative health clinic for miles and we don't want standards slipping.'

Her former career had been as a nurse and she had spent enough years in a uniform. Now it was a relief to wear colour and texture and she favoured ethnic clothes, far in image from the power-dressing that Sebastian Kingsley seemed to favour. She felt humiliated and angry — and worried. This would be the worst time for her to find herself out of work. Jenny, not as fond of Prior's Court as she was, had persuaded her to find time today to visit the building society and discuss a possible mortgage for a house that she was set on moving into. It would be much too big for them and much less convenient for her work at the clinic, and would involve a considerably larger mortgage.

Damning Sebastian Kingsley, Anne crossed one of the walkways of the development and took the stairs to the second floor. Jenny would be later tonight because of a demonstration workshop with students from the college. They were supposed to be going to the film club at the Corn Exchange Arts Centre to watch two films by some Russian director whose name she couldn't remember. Jenny was the film enthusiast.

The rooms were a mess, the washing-up not done from this morning, Jenny's clothes strewn around the bedroom, and the living-room untidy with magazines and CDs on most surfaces. By the time she heard her partner's key turn in the lock, the flat was tidy, the table was laid and the meal nearly ready. Jenny came to the hob and planted a kiss on her cheek.

'Smells wonderful!' she breathed into Anne's ear. 'Everything all right?' she asked lightly, seeing Anne's apparent concentration on stirring the sauce.

Anne felt a wicked surge of feeling closer to anger than to irritation, but she took a breath and rewarded Jenny with a smile.

Jenny smiled back, tilting her head upwards, showing her perfect teeth and lifting her expression dramatically from the sullenness that had begun to form. Anne thought how pretty she was, how perfect, how groomed from her hair to her manicured toes. She lectured in beauty therapy, so it was a requirement of her job to present herself well but Anne felt unhappily shabby in comparison, reminded again of Sebastian Kingsley's criticism.

'Have I got time for a quick shower?' Jenny asked, giving her another brief kiss on the cheek.

Anne bit back a waspish reply. 'Five minutes!' she said brightly and Jenny was through the door.

Anne continued to stir the sauce, turning down the heat. She saw things clearly enough in this relationship: that she was the essential provider both emotionally and financially, as she had been with her husband, who had done the conventional thing and had an affair with his secretary. It was shortly after she had started work at the Cathedral Clinic that she had met Jenny. There had been nothing dramatic in the encounter initially; both of them had been shopping and had stopped for a cappuccino and Danish in a new stylish café near the city centre.

It had been with a rising sense of delight that she had experienced the lively young woman's flattering interest in herself as they had sipped coffee, begun talking about their lives, and ordered more coffee. Jenny told her that she too was divorced, though unlike Anne she had not mentioned any cause for the breakdown of her marriage. She had not referred to the fact that she was gay and had had two such relationships since the divorce, and she had begun her subtle seduction of Anne.

It had been after a meal in Anne's flat that the relationship had at last become physical. They had had too much wine to drink. Usually they had restricted themselves to one glass plus an occasional half because Jenny had to drive home. On this night Jenny had provided the wine, two bottles of it, and had continually refilled their glasses, amid much laughter, hiccups and giggles. Inevitably she had had to stay the night. Anne had made up a bed in the spare room and, still giggling, Jenny had had her shower and retired to bed. Anne had been on the verge of sleep half an hour later when Jenny had crept into her room. 'I'm feeling cold', she had whispered. 'May I cuddle up?'

For Anne, at first dismayed and confused, it had turned into a night the like of which she had never known. Aroused, overwhelmed with sensation, sexually satisfied in a way she had never been before, she found herself regarding Jenny with nothing short of awe — that this slight, even superficial, pretty creature could so completely and swiftly overturn her life. Her former consciousness of Jenny had never been rationalized by her into what it truly was. She had never thought of women as potential sexual partners and so she had thought she had merely found a loving and important friend. Now, she was enslaved.

It was a while before Anne had realized that she was not 'the first'. She had been very naïve. Now, a few years later, with more knowledge of the gay scene and Jenny's gay friends and her own bewildered acknowledgement that she was now one of their ranks, time and experience had not diluted her passion for Jenny and she laid the table, listening for when she would join her.

As Anne served their meal, Jenny, freshly dressed for the evening ahead, said:

'I'm so excited about our house! We can have a dog! I've always wanted a dog. You'd like a dog, wouldn't you, darling?'

Anne would prefer a cat.

'Are you saying we can't?' Jenny asked flatly.

Anne swallowed. 'So long as I can have a cat,' she said with an uneasy smile. 'I suppose you can get cats and dogs that get along?'

3

Ruth Maguire closed the door on her last client of the day and did a quick tidy of her desk, returning reference books to the shelves and stacking papers ready to be filed in the morning.

Her decision to train in medical herbalism had been prompted by personal experience: her late husband had died as a direct result of taking a prescription drug which had meant eight years on dialysis before his premature death. She had cared for him through those years while raising a family of two children and managing to run a computer consultancy from home, keeping the family solvent at a time when it had seemed they might lose everything. But she had lost her husband and that had been bad enough. Despite experience she was not entirely prejudiced against orthodox medical treatment, though many clients came to her as a last resort, after failing to find relief from prescription drugs.

She had been at the clinic now for three years and her life was beginning to come together again. The children were both in London, one at university, the other working in a city bank; she was still living in the family home and, despite being a single middle-aged woman, had a good social life. However the fact that she was not as single as she appeared to be had made all the difference to her life in the last year.

After collecting her coat from her cloak-room she took a last glance around her consulting-room, switched off her computer and stepped out into the first floor corridor. As she approached the open space of the landing at the head of the stairs, Sebastian Kingsley turned the corner and filled her vision.

'Ruth!' he exclaimed, as if they had met unexpectedly in a distant desert land.

'Sebastian,' she acknowledged, edging past him. She got along well enough with Sebastian herself but knew enough of him not to seek his company.

'I was just coming to see you,' he said in a manner that suggested she must be delighted.

'Sorry, I'm in a hurry.' She tried again to get past him.

He stayed blocking her path, a look of pained disappointment on his face.

'Is it important?' she sighed.

'Well, I rather think it is. And so should you as a member of this clinic.'

She pulled back her coat sleeve and looked at her watch.

'Five minutes?' she said.

He waited for her to unlock the door of her room and followed her in, immediately going to the window to look out at the lit-up cathedral.

'We are very fortunate to have this location for the clinic,' he said.

'*You* are very fortunate to have the dean of the cathedral as your uncle,' she observed.

'Which makes us all very fortunate then, doesn't it?' he said turning back to face her.

'What's this all about, Sebastian? I've had a long day and I have to get home.' Ruth perched on the edge of her desk, determined not to adopt a more permanent-looking posture by sitting down.

'OK.' He swiftly sat in the client's chair and placed his highly polished shoes on the desk beside her. A trouser-leg of his well-tailored pin-stripe suit slipped back to reveal dark curling hairs above his socks. Ruth was not sure if she would have been more repelled to have seen that his legs were hairless. There was something about Sebastian Kingsley which, despite his overt dark good looks, she recoiled from, and she had never been quite able to clarify what quality it was in him that produced this

42

reaction in her. She shifted slightly, moving her body away from him.

'It's about the clinic gremlin,' he said.

'Has there been another incident?' she asked.

He gave a snort. 'I thought it might have visited Anne Stillings when I called into her room today. Paperwork all over the place. But of course it was just Anne's usual inefficiency. But more of that later.'

Ruth stiffened. She liked Anne, knew she was good at her job and conscientious in the extreme. Her wariness increased.

'All the incidents have happened after an evening class the night before,' she said. 'I thought we were assuming that someone from one of the classes had some sort of grudge.'

'The point is, there has been another incident,' Sebastian said flatly. 'Today, a client of Hannah Crossley was stuck with acupuncture needles when she sat in Hannah's relaxation chair.' Hannah was the clinic's psychotherapist.

'That's terrible!' Ruth got to her feet. 'I didn't hear anything about it.'

'We kept it quiet. Didn't want other clients hearing about the fuss. Fact is,' he said, also standing, 'it's going to be bad news for the clinic if this kind of thing carries on. If people think they are in danger of injury or worse by coming here it's going to finish us.'

'But what about Hannah's client?'

'We managed to cover up, I think. Told her some story about the chair having been re-covered recently and that the upholsterer must have left some pins that had worked their way out. Hannah's going to give her a couple of free sessions in compensation and she went away happy enough.'

'But she *was* hurt?'

'The needles were embedded in her thighs and her left buttock.' Sebastian gave a quick sardonic laugh. 'She went off to Hannah's cloakroom to sort herself out, too embarrassed to want any help. But apparently it was all just skin deep and nothing too serious, just painful.'

'So long as the needles weren't infected in any way,' Ruth commented.

'Perish the thought.' Sebastian sat down with a thump in his chair again.

'There was a meditation class last night, wasn't there?'

'I just can't imagine anyone sneaking around the clinic after an hour or so of relaxing meditation intent on inflicting damage on some unknown stranger,' Sebastian said.

'But that's not the point if the intention is

to damage the clinic, is it? Had Hannah locked her door?'

'She says she did.'

'The set of spare keys is kept on that hook at the back of the hall, under the stairs. Easy enough for anyone to get hold of.'

'But they're not obvious to anyone who doesn't already know they are there.' Sebastian got up restlessly and went over to the window again.

'So, if it's not someone who comes into the building because of evening classes, that leaves one of us. Or Jock.' Jock was the caretaker and cleaner who lived with his invalid wife in the basement flat.

Sebastian turned to face her.

'Can you really imagine old Jock doing these malicious things?'

'Can you really imagine any of *us* doing them?' Ruth arched an eyebrow.

Sebastian shrugged.

Ruth picked up her bag, angered at his implicit acceptance that one of his colleagues might be behind it all.

'Sebastian, I don't know why you've brought this to me tonight. We obviously need to have a staff meeting and discuss security. One obvious step is to ensure that all the evening-class teachers supervise people leaving the building at night. Perhaps Jock

45

could keep an eye on them as well.'

'Yes, you're right. The more we can tighten things up the more obvious it's likely to be who's behind all this.'

Ruth adjusted her bag over her shoulder and wound her scarf around her neck but Sebastian ignored the hint, turning back to the view from the window again.

'I've really got to go, Sebastian.' Ruth insisted.

'Mmm. Me too. I've got choir practice tonight.' Sebastian was a member of the cathedral choir. He swung back suddenly. 'You don't think it's Anne Stillings, do you?'

'Anne? Why on earth would I think it was Anne? She's one of the gentlest, kindest creatures.'

'You think so? I'm not so happy with her.'

'Well, I think you're wrong.' Ruth compressed her lips and stared hard at his back.

'I was thinking of getting rid of her.' He spoke almost idly.

'Sebastian, I thought that the policy of the clinic was that decisions about the professionals who work here are made by the clinic as a whole.' Ruth could not keep the coldness and resentment from her voice. 'And, anyway, why should you want Anne to leave. She is very good at what she does. She's successful, clients like her and are very grateful for the

46

help she has given them. She's helped some people quite dramatically.'

'She's . . . shambolic,' Sebastian said.

'You don't think she fits the image of the clinic?' Ruth said sarcastically. It was true that Anne favoured a more colourful and relaxed style of dress than the rest of them, that her hair was unruly and free of any hairstylist's control and that these facts might irk the highly image-conscious Sebastian, who regarded the clinic as entirely his own.

'No, she doesn't.' He pressed his full lips together as if in final statement.

'Well, I'm afraid I don't agree with you. And I don't think the others will either.'

'I saw you in London last weekend,' he said quietly, picking a book from the shelf.

Ruth felt herself freeze and her heart lurch. Even as it happened she was aware that the shock she felt was as much due to the menace that Sebastian intended by his remark as to its meaning.

'All very discreet, of course, with this by-election coming up.' Sebastian smiled at her, carefully replacing the book on the shelf.

They had indeed been discreet. There had been months of secret meetings in out-of-the-way places since she had first met James Flamborough. She had become involved in a local organization concerned with the effects

47

of herbicides and pesticides on the water-table in the area, as well as their general effects on health. James, as prospective parliamentary candidate for the city after the resignation of the sitting MP, had visited the group as part of his efforts to get to know the local electorate in all its manifestations. He had professed great interest in the work they were doing and had spent a significant amount of time with her in her capacity as chairperson in that first meeting. This had been followed by his contacting her by phone.

She had known he was married, his children, like hers, grown and departed, but there could hardly have been a worse time in his career to begin an adulterous relationship. The strength of their feelings for each other had, despite their efforts to stay apart, made it impossible to keep to their frequent promises until the election was over and his political career properly established.

'Oh?' was all she could say, unsteadily, to Sebastian.

'Not really the most discreet of places, The Garden.' He smiled again, his eyes narrowing. 'Neither of you would want the news of your relationship getting about at this point in time.'

'Are you,' she said, her voice rising,

'blackmailing me in some way, Sebastian?'

'What a thing to say!' He looked down at her patronizingly. They stood staring at each other for a moment. Then Sebastian said easily: 'But you will back me up over Anne, won't you? Oh, and do bring that lovely daughter of yours to our next open day. Such a lovely girl, Cassie.'

He smiled again and patted her on the shoulder. 'Sorry to have delayed you this evening, Ruth.'

He left the room abruptly. She was sure she could smell the lingering sulphur. She had known he had been responsible for Cassie's confusion last summer when she had been threatening not to go to university. She had even wondered whether Cass had formed an unhappy attachment to Kingsley. But at the last minute Cass had relented and taken herself off to London, much to the mixed relief and sorrow of her mother.

James was calling her this evening. Even in the matter of phone calls they were exceedingly discreet. She checked her watch again and left her room, remembering to lock the door, wondering uneasily what Sebastian had been doing in London last weekend.

★   ★   ★

Jock Patterson, caretaker, cleaner and odd job man for the Cathedral Clinic started work on the third floor of the building. The duties were usually light in the consulting-rooms themselves but the third floor contained the library and the staff rest room, areas which were more intensively used and needed extra effort.

When he had first moved into the basement flat with his wife Valerie after the clinic opened, the arrangement had been for his wife to carry out most of the cleaning duties while he did the caretaking and any other jobs, inside and out. But his wife had soon become ill and though she had struggled on for some time it was obvious she could no longer keep her side of the contract. They had been worried that they would lose their home as a result, but Jock had insisted that he would manage both their jobs and so far they had kept going. The arthritis that had begun as what his wife had thought of as 'just middle-aged aches and pains' had developed into crippling incapacity.

Kingsley had surprised him and others with his sympathy and practical help. Even before Valerie had eventually had to succumb to the use of a wheelchair, Kingsley had had the area at the back of the flat redesigned so that it was easier to move the wheelchair around. He had even suggested that Jock build the raised beds so that she could do light gardening, grow flowers and brighten her life a little.

And from the beginning Sebastian Kingsley had funded her treatments at the clinic. Just about every therapist had treated Valerie and none had cured her. There had been a cheering respite during her consultations with Anne Stillings: the dietary route had seemed to produce some dramatic improvements in Valerie's health. But the good effects had fallen away as Valerie claimed she found it difficult, and expensive, to stick to the foods that Anne said were required.

Jock had found it hard to repress his anger with her. But she was in very real pain and he had contained his impatience. Kingsley, and Anne, had obviously been disappointed too with Valerie's relapse and when Valerie began an even greater decline in health, Jock had expected their tenancy to again be under threat.

But it hadn't happened that way and Jock was increasingly anxious that he might be unable to manage all the duties alone, that he was going to fail in his job in some significant way and they would be homeless again. They no longer had Kevin, their son, living at home able to help out occasionally. That was another source of heartbreak altogether, Kevin running off like that a year ago at only thirteen. It had been all the worry and stress over that which had made Valerie's pain more acute than ever.

Jock dumped his things beside the sink in the staffroom and began a thorough polishing of the stainless steel surfaces. The therapists were a considerate lot on the whole, didn't make a mess and expect him to clean up after them.

It was a pleasant, relaxing room with windows looking out to the cathedral and the warm glow of its statuary, in clear relief from the lighting that surrounded it. That soaringly beautiful building had stood for over 700 years as a monument to God's love and it comforted him. It was a vital part of Jock's attachment to the place. He was not overtly religious, though he visited the cathedral often, just to feel its peace envelop him, to feel the power of 700 years of patient prayer. He had visited more regularly when Kevin had been in the choir but his son's voice had broken not long before he had disappeared and the boy had shown no further interest. He had become moody and withdrawn. Jock had put it down to his age, being a new teenager, and had adopted a tolerant attitude, prepared to wait out the storms and moods.

He left the room, checking the state of the stairway up to Sebastian Kingsley's flat, then went on to the second stairway to the staff meditation room on the top floor. He wasn't quite sure what went on in here but he could sense the different atmosphere this room held, the air clean and pleasantly cool, faintly scented, a feeling of peace. Here the dormer windows gave on to a parapet and a higher perspective of the cathedral, so that, lit up as it was, it appeared to float in the dark crisp air.

He was frowning as he went back down the stairs, the thought of the clinic gremlin was never far from his mind and the issue was beginning to prey on him as the one responsible for the security of the clinic and those who worked there and visited there. There was no guarantee that it was necessarily someone at evening class who was doing these things; it could be anyone with access to the clinic.

When he had finished his cleaning duties Jock did a final check of the doors and windows on the ground floor and unlocked the door at the rear of the building which led down internally to his flat. Until recently he had left the door unlocked and sometimes one of the therapists would call in on Valerie to see how she was, bring her some little gift such as a plant or flowers. Since the happenings in the clinic he had felt concerned enough to make sure that Valerie was secure.

He locked up behind him; there were no classes tonight and they had the evening to themselves. As he went down the stairs he registered that the flat was absolutely silent. He immediately worried that Valerie had had a fall and rushed down pushing open the door at the foot of the stairs.

'Val?' he called. The place was in darkness and he began to panic. Then he noticed the light under the living-room door.

He called her name again as he pushed the door open then stopped in amazement and disbelief at the sight of his wife and his son sitting together on the sofa, his son's head resting on his wife's shoulder. It was obvious that they had both been crying.

'Kev?' Jock had no idea what to say. He had no words to express the utter joy he felt in seeing his son safe and at home again. He went behind the sofa and leaned forward, his arms around them both. 'Thank God you're all right!' he breathed.

They stayed like that for a minute or two until Kevin stirred and got up.

'Why, son, why did you go off like that?' Jock couldn't hold back the question, however much it sounded like reproach. Now that he knew Kevin was safe he could for the first time in over a year give vent to emotions he had held in check for so long: the fear, the terrible anxiety, watching Valerie become more ill and sink into indifference over her health.

He came round the sofa to put an arm around his son's thin shoulder to soften his words. The boy had grown scarcely any taller, he was still small for his age. Neither had he grown in substance, his shoulders were thin and bony, his face drawn and pale. Jock was afraid to ask what had happened to him while he'd been away.

'Leave it, Jock,' Valerie said gently. 'Kev's told me all about it. We'll talk about it later after we've all had a cup of tea.' Her voice was hoarse with the tears she had shed.

Jock felt his anxiety increase again. He needed to know why his son had disappeared like that.

'Was it something we did?' he asked his son, his voice sharpened unintentionally.

'No! Leave it, Dad,' Kevin repeated, his red-rimmed eyes, dark-shadowed, looked injured.

Valerie raised her voice a note, summoning some energy and a little cheer.

'Do you know, we've neither of us had a

cup of tea yet. Put the kettle on, Jock, there's a love.'

He felt excluded, shut out from what mother and son had obviously shared while he had been doing his rounds of the clinic. But he did as he was bid, clumsily spilling the boiling water over the worktop, scalding his hand — though he barely noticed.

When he returned to the sitting-room carrying the tray and longing for a drink of whisky rather than tea, Kevin had taken the seat opposite the sofa and was head down, examining his hands. They were grimy, the nails bitten to the quick. An image of the boy, angelic in his choir robes, came to Jock's mind and he swallowed hard on the lump in his throat.

He couldn't stop himself asking the question: 'Is it drugs, Kev? If it is, we'll do all we can. There's a good clinic we can get you into and — '

'It's not drugs, Dad,' Kevin interrupted, shifting abruptly in his seat. He began biting at a gnawed finger.

Jock felt an immense surge of relief at Kevin's assurance. That, surely, was the worst that could have been going on. If it wasn't drugs it must be something they could sort out between them.

'We'll get you a nice hot bath in a minute,'

he said. 'You'll scrub up. And you'll be wanting something to eat.'

But neither his son nor his wife responded; they sat staring silently into their tea. Jock resisted the wave of fear that began to overwhelm him again. They were all right, he said to himself; he was just so grateful that they were all safely together again.

★ ★ ★

Hannah Crossley stood that Thursday night at the window of her apartment looking down at one of the tall ships in the dock basin below. Had it not been for the electric globe-lights reflecting in the sinister oily water she could have imagined herself to be living in a much earlier age. She was realist enough to know that she preferred her sanitized existence on the fourth floor of this converted docks warehouse to anything the past had to offer, but her feelings of discontent were dominant tonight.

It occurred to her that the degree of control she had in her life was their source; her life's easy predictability the cause of her malaise. She was a well-qualified psychologist with a good job at the Cathedral Clinic as their resident psychotherapist. She owned this highly desirable property she lived in and she had an equally desirable and expensive car. Both owed more to her antecedents than to her personal efforts and perhaps they would satisfy her more if that were not the case. But life had never presented her with many problems: her childhood had been bland and without any trauma, her teenage years happy and her university time successful both socially and academically. She had had a number of relationships with men during and after that, none of whom she had cared for deeply enough, nor needed enough on any level, to marry. Her parents, of whom she had been fond, were dead and she had no siblings. Her life, she reflected, feeling the warmth of alcohol in her stomach, was indeed sanitized on every count, except one.

Her relationship with Sebastian Kingsley had begun earlier in the year, not long after she had begun working at the clinic. At first it had seemed to follow the usual pattern with herself in the comfortable role of the pursued. She had lapsed into her habitual casual manner, as she had in all previous relationships, a fact that had not in the least put off previous suitors, quite the contrary. But with Sebastian she had found herself in a different game altogether and her usual pose of cool indifference had done the opposite of increasing his interest. She was not used to being on the receiving end of the emotional games people play, and of which she as a psychologist had been so serenely aware, and she was, perhaps for the first time in her life, deeply troubled.

Tonight he should have been here. Dinner was drying in the oven, the lit candles on the dining-table were already guttering, and she had drunk too much. She was angry. She couldn't remember when she had last felt so incensed. She didn't know any more whether she was upset because she cared about him too much or whether she was simply experiencing fear of rejection — and she couldn't bear to believe it was the latter.

She tossed off the last of her vodka and picked up the phone.

It rang several times before he answered.

'Hannah? What's the problem?' he sounded mildly irritated.

Her anger increased, though she tried to disguise it.

'You said you were coming over this evening,' she said, her teeth clenched.

'So? It's not over yet, is it? Tonight, I said, anyway.'

'What time?' she asked, her voice sounding unnatural to her.

'I don't know. An hour or so do?'

'Where are you, anyway?' She bit her lip.

She had not meant to ask.

'None of your business, my dear. But if it will mollify you, I am with my uncle, the dean. Came here after choir practice.'

She knew perfectly well that his uncle was the bloody dean. His saying so would increase the impression to anyone listening that she must be a mere acquaintance.

'You must have been there a while so there's nothing to delay you, then,' she said, her voice clipped.

'Not a very kind reflection on my dear uncle.' She heard him laugh softly. 'Actually, I have to pop into the clinic before I come on to your place.'

'Why?' she asked.

She heard his soft laugh again. 'Just a couple of things to finish up. Won't take long though. 'Bye.' The line went dead.

4

The only view of the cathedral from the basement was of the tall spires of the western towers. Jock Patterson stood on the first-floor landing absorbed by the greater view of the cathedral and the frost, white as a fall of snow, on the green. He would have been happy to stay where he was, gazing mindlessly, but there were things he had to do. Feeling calmer after the stormy emotions of the night before, he moved on, unlocking the doors of consulting-rooms and checking that all was as it should be. He hesitated when he came to Sebastian Kingsley's room: the door was slightly ajar. Using his right index finger he slowly pushed it wider and entered. The heavy curtains were closed and the room was in almost total darkness.

Jock moved slowly to draw the curtains aside, seeing his way by the light from the upper hall that came through the open door. He paused before turning to look at the room. Kingsley's desk was close by, turned at a right angle to the window, positioned so that he could see the best of the view. But it was an image he would never linger over again, though his sightless eyes stared in its direction. The right side of his head was pressed against the surface of his desk, blood pooled and congealed over its surface.

The caretaker moved stiffly around the desk to where he could see the back of Kingsley's head, the pulpy mess of blood, matter and splinters of bone. Jock knew there was no need to check if he was dead. He reached shakily for the phone and pressed 999.

*   *   *

The room had been cleared for the moment of technicians and photographers, leaving Detective Chief Inspector Christopher Simon and the pathologist Evelyn Starkey a moment's freedom to survey the scene. From where they stood, and apart from the blood on the surface of the desk, Kingsley might almost have fallen asleep there, his arms bent, his head resting partially on his right hand. But some of the surface contents of the desk appeared to have been swept by his elbows on to the floor, a file of papers had opened in its fall and some of the sheets had caught the spillage of blood that had seeped over the edge of the desk.

The murder weapon — there seemed no

doubt that that was what it was — had been flung down in the middle of the room, as if the killer had thrown it from him before leaving. It was a heavy stone African head, the features carved sharply and adding to its potency as a weapon, the dark blood scarcely showing on its black surface.

'The carved head belonged to Kingsley?' Evelyn Starkey asked. 'It was kept in this room?'

'Apparently,' Simon said. 'He kept it on his desk. Something he brought back from working in Africa.'

'Likely that it was a heat of the moment killing then,' Evelyn Starkey observed.

'Quite probably, I suppose. But if the killer knew the thing was here he or she could plan on using it. Easy enough to pick it up and handle it during the course of a conversation and then quickly get behind him and strike him hard.'

'Only one blow. But it's a very heavy object.' The pathologist moved over to the murder weapon and lifted it from beneath with a pen, managing to shift it only slightly. 'So, it's either someone who knew what was in the room, and knew he could be easily killed with what was to hand, or a spur of the moment killing — either by someone he knew or a stranger, perhaps someone surprised by

Kingsley's finding him in his room.'

'I don't think the latter scenario is likely,' Simon said quietly. 'There is no sign of a break-in anywhere. And it's hard to imagine why a common thief would imagine there was anything here likely to be of use to him.'

'He's got some nice pieces, though,' Evelyn Starkey said, looking around the room at the Middle-Eastern rug hangings and the fine Chinese vases on the mantelpiece.

The room was altogether more expensively furnished than Jonathan Hadden's, Simon thought. Hadden's had been functional and modern while Kingsley's room was more in keeping, in expense if not entirely in style, with the grandeur of the building and of the room. The floor was of polished wood overlaid with a very beautiful rug, the desk looked period Georgian, as did the chairs.

'Alternative medicine must be paying well,' Evelyn Starkey observed. Simon remembered some remark Jessie had once made about Kingsley.

'I believe there's money in the background anyway,' he said. He asked Evelyn Starkey the first important question: 'Can you give me a time of death?'

'Approximately ten hours I should say. Apparently the heating was left on all night, has been recently because of the cold weather.'

Beneath the window and in close proximity to Kingsley's body, there was a large old-fashioned tubular radiator. 'He would have been kept pretty warm,' Simon commented.

Starkey nodded. 'I have, of course, taken that into account,' she said with a slight smile. 'Unless there are factors we don't know of, the steady temperature makes it easier to be fairly confident about the likely time of death. To be on the safe side I'd suggest you look for alibis for between nine-thirty and eleven-thirty.'

Simon nodded, 'But he probably died closer to ten-thirty last night.'

'Around then. But you know this is not an exact science.'

'Can you make any judgement about the assailant from the position of the wound on his head? How tall they were for instance, or whether they were likely to be strongly built?'

Evelyn Starkey moved behind the body.

'It's something that may be clearer from the post mortem itself, but I'm not sure it will tell you anything reliable because it would depend on how Kingsley was holding his head at the time the blow descended. If he was leaning forward over the desk then the position of the blow near the top of the skull is not particularly indicative — the person could have been of average height or taller.' She shrugged. 'As for the amount of force used — that weapon has enough weight to carry its own momentum and do plenty of damage even if used by someone who isn't a heavyweight themselves.'

'Not much help there then,' Simon said, turning his attention to the items that had fallen from the desk. They seemed like nothing more than clinical notes. 'He has a flat at the top of the house. I wonder what he was doing in his consulting-room at that time.'

Evelyn Starkey returned to his side. 'Perhaps he was just catching up on some paperwork,' she said, bending to look more closely at some of the papers. 'I know from experience that medical records are best kept well up to date. Anyway, that, no doubt, will form some part of your investigation.' She straightened up. 'I'll be ready soon for the removal of the body if that's OK with you?'

Simon would be only too glad. He had seen all he wanted to see of Kingsley and his bludgeoned and bloody head. Scene of crime officers could continue with their work. The photographers had taken every conceivable picture of the body from every possible angle.

He could leave the room for the time being and attend to what was happening in the rest of the building.

'Post mortem?' he asked her.

'Tomorrow. I'll let you know when.'

'I'll look forward to it,' he said, his expression making it clear that he would not.

She gave him a sympathetic smile and waved him away.

The staff arriving at the clinic, bewildered at seeing a police officer on duty outside, had been ushered into the large room to the right of the front door, the room normally used for evening classes. Simon checked that everyone had arrived and entered the room to a buzz of speculation and questions. They had not yet been told the reason for their unusual reception at work this morning. He stood with his back to the window, taking a moment to scan their faces.

As Simon began to speak all eyes turned to him.

'I'm very sorry to have kept you waiting. Clients arriving for appointments will be turned away and told that they will be contacted to make future arrangements. Miss Fulton can telephone people expected later in the day to put them off.'

'Perhaps, Chief Inspector, you could explain to us exactly what is going on?'

Jonathan Hadden spoke quietly and there was a quiet buzz of agreement. It occurred to Simon that they were all behaving in a surprisingly muted way, given the circumstances.

'I was about to,' Simon said. 'Sebastian Kingsley was found dead in his consulting-room earlier this morning. He had been killed with a blow to the head.'

The faces showed a mixture of horror and blank incomprehension. Then there was a series of low-voiced exclamations. Simon could discern no sign of guilty knowledge in any of their expressions, some sitting apparently stunned and silent, others turning to someone nearby, generally with looks of dismay on their faces. No one ventured any questions immediately, then Jonathan Hadden spoke again.

'Do you know when he died, when he was attacked?'

It was more useful to be vague on the issue at this point.

'It was some time last night,' Simon answered. 'We shall know more for certain when the pathologist has completed her investigations.'

As the spectre of a post mortem examination sank in they all fell silent again, the reality of sudden death reinforced.

A tentative voice then spoke up, belonging to a woman with flowing ethnic clothes and a mass of long wavy hair.

'Was it a break-in. A burglary?'

'Why on earth would a burglar want to break in to a health clinic?' A striking blonde woman, very slender in a black designer suit turned to the speaker, her voice shaky.

'There is no sign of any unlawful entry,' Simon said.

All eyes turned to him again and regarded him solemnly. Frances Fulton expressed what was probably in all their minds.

'That means you think one of us did it?'

'It's far too early to express any opinion at this stage,' Simon said. 'But obviously we will need to speak to you all individually, along with anyone else acquainted with Sebastian Kingsley. If anyone does know anything they think may be helpful to our inquiries then I hope they will come forward sooner rather than later and say so.' He glanced around the room but their faces remained blank.

'What about the clinic?' Hadden asked. 'Are you going to close us down?' He looked very pale and tense, a small tick showing in his cheek as he clenched his teeth.

Simon supposed it must be a natural anxiety, given that their livelihoods depended on the clinic's remaining open. He wondered what might happen to the clinic and its employees with Sebastian Kingsley gone. He had understood from Jessie that it had been very much Kingsley's set-up, though Hadden had been with him from the start.

'It's Friday today,' Simon said. 'Do clients visit over the weekend?'

Various heads were shaken.

'We shall obviously need time to complete our examination of Mr Kingsley's room, and that may take more than the weekend. I'll discuss it with you later, Mr Hadden, if that would be appropriate?'

Hadden nodded and began examining his hands again.

'Meanwhile, for now,' Simon addressed them all again, 'we shall ask you to remain in this room until you are called to answer some questions. For the purposes of elimination, officers will be asking you all for an account of your movements last night. Tea and coffee can be brought in.'

'Shall I start telephoning people who are to due come for appointments today?' Frances Fulton asked, her face impassive.

'Please do,' Simon said.

'What do I say to them about alternative appointments?' she asked.

'Say that you will contact them as soon as possible. We hope we'll soon have a clearer idea of when the clinic can start functioning again.'

'They may not want to come, Franny, after this happening,' the woman in the colourful ethnic clothes said.

'Can't we wait in our own rooms?' The blonde woman spoke, her voice high.

'Later perhaps. Mr Hadden, it would be helpful if we could use your room in which to interview people.'

Hadden stood up. 'I'll come and clear my desk for you.'

A general low murmur of protest broke out, no doubt at the prospect of their temporary incarceration. Simon thanked them, not without a hint of irony, for their patience, and joined Hadden who was waiting for him at the door.

5

'Do you know what may happen with the clinic now that Mr Kingsley has died? I understood the building was leased by him through the offices of his uncle the dean,' Simon asked Hadden as they entered his room.

Hadden looked up blankly and passed a hand through his light wavy hair. He frowned.

'I just can't believe it, you know. I've known Sebastian for years. He was so very much alive, so much a presence.' His voice trailed off. He looked directly at Simon. 'I'm sorry, you asked me something.'

Simon repeated his question. Hadden sat down behind his desk.

'Sebastian included my name on the lease a while back. He was making his will at the time and he said that he might as well make sure he left everything tidy in case anything happened to him. So I suppose we are all secure enough in continuing our work here. That is, as Anne remarked just now, if anyone wants to come to a health clinic where there has been murder done.' He leaned forward and put his face in his hands. 'What a terrible thing,' he said, his voice muffled.

'Was he expecting anything to happen to him, then?' Simon asked, 'When he made the will.'

'What? No, not really. This was a couple of years ago. He'd had a minor car accident. He always drove a bit too fast and it could have been much more serious. He said it had reminded him that we are all mortal.' He pressed his hands over his eyes.

'What about the broader business side of the clinic?' Simon asked. 'Did Mr Kingsley sub-let rooms to therapists and were they self-employed or were they employed by the clinic?'

Hadden looked at him curiously.

'I'd have thought Jessie would have told you about the arrangements.'

Simon made no comment. In fact he did not concern himself with Jessie's income and the subject of the clinic in this respect had never been discussed.

'The clinic employs them,' Hadden said. 'Fees are paid to the clinic and they are paid a salary.' Hadden looked vaguely through the window looking over the green. 'Actually, it was a different arrangement for Jessie as she was only part-time.'

'So what happens to the business now?' Simon asked.

'It's mine,' Hadden said flatly. 'At least I suppose so, unless Sebastian recently changed his will.' His light-blue eyes rested on Simon again. 'You see we more or less started this together. I helped out with the cost of the lease and there were just the two of us right at the beginning. It was the logical thing for Sebastian to do, to leave the whole thing to me if anything should happen to him. Besides, we were close friends, had known each other since school.' His eyes momentarily filled with tears and he turned away, brushing at them with his hand.

Simon, uncomfortable, turned to more practical issues.

'I'll speak to you again later, of course, but would you mind giving me a list of everyone who works in the building, names, specialisms, how long they have been employed here, room numbers?'

Hadden silently pulled out a sheet and began writing. After a moment he looked up.

'I forgot to mention the occasional therapists, like the reflexologists and aromatherapists,' he said. 'But that side of the business is building only slowly and at the moment they are working on a consultancy basis with the use of their room and their appointments arranged through the clinic. None of them has worked here for long. And none of them is due in today.'

'Do they have their own key to the clinic?'

'No. Even their consulting-rooms are shared with each other at present. It's very much in its infancy, all that side of things.'

'So do you think any of them should be interviewed, or are they not really sufficiently part of the set-up yet?'

'Sufficiently so to wish to murder Sebastian, you mean?' Hadden looked coldly at Simon.

'I suppose that is exactly what I mean,' Simon said. 'We need to know who might have been involved sufficiently with Mr Kingsley to have lashed out at him in anger, as appears to have happened.'

'Then no. None of them really knows him as yet — knew him, I mean. Sebastian had had nothing to do with them much. Franny and I arrange that side of things between us.'

Hadden finished writing the list and passed it, written in a neat hand, across the desk.

'Do you have a spare set of keys for the front door and the rooms that you can let me have?' Simon asked.

In response Hadden stood up. 'We keep a set in Franny's desk. You can have those.' He left the room and returned quickly, handing the bunch of keys to Simon.

Simon dropped them into one of his capacious overcoat pockets.

'I have to ask you the inevitable question: do you have any idea who might have attacked Sebastian Kingsley? Do you know of anyone who might have had any kind of grudge against him, anyone he was in some kind of conflict with, Mr Hadden?'

Hadden said: 'I was going to suggest you call me Jonathan. It seems so coldly formal, knowing Jessie as I do, but I suppose formal is exactly what you have to be in the circumstances.'

Simon gave a slight smile of acknowledgement.

'Even after you have seen me at my most abject. I can't tell you how grateful I still am.'

Hadden gave a brief smile in response.

'No. I can't think straight at the moment. I can't think of anyone obvious who might attack him. Good God! How could I? If I'd thought anyone bore him that much of a grudge or whatever, I'd have looked out for him.' He went silent, his hands over his eyes again.

After a moment he removed them. 'Look, you'll find, as you question people that Sebastian wasn't any kind of ministering angel, however good he was at his job. He

76

could put people's backs up. He could be arrogant and overbearing and he didn't suffer fools. And he thought a lot of people were fools.' A slight smile twitched at his mouth. He shrugged. 'Anyway, I don't know all the details of Sebastian's life. We didn't live in each other's pockets or anything like that.'

'You'd know if he was in a relationship with anyone, though?'

'I think he was seeing Hannah Crossley,' Hadden said briefly and without hesitation. His eyes fell to his hands, linked on the surface of his desk.

'Who is Hannah Crossley?' Simon asked.

'Sorry.' Hadden indicated the list in Simon's hand. 'She's our psychotherapist, a full-time replacement for Jessie. I'm not sure if Jessie's actually met her.'

Simon glanced through the list. 'No one else, either at the clinic or elsewhere that you know him to have been involved with?'

Hadden shook his head.

'Are there any next of kin we should be contacting?' Simon asked.

'There's only his uncle, the dean of the cathedral. He lives on the other side of the green in Precinct Row.' Hadden looked towards the window. 'It's the tallest building in the row. I should let him know what's happened. He'll be devastated.'

Simon turned to the view and easily identified the dean's house, a large and imposing pre-Regency building with elaborate mouldings above the windows and a porticoed front door, standing out from more discreet Georgian buildings in the row.

'We'll send someone across to notify him. Uncle and nephew were close, then?'

'Pretty much so. They were the only family each of them had.'

'Thank you Mr Hadden,' Simon said turning back to him. 'I'll speak to you again later, after I've interviewed the others. I suppose that you are now in the position of head of the clinic and will expect to be a liaison between the police and your co-workers.'

'I suppose so.' Hadden's mouth twisted. 'So you'll let me know what decisions are being made so that I can keep them informed?'

'When the decisions are made,' Simon agreed. 'Perhaps you'd wait with the others for now.'

'How long is all this going to take?' Hadden asked.

'You can expect today to be fully disrupted. We're hoping to do an initial interview of everyone who works here. After that you can all go home and we'll contact you as and when we need to speak to any of you again. It may be that next week it will be only Mr Kingsley's room that will be off limits and you can all resume occupancy of the rest of the clinic.'

Hadden nodded and stood up.

'Oh, Mr Hadden,' Simon said with a belated afterthought. 'Do you know whether Mr Kingsley had any particular purpose in being in his consulting-room last night? After all, his flat is within the building. It's not likely he was seeing a client so late, is it?'

'I wouldn't have thought so,' Hadden said wearily. 'Maybe he was keeping his notes up to date. He was very particular about that.' He opened the door and went out without a backward glance.

Detective Sergeant Longman came into the room before the door had closed.

'I've been talking to Jock Patterson, the caretaker,' he said. 'He says he didn't hear anything unusual last night. He was with his family in the basement flat and they were watching television.'

'And everything was normal when he did his rounds last night.' Simon nodded. 'He said he finished at around eight thirty. Yes, I spoke to him when I arrived, as he was the one who discovered the body.'

'He did all the right things,' Longman said.

'Just rang 999 and left things as they were.'

Simon wandered over to the window and looked out. Brilliant sunshine was melting the overnight frost and beads of moisture hung like pearls on the shrubs in the foreground.

'He didn't ring Jonathan Hadden, did he? You'd have thought he might have done so, given his senior position at the clinic.'

Longman joined him. 'I think he was pretty shocked. Who wouldn't be? And his first thought was for his wife, because she's ill, perhaps. He went down to let her know straight away.'

'Understandable enough, I suppose,' Simon said. 'They've found no evidence of any break-in, but what about footprints? It was a hard enough frost to leave evidence of anyone coming and going last night.'

'There's no sign at the rear entrance to the building that anyone has been in or out. The thin layer of frost there is undisturbed. On the other hand the paved area at the back around the Patterson's flat shows footprints where they've been out in their utility area. So, if the killer didn't break in it seems most likely he or she came in through the front door.'

'And the front steps were well trodden by the time I arrived. Who got here first?'

'Sergeant Mann and PC Anderly. Patterson

was waiting and let them into the hall. They say there was again a thin layer of frost and no prints on the steps at the front.'

'So the killer could have brushed away any marks of his footprints and there was plenty of frost last night so that the frost could re-form. But the same could apply to the entrance at the back as well.'

'Wouldn't take half a minute to brush frost off,' Longman observed.

'It seems likely that the killer has a key and must be someone who works here.'

'Unless Kingsley let him or her in.'

Simon turned back to the room.

'Let's begin with the inmates, shall we?'

A loud altercation suddenly began in the hallway. The deep reverberating tones of a man could be distinguished in confrontation with one of the police officers guarding the front door. The door to the room suddenly burst open and a distinguished-looking man with grey hair and a dark clerical suit stood on a threshold, his face red with anger or exertion, or both. PC Broath hovered anxiously at his shoulder muttering:

'Sorry, sir, he pushed his way in.'

Simon guessed immediately who this must be.

'That's fine, Constable,' he said, waving him away.

'I am Alistair Kingsley, Dean of the Cathedral,' the man announced. 'I am Sebastian Kingsley's uncle. What is going on here, and where is my nephew? I looked out of my bedroom window after going up from breakfast and saw police officers milling around and police cars in the carpark.'

'Mr Kingsley, please take a seat.' Simon indicated one of the armchairs near the window.

Kingsley remained standing. 'Where is my nephew?' he repeated.

Simon was uncomfortably conscious that Dean Kingsley should have been notified of his nephew's death more swiftly. If they were as close to each other as Hadden had suggested the news was likely to be a considerable shock.

'Please, Dean Kingsley, take a seat,' he repeated, sitting down in the one opposite.

The man seemed suddenly to become properly aware that he might be about to receive news likely to affect him personally; his face paled markedly and he reached out a hand for the arm of the chair, lowering himself slowly, his eyes on Simon's face.

Simon briefly introduced himself and Detective Sergeant Longman.

'I apologize that we haven't contacted you sooner, Dean Kingsley. I was about to send

82

someone over to you.'

'Something's happened to Sebastian!' The dean put his hand to his mouth. They were very white, square hands with carefully manicured pink nails.

Simon gently described the discovery by the caretaker of Sebastian's body earlier that morning.

Dean Kingsley looked appalled, his hand going to his large pectoral cross.

'Did someone break in? Was it a robbery? Sebastian had some very nice things. But you say it was in his consulting room? But then he had some very nice expensive things there, too. But surely no one, no casual thief would be likely to know that . . . ' Dean Kingsley broke off suddenly, as if aware that he was gabbling.

'It is not looking like a break-in. There are no signs of unlawful entry.' Simon's voice was sympathetic, aware that the implications that a loved relative might have been killed by someone they knew was often harder to bear than the idea of a stranger doing the killing.

'I see.' The Dean's voice was heavy. 'And you say he was killed by a blow to the head?'

'A single strong blow. It might suggest that the murder of your nephew was unpremeditated, something that happened in the heat of the moment, when the murder weapon was snatched from his desk.'

'What was it?' the Dean whispered, the image obviously more vivid and unwelcome.

'It appears to have been the carved-stone African head.' Simon's instinctive caution when it came to opinions of any kind early in an investigation kicked in. 'But we have hardly begun our inquiries yet. We shall, of course keep you informed of any progress. And I shall be grateful if I may come and speak to you later in the day.'

'Yes, of course,' the dean said vaguely, running a finger absently around his clerical collar.

Simon thought he was probably in his early sixties, though his manner, and dignity of office, made him seem older. He was a handsome man; good looks must have run in the family, Sebastian Kingsley having been strikingly good-looking. But whereas the nephew's eyes had been a piercing blue, those of his uncle were a pale hazel, so that he lacked the former's intensity of expression.

'When did you last see your nephew, Dean?' Simon asked.

'Last night.' The dean gripped both hands tightly. 'We had choir practice and he came to my house with me afterwards for a whisky. We sat and talked for a while. I was very interested in his work, so glad it was all working out so well after he decided to leave his GP practice.'

This was news to Simon. 'I had no idea Mr Kingsley was formerly a GP,' he said.

He was regarded a little haughtily.

'Why would you?' Dean Kingsley said. 'He retrained in homoeopathy because of his dissatisfaction with the obsession the health service has for drugs as the preferred treatment for almost any ailment.'

Simon wondered if 'obsession' was perhaps too harsh a term, but he could sympathize with the sentiment.

'How did your nephew seem? Was he troubled by any problems with any particular person?'

'Not at all. At least, he seemed to me to be in good spirits.' Kingsley pursed his well-moulded lips, sucking in the corners as if suppressing emotion.

'What time did he leave you?' Simon asked quietly, anxious not to demand too much of the man.

'Around ten.' The dean swallowed, his Adam's apple moving convulsively above his clerical collar.

'Was he planning to see anyone else that night, do you know?'

The dean's pale eyes refocused on Simon.

'I'm not sure. He had a telephone call from

someone. I think it was a lady friend and he did say something about seeing her later.'

Kingsley's cell phone had been in his pocket. They would be tracing his calls, though last night's might well turn out to have been from Hannah Crossley. Simon debated asking the Dean a few more questions but decided that it would be kinder to allow the man a chance to recover a little in the privacy of his own home for a while first.

'Dean,' Simon said, getting to his feet, 'I shall speak to you later.'

'I hope you will.' The man straightened stiffly in his chair and clutched the arms. 'I hope you may have some news for me.'

'There will be a post mortem, of course,' Simon said. 'But we shall need an official identification. I understand that you are Mr Kingsley's nearest relative?'

The dean bowed his head.

'I am the only one left.'

Simon made arrangements for him to be taken to the mortuary to view the body and assured him he would call on him later.

Longman showed the dean out, a much-shrunken figure compared to the one he had cut when he had entered the room.

6

Simon watched from the window of Jonathan Hadden's room as the dean turned left along the narrow lane then followed its curve to the right and disappeared momentarily behind the evergreen tree. Detective Sergeant Longman was waiting, perched on Jonathan Hadden's desk.

'I think I'll interview them in their rooms after all,' Simon said. His experience was that people were more likely to talk freely in familiar surroundings. 'Find out who has given an alibi statement so far and ask Rhiannon to join me.'

Longman returned with DC Jones within a couple of minutes.

'Mrs Stillings and Mrs Maguire have given their statements and Mr Hadden asks if he can come back to his room if you won't be needing it.'

Simon agreed again and accompanied by Rhiannon went up the stairs to see Anne Stillings, the dietary therapist.

Her room was on the first floor at the back of the house overlooking the long grassy garden. It was a contrast to the clean lines of

Hadden's room, with more upholstery and cushions and with richly patterned curtains framing the window. It was also untidy.

Anne Stillings sat behind her desk, which she had placed at an angle to the window, giving her a view of the garden and the door. She stood up as Simon came in with DC Rhiannon Jones and clutched her hands.

'Would you like some coffee or something?' she asked, her face flushed.

'Thank you,' Simon said gently, 'but we'll have some a little later.'

She regarded him wide-eyed, hands holding on to the arms of her chair, obviously thrown by their alien presence in her room.

'Relax, Mrs Stillings,' Simon said, smiling. 'We're just here to ask a few questions of everyone — about the clinic and Mr Kingsley and who works here, to give us a general picture of things. Nothing too demanding.'

She gave an apologetic smile, lightening her slightly heavy features, and relaxed a little, letting her hands fall to her lap. She was attractive, Simon thought, even a little exotic in her flowing ethnic robes. She certainly added a little colour to the rather austere atmosphere of the clinic.

He glanced down at the papers that had been handed to him.

'I see that you were out with a friend last night.'

'My partner,' she corrected, nodding. 'Jenny Knowles. We went to see a couple of films at the Corn Exchange Arts Centre.'

'And you left at about a quarter to eleven and went straight home with your partner to where you live in Prior's Court?'

'That's right.' She turned her head to gaze out at the garden.

'And you didn't deviate to the clinic on your way home for any reason?'

She turned her eyes rather than her head, brown eyes that reminded Simon of the colour of milk chocolates.

'No, we didn't.'

'I'm not suggesting that you might have killed Mr Kingsley,' Simon said quietly. 'But if you had come this way you might have seen someone entering the clinic perhaps, or leaving it.'

'Either way,' she gave a slight smile, 'we didn't.'

'But isn't this a reasonable route to take on your way home? It's a short cut, isn't it, cutting through from the West Gate across Cathedral Green and under Martyr's Arch.'

'And a route I take every day on my way home from the clinic, Chief Inspector. For variety and excitement I like to follow the

89

West Gate further down and enter Prior's Court from there.' She smiled, lightening her features again.

'Which was what you did last night?'

'Which was what we did last night,' she confirmed. She pushed her abundant hair back from her face.

'What did you think of Sebastian Kingsley?' Simon asked.

She blinked rapidly. 'I can't say I liked him overmuch,' she said, pressing her otherwise shapely lips into a thin line.

'Why was that?'

'He was a control freak. He was manipulative, he liked to . . . ' she paused for a word, 'shake people up a bit, keep them on edge.'

'And did he do that to you, Mrs Stillings?'

'At times. I don't think he liked my image very much.' She lifted her arms and spread them, displaying her sartorial splendour. 'He was very image-conscious, was Sebastian. I think he was concerned that we didn't get labelled as some irresponsible fringe set-up, so he preferred us to dress very professionally. But I've had twenty years in a nurse's outfit and I'm off uniforms.'

'How long have you worked here, Mrs Stillings?'

'Three years. I started a new life after my divorce, and retrained.'

'And have you been happy here, despite Mr Kingsley's provocations?'

She smiled. 'I love my work.'

'The clinic appears to be a great success,' Simon said. 'Do people who work here get on well generally?' It was an open question, designed to allow her to comment on any difficulties she might have experienced, despite her stated satisfaction with her job. She hesitated.

'I suppose I may as well mention it. You're bound to hear about it in your investigation.'

'Yes?' Simon said encouragingly as she paused again.

'We've got a gremlin,' she said.

'I'm sorry?' Simon had a sudden vision of a malevolent goblin haunting the building.

'Things going wrong, you mean?' Rhiannon said at his side. 'Someone making trouble?'

'That's right. It began a few months ago, but it's got more unpleasant. Yesterday a client sat in her chair in Hannah Crossley's room and some acupuncture needles stuck in her.' She looked up at them. 'I've only just been told about that one. But other things have happened too.'

'Does anyone have any idea who might be doing these things?' Rhiannon asked.

'No, we don't. Though they do seem to

happen after there's been an evening class so it's possible it's someone from outside the clinic.'

'Or someone inside wanting it thought that it's someone from outside,' Simon murmured. Anne Stillings looked surprised.

'I suppose so,' she said slowly.

They would have to follow it up, Simon thought. If the so-called gremlin had a grudge against the clinic it might equally be against Sebastian Kingsley himself. But it was difficult to believe that any employee would wish to jeopardize their own career by putting the clinic and its reputation at risk.

'Tell me about the people who work here,' he said. 'I have yet to meet most of them and your views would be helpful.'

Anne Stilling sat back, pushing the palms of her hands against the edge of her desk. He had, partly under the benign influence of Jessie, become more aware of body language. It was not surprising that Anne Stillings should balk at having to report on her colleagues.

'Nothing to feel concerned about,' he said. 'Just tell me what you feel comfortable with.'

'Well, there's Jock Patterson,' she began. 'He lives in the basement flat with his wife Valerie, who has very bad arthritis. She's in a wheelchair most of the time now.' Her voice quickened. 'I did treat her for a while and she got very much better.' She sighed. 'But people find it so difficult sometimes to stick to a strict diet. So Valerie is back where she was. In fairness though, I think that all the stress over Kevin didn't help matters. Stress is poison where arthritis is concerned.'

'Kevin?' Simon queried.

'Their son. He ran off about a year ago when he was thirteen.'

'Do they know why Kevin ran away?' Rhiannon asked.

She shrugged. 'I don't think so. Jock doesn't seem to know why. They've been nearly out of their minds with worry, of course.'

'And what is Jock like? Is he good at his job, well liked here?'

A smile lightened her face. 'Oh everyone likes Jock. He's a lovely man. Very conscientious, very thorough in his work.' The smile faded. 'Of course, he's very worried about the gremlin, feels it reflects on him.'

'And other colleagues?' Simon asked.

She pulled a face. 'I hope you are not expecting me to dig the dirt on people, Chief Inspector.'

'Is there some, then?'

She flushed. 'Not that I'm aware of. Let me see, there's Ruth Maguire, our medical herbalist. Very pleasant, very good at her job.'

Simon remembered it was she whom he had met the day before in the company of Jonathan Hadden.

'How did she get on with Mr Kingsley?'

'Fine, as well as I know.' She closed her eyes briefly. 'Who else? Hannah Crossley, the psychotherapist.' She gave them both a conspiratorial smile. 'She's much more Sebastian's idea of the right image, as you'll see. In fact the two of them seemed to have something going between them. And I'll leave her to tell you about that, if you don't mind,' she said firmly.

Simon glanced at his list. 'Anil Patel?'

'Our lovely Anil,' she said. 'Nice boy, engaged to his Indian bride. Very professional in his work and well thought of.'

Thumbnail sketches didn't come much smaller, Simon thought, but didn't press her; he had asked her opinion of her colleagues more to gain an impression of her attitudes to them than in expectation of any meaningful psychological insight. 'Did he have any problems with Kingsley?'

She sighed. 'I'm not aware of anyone with a particular problem with Sebastian, apart from the fact that we all felt his arrogance from time to time.'

'Frances Fulton?' Anne Stillings gave a quick frown.

'I always think she's a bit of a dark horse, our Frances. Doesn't say a lot. I suppose it's understandable in a way because the rest of us, when we gather in the rest-room, talk about cases, share ideas, and she's doing a different job. She's perhaps a bit shy. Sebastian could be pretty hard on her at times. Terrible snob, Sebastian. Had an antediluvian attitude to the servant class and that was where he put Franny.'

'Was he equally patronizing to Jock Patterson?' Simon asked.

'To be honest,' she said, making Simon wonder if this was a Freudian slip of some sort, 'Sebastian was actually rather good to Jock and his wife. He had alterations done to make Val's life easier. Struck me as a bit out of character, I have to say.'

It certainly suggested that Kingsley was not as one-dimensional as first impressions seemed to indicate; unless, as with all manipulative people, some ulterior motive was lurking there.

'And what about Jonathan Hadden?' Simon asked.

'He's a very decent sort,' she said. 'Not like Sebastian, though they were old friends. Jonathan is a deeper person, more sensitive, tactful, kind. He pours oil on any troubled waters.'

As Simon himself had witnessed the day before.

She had relaxed back into her seat again, her eyes once more on the garden, the frost still white on the shaded southern side.

'So, apart from Mr Kingsley's unkindness to Frances Fulton, no one was in any kind of conflict with him?'

She looked at Simon doubtfully, obviously unwilling to expand on what she had already said.

'Let me put it another way. Do you know of anyone whom Sebastian might have angered enough to provoke his death?'

'I can certainly imagine that he might have angered almost anyone enough to provoke an attack on him. But I'm afraid I have no idea about anyone in particular. As I said, he put people's backs up, he was arrogant and sometimes offensive and he never let anyone forget he was boss, but I know of no more than the sort of frictions that occur in any workplace, particularly where someone like Sebastian is boss.' She folded her arms across her embroidered bodice, indicating a symbolic full stop.

'So the clinic will be a happier place without Mr Kingsley,' Simon commented with only a faint interrogative.

'I've no idea what happens now. I hope there will continue to be a clinic.'

'It has a very good reputation,' Rhiannon said, the Welsh lilt in her voice adding weight to her sincerity. 'I'm sure it will survive. People soon forget other things in the face of their own aches and pains.'

It was typical of Rhiannon to be so quick to sympathy and the gesture was appreciated by Anne Stillings who gave her a warm smile.

'I hope you're right,' she said. She turned to Simon. 'May I go home now? I've told you all I can and there's no point in keeping us hanging about here once you've spoken to us.'

'I'm happy enough for you to go home but I'd appreciate it if you would stay there for the rest of the day in case I have anything else I need to ask you,' Simon said.

'Thank you.' She stood up, a fine figure of a woman, as Longman might put it, tall, well-covered without being fat, and with that splendid mane of hair that Sebastian Kingsley had no doubt disapproved of.

She picked up her coat and bag and joined Simon and Rhiannon as they reached the door.

'When did Sebastian die?' she asked him. 'What time?'

'Is this curiosity, or do you have a reason for asking?'

'I'm just curious,' she said, arching her eyebrows.

'As I said earlier, we'll have to wait on the post mortem results,' Simon said firmly.

'I suppose,' she said slowly, 'you'd rather we didn't know so that we are not sure when our alibis should be focused on.'

'No flies on you, Mrs Stillings,' Rhiannon commented, holding the door open for them.

'But the murderer wouldn't need to know, or ask, would he?' Anne Stillings said closing the door behind them and locking it.

7

Ruth Maguire had chosen to forgo the barrier that her desk offered and sat instead in an easy-chair near the marble fireplace. As Simon and Rhiannon entered the room she calmly offered them coffee.

The room felt lighter and airier than Anne Stillings's, partly because it was at the front of the house, simply furnished and very tidy. Ruth Maguire quietly poured and handed their cups to them, then sat back and eyed them, very much in command.

'Well, what a shock,' she said wryly.

'Not a fate you would have predicted for Sebastian Kingsley, then, Mrs Maguire?' Simon asked, tasting his coffee and finding it good.

'Not a fate I'd predict for anyone, Chief Inspector, lest it came to pass.' She cast him a look of some amusement.

'But Mr Kingsley was apparently a man who was not averse to upsetting people, it seems.'

'True.' She nodded slowly, her sleek bob of hair sliding forward on her cheeks.

Simon referred to the alibi information he had so far.

'I see you were at home on your own last night, Mrs Maguire, and you received two phone calls during the evening, both conveniently late.'

'I take exception to the word 'convenient', Chief Inspector. Convenient or not, I had a call from my daughter at a quarter past ten and spoke to her for about twenty minutes. And I have no idea when it would have been 'convenient' for her to have telephoned me, if, by using that word you are referring to the time that Sebastian was killed, since I don't know when that occurred.' She had a smile on her face as she spoke, robbing her words of any hostility, but she had conveyed her determination to keep control of the situation she found herself in.

Simon, for a moment nonplussed, glanced down again at the paper in his hand.

'And the other call you received, Mrs Maguire?'

'From a colleague about some committee work I am involved in, as I told your officer. That was just after I finished speaking to my daughter.'

'James Flamborough?'

'That's right.'

'You've worked here for just over four years, Mrs Maguire?'

'Yes. As I said when I met you yesterday, I

know Jessie Thurrow, your partner. I imagine she will be helpful when it comes to inside information on those of us still working in the clinic.' Again the calm smile, with the sting behind it.

'If you think that, you apparently didn't know Jessie very well,' Simon said, duly stung. 'I think discretion is habitual to her.' Quickly he moved on. 'When did you last see Mr Kingsley?'

'Yesterday evening, just as I was leaving work. He came to my room to speak to me about something.'

'And that was?'

'He wanted to get rid of Anne Stillings.'

So much for her own reserve where colleagues were concerned, Simon thought.

'Did he say why?'

'He didn't think Anne's image was good for the clinic.'

'Mrs Stillings seems to have had that impression, but I can't understand why,' Rhiannon said.

It was evident that Ruth Maguire's choice of a well-cut grey suit would have been in keeping with Kingsley's taste for the professional image, perhaps why he had thought he would find in her a sympathetic ear when it came to Anne Stillings's perceived sartorial shortcomings.

But Ruth Maguire obviously agreed with Rhiannon.

'Ridiculous, isn't it?' she said, smiling appreciatively at her. 'Anne is very good indeed at her job, and a real asset to the clinic.'

'What did you say to Mr Kingsley when he approached you about Mrs Stillings?' Simon asked.

'I told him I didn't agree. I reminded him that appointments and expulsions from the clinic were supposed to be taken with the agreement of us all.'

'And what did he say to that?'

She shrugged. 'He said something about having to go to choir practice, I think.'

'And apart from that he didn't seem troubled by anything?'

She gave a brief spurt of laughter. 'I don't think Sebastian ever seemed *troubled* by anything. He was easily irritated, and I think that that was what it was with Anne. She didn't *conform* in quite the way he wished, that was all.'

'Was there anyone else whom he was in conflict with?'

She considered his words. 'Conflict would be too strong a word. He could be unkind to Franny, the receptionist. But that was his seigneurial way with underlings.'

'He was close to Mr Hadden, I understand?'

'They went back a long way, I believe, and set up the clinic more or less together.'

'Tell me about Mr Hadden.'

She raised her eyebrows at that, as if he had committed some social solecism.

'I hope you are not expecting us to implicate our colleagues in the matter of murder. That's a bit much to expect.'

'I'd just like to know what you know about him, think about him.'

She shrugged, as if humouring him.

'He's a decent man, much less flamboyant than Sebastian. Good at what he does, as you no doubt experienced?'

Simon nodded. 'Indeed.' He blessed the man for the unbelievable relief from pain that even now made him feel quite lightheaded. 'What about his personal life? Is he married?'

'I really think these questions are better put to the individuals concerned, but I suppose there's no harm in telling you the obvious. Jonathan was married but he divorced about a year after the clinic opened, shortly after I arrived here. I got the impression that his ex-wife is a bit of a bitch. She struck me as a narrow-minded, rather limited person on the few occasions I met her, mean-spirited, if you know the type. They have a son whom

Jonathan absolutely dotes on and is the centre of his universe.'

'They live nearby? Haven't moved away?' Simon finished his coffee, which had been excellent, and placed his cup and saucer on the tray.

'Perish the thought! No, so far she hasn't visited that particular torture on him. I believe she has a new boyfriend who is a policeman,' She gave a quick smile. 'So that may keep her here a while longer, unless the traffic cop moves on, that is. She lives in what was the marital home in Madderley, a village just over the river. Jonathan has bought himself a nice bachelor pad in the West Gate, handy for work and for his son.'

'Do you know of any friction, serious friction, between Mr Kingsley and anyone else?'

'Enough for someone to want to hit him over the head, you mean? No, I can't say I do. He got people's backs up, for sure, but I don't know of anything that might have provoked the kind of murderous rage that might have ended his life.'

Her indifference to Kingsley's death was on a par with Anne Stillings's, Simon thought, though it was possible that it was this woman's studied self-control that conveyed that impression in her own case.

'I understand you have been having trouble in the clinic, some unpleasant things happening. Do you have any idea who might be behind it?'

'The clinic gremlin, you mean? No, I've no idea. We've assumed it might be someone attending evening classes, but that may be what we are intended to assume. Sebastian was going to raise the issue at the next meeting.'

'Have there been any other problems in the clinic? Has anyone caused trouble before?'

She visibly cast her mind back, raising her eyes to the moulded ceiling-rose above them. Light dawned in her eyes and she gave that curious half smile.

'Yes, there was some trouble a bit back. It was the husband of a woman who was treated here. She mainly saw Sebastian, though he drew others into her treatment.' Her smile faded and she looked less comfortable. 'The woman had cancer and didn't want orthodox medical treatments like chemotherapy and radiology. She'd insisted that she had seen enough of them to know that that was not the way she wanted to go.'

'And she died as a result?' Simon could understand that a spouse might be angry in the circumstances. Ruth Maguire gave a slight shrug.

'It's impossible to know that. She might have died anyway. The cancer was quite advanced before she did anything about it. Her husband was a GP, so perhaps that was part of the issue, like builders' houses always being the ones that most need attention.'

Simon thought he understood what she meant. Perhaps the husband's anger was mixed with guilt that he had not noticed that his wife was becoming ill, being too busy with other people with medical problems.

'In what way did the husband cause trouble?'

'He got in the door by pretending he was a patient, having made an appointment to see Sebastian using a fake name. He chose what was a busy time of day and as soon as he was through the door proceeded to denounce the clinic and all its works to the waiting patients.' She sighed. 'He made such a noise that we were all out of our rooms wondering what on earth was going on.'

'What happened then?' Simon could picture the scene and the likely reaction of Kingsley.

Her half-smile was back. 'Sebastian made the mistake of coming down the stairs and remonstrating with the man, arguing with him about the issues involved. The worst thing he could have done, of course.' She shook her head, and tucked her hair behind her ears. 'The man took a swing at Sebastian and caught him on the chin. It was all very unpleasant. Fortunately, when Sebastian saw what was happening he'd had the sense to ring for Jock to come up and help with the situation and he soon sorted things out and saw the man through the door.'

'When was this exactly?'

'I couldn't give you the date, but it was in the spring sometime, before Franny came, anyway, because I remember the receptionist we had then getting in a bit of a state.'

'Did this doctor cause any further trouble?' Simon asked. It was possible the man had come back again and made his attack on Kingsley more lethal, but the gap of almost nine months since his initial assault seemed a longish time to wait.

'He wrote angry letters, threatened us with legal action and so on, but there was nothing he could do. His wife was in her right mind and made an informed choice about how she wanted to be treated. I don't think we've heard from him for quite some time.'

'It's not likely he's behind the sabotage the so-called gremlin is carrying out?' Simon suggested.

'You tell me!' She raised her eyebrows. 'But I wouldn't have thought it was his style. He was confrontational.'

'But it seems that the activities of this gremlin have advanced a little in seriousness,' Simon said. 'Leaving needles in a chair to injure a patient seems a bit more aggressive in intent.'

'I suppose so.'

'Do you have a name for this unhappy doctor?' Simon asked Ruth Maguire as she made a fresh pot of coffee.

'Sebastian will have it,' she said unthinkingly. 'Ah,' she said, turning back to them, her face flushed, 'he won't be able to help you there, will he? It will be on his files though. Jonathan will be able to tell you, I'm sure.'

She returned with the tray, this time with biscuits added, and sat down again.

Simon asked her a few more questions of a general nature, such as he had already asked Anne Stillings, and learned nothing more.

'What do you know of Sebastian Kingsley's private life?' he asked in conclusion.

Ruth Maguire curled her rather narrow lips in obvious distaste.

'What an unpleasant job you have, Chief Inspector! I suppose we can all expect this kind of prurient interest in our lives before, or if, you catch whoever killed Sebastian?'

She had touched one of Simon's sensitive nerves. He was vulnerable to such accusation, having an unhappy reserve when it came to some aspects of his work. He annoyed himself by responding defensively.

'I assure you, Mrs Maguire, that I take no pleasure in intruding into people's lives in such a way. But can you suggest an alternative route? People's personal relationships often have a strong bearing where murder is concerned, and it would be irresponsible of me not to take into account what was going on in Sebastian Kingsley's life.'

'I'm sorry,' she said, surprising him. 'That was a cheap shot. Of course you have to delve into Sebastian's life. But there's not much I can tell you, not much that I know.'

'Sebastian was seeing Hannah Crossley I believe. But he seemed to spend a lot of time in London, so I assume he had friends there.' She shifted in her seat, smoothing down her narrow skirt. 'Sorry, that's all I know. He was a private person who did, however, like to know as much as he could about what was going on in other peoples' lives. He had a salacious streak, I'd say.'

And that could have sown the seeds of trouble, Simon thought.

8

Longman was hovering outside the door as they left Ruth Maguire's room. 'Detective Superintendent Munro wants to see you,' he said, giving her her full title, as people tended to do.

'Has the dean done the formal identification?' Simon asked.

Longman nodded. 'He's back at the deanery when you're ready.'

Which meant an even longer wait for the people at the clinic, if this was the veiled summons from Munro that Simon assumed it was.

'Have they completed the preliminary statements?' Simon asked.

'Yes. And they're getting restless.'

Simon looked at his watch. 'They may as well all go home now. But impress on them to stay in their homes because I want to speak to as many of them as possible before the day's end.'

Longman turned away.

'Anything yet on the first house-to-house calls?' Simon asked after him.

'I'd have told you if there had been,'

Longman said. 'There's not much to call on in the usual sense, anyway. The building further along the lane is a church or cathedral office of some sort. Beyond that you probably know it leads into the grounds of the cathedral school. The buildings facing the carpark are also offices of one kind or another and apparently no one was working that late last night. Which leaves only the Precinct Row, which the dean lives in and the few houses that join it. There are no security cameras installed around here, so no hopes in that direction. So far nobody in the houses saw or heard anything.'

'And nothing leaps out from the statements that have been taken from the staff?'

Longman rolled his eyes beneath bushy brows.

'Nobody confessing to have been at the scene. All spending blameless evenings, as we might expect.'

They walked down the sweeping staircase to the ground floor, Simon doing a mental survey of his sartorial shortcomings in prospect of an interview with Detective Superintendent Munro, who took an unfortunate interest in them.

In fact, the sartorially impeccable Detective Superintendent Munro for once showed not the slightest interest in Simon's perennially dishevelled appearance. He realized, admiring the way the soft yellow of her suit made her dark skin glow, that in truth he probably took as much interest in her appearance as she did in his, if for different reasons.

'Any likelihood that the killer of Sebastian Kingsley is going to be arrested quickly?' she asked.

'No sign of it so far. No one who worked with him so far appears to have any idea of a real motive, and no one seems to know anything useful.'

'What do you mean, 'real motive'?' she asked.

She never missed the slightest nuance, Simon thought.

'I mean, beyond the fact that he was the type to put people's backs up, no one seems to have any idea why he was killed.'

'So you think we might be in for a long haul?'

'I've no way of knowing. I haven't spoken personally to them all yet. Who knows what might turn up? But he kept his private life private and that could take time unravelling.'

'The bishop has been on to the CC,' she said, unsurprisingly. 'He's anxious that this is kept as low profile as possible. Doesn't want the cathedral and its environs tainted with scandal of any sort.'

'It is rather vulgar to go and get yourself murdered I suppose,' Simon observed acidly. 'Too much to expect a little Christian compassion as the first reaction, I suppose?'

'Yes, well, I take your point,' Munro said, sliding into her seat behind her desk. Simon wondered if this was body language hinting that she might now start directing the case. He should not have doubted her. 'I understand your reaction, Chris. None of us responds too happily to string-pulling and influence from on high. I trust you to carry on the investigation with your usual integrity and efficiency. I'm just warning you to keep a close watch on junior officers and their relationship with the media.

'The bishop is ordering the cathedral precinct gates and all other entrances to the area to be locked for the duration.'

Simon suppressed a smile. It sounded positively mediaeval.

'I know,' she said, acknowledging his amusement. 'But it could be helpful to you. It will keep the media out of your hair.'

Simon could picture them hanging on to the huge barred gates in the cathedral approach, more than ever like animals at a zoo. 'It's going to be inconvenient for my officers. I know it's only a short distance but it means walking to HQ to pick up their cars

113

every time they have to go anywhere.'

'He's arranging for a cathedral attendant to man the gates and let appropriate people in and out.'

Simon shrugged. 'What about the exit into the precinct from Candlemaker Lane?'

'That has an old barred gate, too, apparently, and it's kept in working order. Have you ever noticed it?'

Simon admitted he hadn't.

'Neither have I. However it will add to security. And Martyr's Arch is likewise gated. Other means of access are at the discretion of the headmaster of the cathedral school and he's drawing up the portcullis as well.'

So apart from getting through the madding crowd that was likely to congregate at the approach gates, there should be none of the usual frustrations with onlookers.

'Is the bishop closing the cathedral for the duration, then? Surely not.'

She shook her neat head. 'No. Individuals on foot or in wheelchairs and authorized coach parties can still gain admittance.'

'So the gatekeepers will have to learn to discriminate between those who come to worship and those who come to ogle.'

'If they can. It's a bad time of year for them to have all this on their hands with Christmas approaching.' She stood up. 'I shouldn't keep you. I understand the dean is expecting a visit from you.'

'I hope he's not expecting me to produce the murderer for him immediately, perhaps dragging him along by the scruff of his neck to be burned at the Martyr's Monument.'

'He's upset, Chris,' Munro said. 'This was the only relative he had. It's understandable that he wants to know what's going on and see that things are done right.'

Simon felt duly admonished but said; 'All the same I get a bit edgy when people use their influence to get preferential treatment, over and above what our 'ordinary' citizens can expect. Most people can't pull up the drawbridge to protect them from the mad media and demand the attendance of the investigating officer when it suits them.'

'But you can be sure they would if they could,' she said, smiling. 'Wouldn't you?'

He had to admit that he would.

'I'll take on the press conferences as usual. Keep me thoroughly up to date on this one, Chris,' she said warningly. 'I don't want to be caught on the hop when I'm asked for information on developments in the case.'

'Let's hope there'll be some,' he said, closing the door behind him.

* * *

It was good to have the chance to be on foot for a change. Simon crossed the pedestrianized West Gate and entered Cathedral Approach. The media had already begun to gather but he slipped around them and through the side gate, showing his identification to the attendant before any of the crowd realized who he was. In the short time that Simon had been with Munro, the bishop had carried out his plan to have the gates locked and Simon was delighted with the effect: the Cathedral Precinct's peaceful ambience had been maintained.

He turned left, passing the few grand houses that formed a right angle with Precinct Row and paused at the gate of the Deanery. He tapped the knocker and the door was opened swiftly by a middle-aged woman in a grey dress, a colourful scarf pinned around her neck, relieving its drabness.

She waited while he showed his identification, then moved back and let him in, closing the door behind him. Only then did she speak.

'I'm Mrs Chambers, the dean's housekeeper. The dean is waiting for you in his study.' She showed him along a stone-flagged passageway to a door on the left, her figure upright and stiff, and tapped lightly.

'Detective Chief Inspector Simon is here to see you, Dean,' she said softly.

Simon heard only a grunt but she apparently interpreted it correctly and opened the door to admit Simon.

The dean was sitting in a leather buttonback chair by the window overlooking an attractive small garden with a birdbath at its centre and a flock of birds feeding from a variety of containers. He was puffing on a cigar, the room filled with smoke which lifted and divided into thin trails as Simon crossed the room to take the chair indicated to him. Dean Kingsley opened a box on a small table beside him and offered Simon one of the long slim cigars that lay there.

Simon was tempted but, having given up in the not so distant past, shook his head.

'We like to encourage others to join us in our sins because we hope we shall not be so lonely when we get to hell,' the dean remarked.

'Perhaps it's because we are lonely because we are already in hell,' Simon said quietly. 'I've often thought that life here below offered a good enough experience of hell at times.'

'And now is one of those times.' Kingsley nodded. His hand was unsteady as he put the cigar to his lips again, and Simon could smell whisky fumes.

'I don't know if I said how sorry I am for your loss,' Simon said. 'You were obviously very close to Sebastian.'

'His face was unmarked at least,' the dean mused, examining the glowing end of his cigar. He looked across at Simon. 'He looked curiously at peace. That was a comfort.'

'He probably had no awareness of what happened,' Simon said gently. 'The blow was in all likelihood unexpected and quick.'

'Not a bad way to go, when you think about it, then.' The dean was decidedly morose. As if suddenly conscious of his behaviour he cleared his throat and sat up straighter in his chair. 'Actually, sudden death is not the best way to go. Ideally one should have the opportunity to prepare to face one's God.'

Simon felt unable to comment and watched the birds through the window.

The dean crunched out his cigar in the ashtray, got up and placed it on his desk against the opposite wall. Simon looked around the room for the first time. It was gloomy at this part of the day, facing north-west, and the colours were mostly brown, dark leather and oak with a dark patterned carpet. The fireplace had a dismal smouldering fire which gave a belch of smoke, making the already acrid air more pungent. The pictures on the wall were of religious subjects, an agonized face of Christ looked down above the desk, and views of the Highlands, with a stag or two and cattle drinking from a loch. A photograph appeared, through the fog, to be of the cathedral choir. He got up to examine it while the dean poured himself a whisky. He joined Simon, pointing to a figure near the back dressed in red-and-white chorister robes, standing immediately behind the two rows of choir-boys.

'That's Sebastian. Beautiful voice he had; taken a couple of years ago.'

Simon could see that it was he, his face expressionless, his hand on the shoulder of the boy in front of him. At the other end of the line stood the Dean in flowing robes.

'Do you perhaps have a photograph of your nephew that we could use in our investigation?' Simon asked.

The dean reached to the shelf above his desk and pulled down a photograph album, opening it near the back.

'Here's a good one I took of him when we went to Snowdonia for a weekend last summer.' He detached the picture and handed it to Simon.

It looked as if it had been taken outside a pub, Sebastian Kingsley looking windblown and tanned, and was a close enough shot to be useful. Simon thanked him and placed the photograph in a plastic envelope in his inside pocket.

'He was a keen choir member,' Kingsley said, returning to his seat, glass in hand.

A tap on the door brought the housekeeper laden with coffee and a rich-looking cake.

'Now, eat a piece of this nice cake, please do, Dean,' she said leaning over him. 'You know you must eat.'

'I did have breakfast this morning,' he said feebly. 'Just as well, before I found out what had happened.'

'Well, you'll need to keep up your strength,' she asserted. She set down the tray and poured coffee then left with a final admonitory look at the dean.

'I should appreciate it if you would keep me informed of anything you discover in relation to my nephew's murder,' the dean said after a moment.

Simon wondered if he was expecting him to supply a blow by blow account of all the people he interviewed; until he had discovered for certain who had killed Sebastian Kingsley, he would probably have mainly negative reports to make. Though inquiries might give rise to more questions for the dean himself.

'Do you have any idea, sir, who might have attacked your nephew? Did Sebastian mention any problems with anyone, any falling out?'

'If I knew of anything I would already have mentioned it,' the man said a little testily.

'You are quite sure that he never spoke of any confrontations with anyone?' Perhaps he hadn't, Simon thought. Perhaps it had not been in the nature of the relationship for Kingsley to confide in his uncle.

The dean lowered his brows. They were black eyebrows, in contrast to the grey of his hair — dishevelled now, as if he had been running his hands through it. 'I can't think of anything. But I will try to recall and I will let you know, of course.'

'He never mentioned, for instance, the man whose wife was a former patient who died of cancer?'

Dean Kingsley nodded. 'That was some time ago, though, back last spring, I think. Sebastian was full of righteous indignation about it, but I could see why the poor man was so distressed. I might have felt the same myself in the circumstances.'

Simon ventured: 'You're not married yourself?'

'I was. My wife died, also of cancer, six years ago. It was one of the reasons I was glad to have Sebastian set up his clinic so close by. The loneliness that comes from loss is not diminished by our faith in God.'

Simon could only begin to imagine the gaping hole in his own life if any such thing should happen to Jessie.

'I'm very sorry,' he said inadequately.

The dean turned his pale eyes on him and nodded acknowledgement.

'You are thinking that this man, he was a doctor himself I believe, may have given such vent to his anger with Sebastian after all this time?'

'It's a line of enquiry we shall have to follow up. I just wondered whether Sebastian had mentioned any encounter with this man since last spring.'

'He never said so.'

'When I asked you about Sebastian and whether he was in a relationship, you referred to a call he had last night on his cell phone. We understand he was seeing someone who works at the clinic as a psychotherapist, Miss Hannah Crossley. But had Sebastian been married or in a previous long term relationship?'

'I'm afraid I got the impression that Sebastian rather played the field,' the dean said hesitantly. 'But he was only thirty-eight and had plenty of time in which to settle down and have a family.' He swallowed, his pale eyes watering.

'He spent a lot of his leisure time in London I understand. Do you know whom he went to see, what he did there?'

'Not in any detail. He used to mention concerts. He loved music. That was why he was in the choir. Choral, church music, he loved best of all. But opera too.'

Simon was curious at the superficial knowledge this man had of the nephew he was supposedly so close to. He decided it would do no harm to express it.

'Despite your closeness to Sebastian,' he said gently, 'you seem to have learned very little from him about his private life.'

Kingsley took a mouthful of coffee followed by some whisky, his hand shaking a little.

'His private life was exactly that. He wasn't one to confide in others generally.' His expression altered, as if he had just recognized something new. 'Yet he loved a good gossip about others now and again. But mostly he and I talked about the choir, cathedral business, the clinic, and enjoyed a good whisky together.'

'He set up the clinic to some extent with

your help I understand, you helping him to obtain the lease on the building. I imagine it took a fair amount of money though to fit it all out. Did your nephew have independent means?'

'He had quite a lot of money left to him by his parents, yes. But Jonathan was involved as well in the refurbishment. He has a monied background too.'

They finished their coffee in silence, the cake ignored.

Simon made movements for departure.

'Do let me know if anything occurs to you, Dean, which might be of help. Meanwhile I'm sure you would be best pleased if I were attending to the matter of whoever killed your nephew.'

The dean gave a faint smile. 'I take the point, Detective Chief Inspector Simon. And I appreciate you calling to see me so soon.'

Simon let himself out of the house, his initial impressions of Dean Kingsley somewhat softened. He had found only an ageing lonely man caught in what seemed genuine grief and bewilderment.

The sun dazzled his eyes after the gloom of the study and the cathedral loomed over him, its vastness completely out of scale with the precinct houses, large by any other standards, and having the effect of comfortingly diminishing mere human concerns. It seemed, by its sheer size and venerability, to point out that everything would be the same in another hundred years, that the hopes and fears of today would be replaced by others of seemingly as great, but ultimately unimportant, proportions.

9

Simon and Longman took the lift to Hannah Crossley's fourth-floor apartment in the dockside development. She kept them waiting a few moments before she opened her door and gestured unsmilingly for them to enter.

Her make-up was immaculate and she had changed from the formal black suit she had been wearing earlier into a long brown skirt and beige cashmere sweater. She had let down her hair and it hung straight and blond to her shoulders. All this should have softened the businesslike exterior she had presented earlier, but somehow it failed to, perhaps because of her expression and the sharpness of her features. Her eyebrows, carefully plucked, arched above deep-set dark eyes from the bridge of her slightly curved nose, giving her the look of a bird of prey. She was certainly a striking-looking woman, Simon thought, but not someone he could readily warm to.

She gestured, again without speaking, to one of the two black-leather sofas facing each other in the centre of the large living-room.

'Coffee? Tea?' she asked.

Longman accepted and they both lowered themselves on to an unyielding black sofa. The room was as uncommunicative as its owner, Simon thought, with not a personal item on display, not a thing out of place, minimalist in the extreme.

Hannah Crossley returned with Longman's coffee and handed it to him without ceremony. Simon suspected she had confined him to the instant variety. He retrieved the crushed notes of the preliminary interviews from an inside pocket of his overcoat.

'Do you have any idea who might have killed Sebastian Kingsley, Miss Crossley?' he asked.

She had sat down, facing them from the other black sofa, leaning back, her legs crossed, a shapely thigh revealing itself under the tight fabric of her skirt.

'None at all,' she said.

'You were in a relationship with Mr Kingsley, which was why you telephoned him last night when he was with his uncle?'

'Yes.' She folded her arms.

'What was your reason for calling him?'

'I was expecting him to visit me last night and when he didn't turn up I rang him to ask why he hadn't arrived.'

'And what did he say?'

'That he would be over in a little while. He said he had to call in at the clinic first.' She made a gesture of impatience. 'Look, I've already said all this to one of your officers this morning.'

'Yes, I apologize for boring you, Miss Crossley, but I like to hear things from the horse's mouth as it were.'

Her bird of prey expression intensified.

'Did he say why he was going to the clinic? This is an important point, as you no doubt understand.'

'Sebastian was never in the habit of explaining himself, Chief Inspector. No, he did not explain why.'

The dockside development was not much of a walk from the cathedral precinct and would take only about ten minutes. 'What did you do when he didn't turn up as expected?'

'As I told your officer earlier, I eventually went to bed.' Her manner was bored rather than defensive.

'You didn't go over to the clinic, to his flat and try to find him?'

'I think I said I stayed in,' she pointed out, a little more sharply.

'How long have you been involved with Mr Kingsley?' Simon asked.

Longman put down his coffee-mug and rather belatedly opened his notebook.

Hannah Crossley cast him a scornful look.

'About a year now, I suppose.' Soon after she had begun work at the clinic then.

'Did he usually come here to your apartment or did you meet in his flat above the clinic?' Simon asked. He had visited Kingsley's flat earlier, where officers were searching for any evidence of the man's private life. It had had the same cold clinical feel as this one, minimalist and all hard lines.

'I've never been into Sebastian's flat,' she said after an uncomfortable pause.

'Why was that?' Simon asked, surprised.

She shrugged, with an edge of embarassment.

'He used to say that it was his little escape from the world. He liked his privacy.'

'Did he ever mention anyone he was in any kind of dispute with?'

She gave a low laugh. 'I think Sebastian was always in dispute with someone or other. It was his way. He was a bit confrontational.'

'Was this at the clinic, with other colleagues?'

'Yes, he liked to keep us all on our toes.'

'Tell me about your colleagues, Miss Crossley.'

'What do you want me to tell you?' she asked, wide-eyed.

'Can you think of any particular clash of

temperaments?' Simon suggested, struggling a little in the face of this woman's derisive manner.

'He didn't like Anne Stillings,' she said.

'Yes, I understand that he considered her image not right for the clinic.'

'He sometimes got his priorities all wrong. Anne Stillings is popular and brings a lot of business to the clinic.'

'Anyone else Mr Kingsley might have threatened in some way?' he asked.

'He was having a row with Ruth Maguire yesterday evening as I was leaving,' she said.

'Perhaps because they disagreed about his plans to dismiss Mrs Stillings,' Simon suggested, remembering Ruth's account of the conversation.

'Perhaps. But the discussion seemed a little heated if that was the topic,' she said. 'Ruth was shouting at him.'

It seemed there may have been more to the discussion than Mrs Maguire had admitted. He would have to ask her about it.

'There have been some unpleasant incidents at the clinic, the latest one involving acupuncture needles in the client's chair in your room, I understand. Do you have, or do you know if Mr Kingsley had, any idea who was behind what's been happening?'

'Not really. We hadn't got any further than

wondering if someone from one of the evening classes was doing it. Seb was pretty angry about it, especially after the needle incident in my room, because for the first time the gremlin caused actual harm to a client. He was planning a staff meeting to discuss better security and so on.'

'Anil Patel has been involved twice I understand, his needles scattered on one occasion, prior to them being found in your room.'

'I don't think that he was being targeted particularly,' she said. 'It's bad for all of us that these things have been happening, because it's bad for the clinic.'

She shifted in her seat, recrossing her legs and gave a short laugh. 'The only person at odds with Anil that I know of was Sebastian, and that was more the other way around really.'

'Oh?'

She looked away from him, towards the black uncurtained windows.

'It was nothing really, just Anil being oversensitive, his honour impugned I think he imagined.'

'Perhaps you would tell me about it all the same.'

'It was nothing,' she repeated. 'We had an open day a little while back and Anil brought his fiancée Salena. She's a sweet little thing and she looked exotic in her beautiful sari, and Sebastian, as was his way, made what might be called a pass at her. He had his arm around her shoulder anyway when Anil spotted him and asked him to step outside. Sebastian managed to laugh it off but Salena, being an innocent, was a bit upset, and so, most certainly, was Anil. He and Sebastian had hardly spoken since.' She gave a tolerant smile suggesting that boys will be boys. Had she not minded herself that her boyfriend was flirting with another woman?

'What do you mean when you say 'Sebastian, as was his way'?' Simon asked. He realized that for all her cool controlled manner Hannah Crossley had probably been vulnerable in her relationship with Sebastian Kingsley, that she had obviously not known where she stood with him. He wondered if, impatient with his treatment of her, and suspicious of him, she had gone over to the clinic last night to find out whom he might be with.

'Had Mr Kingsley upset anyone else in this way, that you know of?' Simon asked.

'At the clinic, Jonathan is the only other male apart from Anil and I gather his ex-wife wasn't too keen on Sebastian. She's a bit of a bitch, I gather, not that I've ever had the misfortune to meet her.'

She shifted impatiently again. 'Look, Chief Inspector, you'll find that Sebastian was not a very nice man, that he was arrogant and abrasive and inclined to boss people around. For all that, I was unfortunately in love with him.' She lifted her chin defiantly and her predatory eyebrows tightened over the bridge of her nose.

Was she adding that caveat in an effort to persuade him that she had loved Sebastian too much to kill him? But a fatal blow to the head was, after all, a common form of attack in a crime of passion.

'He wasn't all bad and entirely self-centred, though, was he?' he suggested, remembering what he had been told. 'I understand he looked after Jock and his wife rather well.'

She gave a tight smile.

'That's a charitable interpretation I'm afraid. Sebastian had some work done because he was planning to increase disabled access to the clinic. It meant they could enter it without having to spoil the steps at the front of the building. And any effort Valerie could put in with the raised flower beds to make the rear entrance more pleasing was fine by Sebastian.'

In love with him or not, Hannah Crossley certainly had no illusions about her lover.

'He upset Ruth Maguire as well,' she said. 'Over her daughter Cass. I don't know much about it, only a few hints from others, but he was probably just doing his usual charm offensive.'

Miss Crossley seemed to be finding this interview vaguely cathartic, Simon thought, in dishing the dirt on her dead lover, her dead disappointing lover. Or she could be deliberately feeding them with as many possible motives for his murder as she could in order to divert attention from herself. Alternatively she might merely be dealing with her grief, reminding herself that the man she had lost was not such a great loss.

It was with this consciousness that he asked her only a few more questions. She had nothing to add about the angry husband who had created a scene at the clinic and she seemed to know nothing more of interest about anyone else connected to the case. He and Longman stood up to leave.

'When do you think we shall be able to resume work at the clinic?' she asked them at the door.

'We'll inform you as soon as we know,' Simon said non-commitally. Since they were not using the clinic for an incident room and Sebastian Kingsley's room and flat could continue to be investigated without disruption to the clinic, he might allow them to re-open as early as Monday.

'Not much love, joy and peace lost between them all, it seems,' Longman commented as the sibilant lift carried them to the ground floor. He sounded aggrieved.

Simon was aware that Longman, with his leanings to the esoteric and his belief in holistic therapies was feeling bewildered and disappointed by what they had learned so far of the reputable clinic. He had to admit to a certain disillusionment himself, partly perhaps because Jessie's former employment there had added a certain lustre to it in his eyes.

'You know how it is,' he said lightly. 'Human nature wherever you go.'

Longman grunted his agreement as they stepped out of the lift into the glamorous lighting of the dockside. It was another clear and frosty night with stars winking in the black waters and a few ragged clouds carried along by an icy wind. They both turned up their coat-collars and made their way out of the dockside area towards the West Gate.

'Bitter sort of woman, wasn't she.' Longman said. 'Didn't seem to have any inhibitions about being judgemental,' he added, echoing Simon's own assessment, 'She's not the sort of person I'd want to pour out my troubles to. Do you think she might have killed Kingsley in a fit of jealousy?'

'She's got no alibi,' Simon said, 'but she seemed used to Kingsley's flirtations with other women, seemed to regard it with a degree of tolerance as just part of his character.'

'Maybe she just wanted us to think that. She might have gone over to the clinic last night and found him with another woman.'

'There seems to be a number of people with possible motives,' Simon said mildly. 'The angry grieving husband could be one such.'

'It's a long time to wait to take his revenge, though. It was last spring that all that happened,' Longman said doubtfully.

'Early days yet. We don't know much about Kingsley since he seems to have guarded his privacy so well. We'll just have to keep an open mind for now. We've got a few things to follow up on already and the initial forensics haven't been done yet, nor even the post mortem.'

'Well, that's not likely to give us any surprises,' Longman said with a degree of sarcasm. 'I don't think we're in any doubt about how Kingsley died.'

'Are you all right, Geoff?' Simon asked. The usually genial Longman had been exhibiting a shortness of temper that was out of character.

'What do you mean?' There was a degree of hostility in the reply that warned Simon off pursuing the matter.

'Just wondered if you had a bit of indigestion,' Simon said lightly. 'Constipation, perhaps?'

Longman glowered up at him through his impressive eyebrows.

'My digestive tract is perfectly sound, thank you,' he said, without the glint of humour he would normally have shown at the suggestion. 'Are we going back to the clinic?' he added without enthusiasm.

'Yes,' Simon decided. 'Now that it's dark I'd like to check the curtains in Kingsley's room, to see if any light would have been showing from his windows last night.'

In Kingsley's room he closed the curtains before switching on the light, leaving them as they hung naturally, without making any special effort to arrange them to avoid any cracks for light to show through. Then he raised the window and called down to Longman, asking if he had seen any evidence of a light being on in the room.

'Sorry, I wasn't looking, I was admiring the

cathedral,' Longman called back. 'Do it again.'

Irritated, Simon repeated the exercise.

'No,' Longman said as Simon looked down to him again. 'I couldn't see any cracks of light. I wouldn't have known there was anyone there.'

'So what does that prove?' he asked Simon as he rejoined him.

'I should have thought it was obvious,' Simon answered a little acidly.

'You mean that it shows that someone might have gone into the clinic last night without being aware that Kingsley was in his consulting room?' Longman said flatly, making it clear that he saw no relevance in the fact.

'And had an unplanned meeting with him as a result, ending in a quarrel which killed him. Or, that alternatively the meeting was arranged.'

'Great!' Longman puffed out his breath, the white vapour showing clearly even in the dim light. 'So now we know that Kingsley was killed by someone who either did or did not have an arrangement to meet him. Very helpful.'

They walked back to headquarters in silence and Longman got into his car offering only a brief farewell. Simon went up to the incident room to file his report.

10

Simon turned on to the narrow road that led to Oxton, the few scattered lights of the village coming into view, little points of warmth strung along the distant turning. Jessie's cottage was a little before the entrance to the village, her car parked on the grass verge.

The kitchen smelled of something good and the table was laid for both of them, so she hadn't gone ahead and eaten before him. She was sitting at the computer in a corner of the sitting-room, her long wavy hair fixed loosely with a comb.

'Hi!' she said. 'I've solved the problem of Christmas presents. They're all getting a whale, a tiger, a wolf or an elephant.'

His mind boggled for a brief moment at images of elephants, tigers and wolves padding around in tidy suburban gardens.

'Sponsorship?' he said, light dawning, trying to imagine the reaction of her mother to the gift she would receive.

'I've done it all on line and it's all fixed up,' she said, closing down the computer.

They went through into the kitchen where

a bottle of red wine had already been opened. Simon poured while Jessie put out the food.

'So what made you so late tonight?' she asked as they sat down to eat.

'Sebastian Kingsley has been murdered,' he said.

'Sebastian? At the clinic?' She put down her loaded fork. 'How?'

'A fatal blow to his skull with a carved stone African head, in his consulting room.'

She was silent for a few moments, then said, 'I can't say I'm entirely surprised.' She picked up her fork and resumed eating.

She wasn't upset then, Simon thought sardonically.

'Oh?' he said.

'Oh, no!' she exclaimed and swallowed quickly, taking a mouthful of wine to help the food down. 'You're not going to pump me for inside information, I hope?'

They had been through this sort of thing before, Jessie always balking at being any kind of informer about friends or colleagues.

'I can't imagine you'll be able to tell me anything I can't get from other sources, Jess,' he said mildly.

'Then ask other sources!' she retorted.

'But it might speed things up a bit, if you helped. It might even mean I could get it sorted by Christmas and we could have some sort of a break.'

'Christmas!' she said with a groan, possibly echoing the feelings of half the country at this time of year. 'You know how I feel about Christmas. I'll be able to have an unChristmastime under the pretext of staying here to keep you company, so you're offering me no inducement at all.' Her face flushed and she pushed back her unruly hair with the back of her hand.

Simon silently resumed eating for a few minutes. The food was good and deserved his attention.

'When did it happen?' she asked eventually.

He told her, and briefly the circumstances they knew of so far.

'So we have a few tentative leads to follow,' he finished, 'including a doctor whose wife was treated at the clinic for cancer. She subsequently died and her husband made something of a fuss, knocking Kingsley on the chin and generally trying to cause mayhem. They had to get Jock to make him leave. Apparently he was very much opposed to her trying the alternative approach but she refused chemotherapy and radiology and so on.'

'Tough for him,' Jessie said, propping her chin on her hand.

141

'I thought so,' he said. 'It must have been bitterly frustrating for him given his own line of work.'

Jessie shrugged. 'She had the right to choose.'

'But don't you think that these clinics are a bit of a health hazard, a bit irresponsible when it comes to serious illnesses?'

She gave him a long look. 'Did you know that from figures available in the US, prescribed drugs are high on the list of causes of death, after heart disease and lung cancer? About a hundred thousand people a year die before their time because of them.'

'But at least the drugs are tested,' Simon objected. 'These herbs and things are not given the same rigorous test trials.'

'And the drug testing *must* be very rigorous,' Jessie said sardonically, 'as I've just pointed out. Whereas a lot of what are called 'alternative' therapies have been around for hundreds of years and they've been tested by time and also not used to torture animals.'

'Glad I ran that one past you, Jess,' Simon said ironically. He quickly changed the subject. 'We've also got a possible suspect in Anne Stillings, and perhaps Ruth Maguire.'

It produced a reaction, as he thought it would.

'Anne Stillings wouldn't kill anyone,' Jessie said. 'And I doubt if Ruth would, either.'

'You see, your inside knowledge might save people a lot of grief,' he said, smiling.

She sighed, and sat back, glass in hand.

'Sebastian was a bit of a bastard,' she said. 'But I can't imagine anyone I know at the clinic reacting in such a violent way.'

'I understand he messed with people's lives. If one of them felt sufficiently threatened they could have been provoked to it.'

She resumed eating. 'You know I wasn't involved with any of them much on a personal level. I really don't think I'm going to be able to help.'

He understood her sensitivity over this. He would feel the same, he thought, in the circumstances, but nevertheless he tried again.

'Jess, I'm not asking you to point the finger at anyone. The opposite, if you like, would be just as useful, like your assessment of Mrs Stillings. Who do you think is least likely to have come to blows with Sebastian?'

She was slow in responding, chewing her food carefully as she chewed over her thoughts.

'An obvious answer would be Jonathan,' she said at last. 'He and Sebastian were quite close, they set up the clinic together with their own money.'

'They were independently quite well off, I understand.'

She nodded. 'Both at public school together as well. I gather that when Sebastian had got in a bit of experience in homoeopathy he sought out Jonathan, who he knew was practising chiropractic and suggested they set up the clinic. Jonathan always seemed able to manage Sebastian and his fits of temper rather well, I thought.'

'Yes, I saw a little of that after my session with Jonathan yesterday,' Simon agreed.

'No more twinges?' she asked.

'Just a bit sore still, but wonderfully better. He's very good at what he does.'

'They all are,' Jessie agreed.

'But you don't know your full-time replacement, Hannah Crossley.'

Jessie pulled a face. 'I met her briefly in town with Ruth last summer. Can't say I was drawn to her.'

'Apparently she and Sebastian were a bit of an item,' Simon said.

'They probably suited quite well,' Jessie said with a smile.

'Do you know anything about Sebastian and Ruth's daughter?' Simon asked, remembering what Hannah Crossley had said.

Jessie put down her fork again and gave him an old-fashioned look.

'I think it was just Sebastian being his usual self, trying too hard to impress any attractive female. I know only what Ruth told me when we had a coffee together in town a few months ago.'

'He seems to have made a habit of trying it on with women. Apparently he did the same with Anil's fiancée.'

Jessie looked up, surprised. 'I didn't know he'd got engaged. Anyone I might know?'

'Probably not. She's recently come over from India apparently.'

'He wouldn't like Sebastian behaving like that. He's a bit of a traditionalist, rather conventional, Anil.' She swallowed another mouthful of food and said; 'But I don't see him making a violent attack on Sebastian, either.'

'That doesn't leave us with many suspects, then,' Simon said wryly. 'What about Jock Patterson? I suppose you are going to tell me he's a dear, too and would never lay a finger on anyone in violence?'

Jessie laughed. 'He *is* a dear. But he is ex-army and wouldn't put up with any messing about.'

Frances Fulton, the receptionist, was the only person they had not touched on, but

Jessie would not have known her as she had begun working at the clinic after Jessie had left.

'That seems to let most of them out, then, according to your assessment,' Simon said.

'I hope I'm right,' Jessie said lightly. 'But I'm sure you'll dig out far more than I am aware of. What about other people in Sebastian's life? He spent a lot of time in London, unless that changed after his involvement with Hannah Crossley.'

'Apparently not,' Simon said.

'You'll have to follow that up, then,' Jessie suggested.

'If we find any leads to it in his flat,' Simon said. Nothing helpful had been found yet. And absolutely nothing useful had been extracted from Jessie. He wondered whether she was being cautious about anything that might be relevant. It was perfectly possible.

They talked generally about Christmas and the possibility of staying at home and then began to clear away the plates and dishes.

'I told you that Jonathan sent you his regards and asked after you?' Simon said.

'You did. How did he seem? Before all this happened, I mean.'

'Fine, I think. I've no way of judging. He's a quiet sort, isn't he.'

'Poor Jonathan,' Jessie said, filling the sink

with hot water. 'I think that ex-wife of his makes his life difficult. But the marriage gave him his beloved Marcus who is a nice child in spite of his awful mother.'

'You've met her then?' Simon wiped a plate and put it back on its shelf.

'Not many times. They were on the point of splitting up when I first met her which, in fairness, probably didn't bring out the best in her in the circumstances. But she was very narrow-minded, even bigoted. She wasn't comfortable around Anil, can you believe?'

Simon had not yet had more contact with Anil than his brief observation of him in the function room at the clinic that morning. He had seen an open attractive face and a slim athletic body, but it would not have been his attractive appearance that Mrs Hadden had apparently reacted to but the colour of his skin. He felt a familiar wave of disgust.

'I can believe it because I come across bigotry and racism often enough.'

'She was equally unpleasant to Anne Stillings, too.'

'Because she's gay, I suppose?'

'Exactly.' Jessie lifted her eyebrows at him. 'Incredible, isn't it?' She plunged her hands back into the water. 'No, that's not true. As you say, prejudice is still rife, particularly among the cowardly and mean-minded.'

147

'You wouldn't be prejudiced about that, by any chance?' he asked, dropping a kiss on the back of her neck where her hair curled in wispy ringlets.

She sighed. 'I know political correctness is a bit of a bore but I think Jean Hadden thinks that it just means voting Conservative.'

11

His attendance at the post mortem had done nothing to cheer Simon's spirits: the preliminary examination had added little more to their sum total of knowledge than the fact that Sebastian Kingsley had had a meal of steak and salad about four hours before he died. Added to which the bright, cold weather had dissolved into dreary fogginess and Longman was as morose and taciturn as the day before.

'Tell me what's the matter, Geoff,' Simon urged as they drove back to headquarters.

'It's nothing,' Longman said gruffly, staring ahead into the grey mist.

'Is it Julie?' Julie was Longman's wife who, despite the sergeant's professed enlightenment about such issues, exercised a lot more independence in the marriage than he seemed entirely comfortable with. Simon wondered what she was up to now.

Longman shifted in his seat, pulling at the restricting seat belt.

'She's all right,' he said, but his tone suggested a degree of dissatisfaction with the fact.

Simon had noted the unusually dishevelled appearance that Longman had presented for the last couple of days.

'She's gone away?' he asked.

'Yes, she's gone away,' Longman agreed testily.

This sounded bad and Simon hesitated to press Longman any further. But if she had left him Simon felt he had some right, as a close colleague and friend, to know. Perhaps Longman could do with some time off?

'Have you had a disagreement?' Simon asked tentatively.

Longman grunted.

'Not really.' He turned his head to stare out of the side window at the increasingly restricted view.

Simon slowed his speed a little more. As they approached headquarters and the west side of the city where it gave way to the river and its notorious fogs, visibility got even worse. It seemed like a metaphor for the case they were involved in and the obfuscation he was suffering from made Simon speak more sharply to Longman than he intended, irritated at being kept in the dark over another little mystery he could do without.

'Well tell me what's wrong, for God's sake!' he said turning to Longman. 'Do you mean you've split up?'

'No!' Longman sounded outraged — to Simon's relief 'No, she hasn't left me. Not in that sense anyway.'

Simon brought the car to a halt at the rear of headquarters. He switched off the ignition and leaned back, unbuckling his seat belt.

'In what sense, then?'

Longman was muttering under his breath as he released his belt with a bit more difficulty. Simon thought he heard him say: 'Mind your own bloody business.'

He felt mortified, and embarassed. Mostly he felt hurt that Longman, usually so open with him on almost any subject, had decided to close against him like this. But he recognized, as Jessie with her habit of analysis would have urged him to do, that Longman's hostility arose from his unhappiness.

'I'm sorry, Geoff,' he said a little stiffly. 'I really wasn't intending to pry, just concerned about you, that's all.' He opened the driver door and put his right foot out. 'I'm glad everything's basically OK.'

Longman didn't move. 'She's gone to her sister's,' he said. 'She and her husband have split up. The kids, Katrina and Joey, are really upset.'

They were probably the main cause of Longman's distress, Simon thought. Julie and

151

he had no children of their own and Longman had often spoken with affection about his nephew and niece.

'I'm very sorry,' he said quietly. 'Does it look as if there is any chance of a reconciliation?'

Longman's mouth twisted doubtfully.

'I shouldn't think so. He's involved with another woman and Sue insists she wouldn't have him back even if he wanted to come home.'

It was such a commonplace story, Simon thought, happening all over the country, all the time. But that didn't make it any easier for those involved to bear, the anguish was as intense however many times it was played out.

'Do you want some time off?' he asked tentatively. It would not be easy to arrange, right at the beginning of a murder investigation: they were short-staffed as it was. Longman shook his head.

'No, it's best left to Julie. I'd probably put my foot in it anyway. Sue knows that Noel and I get on well and at the moment she'd see me as being in the enemy camp.' He opened the car door. 'And I'd be doing all I could to get them to reconcile, for the sake of the kids. It's not something she wants to hear about at the moment, though I reckon she might come to regret it.' He climbed out of the car.

'It's early days yet, I suppose,' Simon said as they went up the steps into the building. 'Things may change.'

'Maybe.' Longman looked sad. 'But I doubt it somehow, she's a fiery piece, is Sue, and full of a lot of noise about women's rights. No use asking her about children's rights. But thanks. We'll see how things go.'

Things were going nowhere very much, investigations being at a very early stage. They called into the incident room for a meagre update and then went on foot to visit Jonathan Hadden, a short distance away off the West Gate in a narrow enclave of former warehouses, another smart property conversion.

Hadden was expecting them: they were hoping to see all the remaining staff from the clinic today. As he invited them in, Simon thought he looked nervy and pale, unlike the relaxed man he had met when he had his treatment. He supposed it was unsurprising: if Hadden and Kingsley had been such good friends it had probably taken a while for the fact of his friend's death to sink in.

They were shown in to a living-room that opened on to a balcony by means of sliding plate-glass doors. Disconcertingly, on such a

153

cold drab day, these were wide open to the seeping fog, a canvas director's chair placed there. The fog obscured the view from the balcony almost completely but Simon could see that it was a good one, taking in the water-meadows so close to the city at this western edge.

'Sorry,' Hadden muttered, hurrying to close the window as Simon and Longman paused in the middle of the room. 'I just needed to breathe some air for a few minutes, and I perhaps shouldn't have bothered, the weather being what it is today.'

Judging by the temperature in the room Simon thought he must have been out there rather more than just a few minutes, but he made no comment and looked round the room as Hadden fastened the doors, which appeared to have every modern security device attached to them.

Simon and Longman sat down, Hadden joining them after a moment's hesitation.

'Have you found out anything yet?' he asked. His voice sounded slightly hoarse and there were dark smudges under his eyes.

'It's a bit soon yet,' Simon said. 'But we do have a couple of questions to ask you.'

'Yes?' Hadden looked Simon straight in the eye. 'I want to help in any way I can, obviously.'

'We understand that the husband of a former patient, a woman who had died after being treated exclusively at the clinic, made threats to Mr Kingsley. We should perhaps have asked to see you at the clinic itself as you may need to refer to files on former patients.'

'No.' Hadden swallowed. 'I know who you mean. It was Dr Woolbridge. He's recently retired, I understand, but he belonged to the Walmcot practice.' Walmcot was a suburb on the main road leading east from the city. 'But it was last spring that all that happened and apart from a few letters I don't think we had any more trouble from him. I'm sure Sebastian would have told me.'

He probably would, Simon thought. But if the man had since retired, he might have had an unhealthy amount of time to sit and brood.

'You don't think Dr Woolbridge might have proved dangerous?' he asked. 'He was violent at the time, I understand?'

'Yes he was. The poor man was bereaved and grieving. He probably felt he should have stopped his wife somehow from opting for an alternative health approach to her illness. But we brought no pressure to bear on her. I know Sebastian urged her to consider conventional treatment.'

'He did?'

'Of course,' Hadden said simply. 'We do have awareness of both the strengths and limitations of what we can offer at the clinic. Mrs Woolbridge opted for a change of diet, homoeopathic support, hypnotherapy and visualization techniques, I believe, with Sebastian looking after her overall care. Sadly, she had come to us at rather a late stage of her illness and she died a few months after beginning treatment.'

'We shall have to speak to Dr Woolbridge. Perhaps you could let us have his address,' Simon said.

'I don't have it here, of course. But the Walmcot practice would give it to you quickly enough.' Hadden held his arms across his chest and grasped his upper arms in a self-protective gesture. 'Have you learned any more about how and when Sebastian died?' he asked hesitantly.

'No more really than we were able to tell you yesterday morning,' Simon said. 'But have you had any ideas about who might have attacked him? I gather from people we've been speaking to that he wasn't averse to upsetting people on occasions.'

Hadden gave a half-smile, almost apologetic.

'I told you, that was just Sebastian's way. I can't believe anyone took that much exception to his behaviour.'

Maybe, Simon thought. Or Hadden's assessment was a particularly tolerant one, understandable in an old friend for whom Sebastian held no fears.

'He was heard having a row with Ruth Maguire that evening. Their voices, or hers, were raised in anger. Do you know anything about that, or the subject of the argument, if that's what it was?'

'No. I didn't hear anything. And Ruth has said nothing to me.' Hadden relaxed his hands and clasped them between his thighs.

'What was his relationship with Mrs Maguire like?'

Hadden's face closed against him resentfully.

Simon understood the look. He said as much, adding: 'But unfortunately, all these little details of people's lives have to be exposed in a murder inquiry. It's very unpleasant for everyone involved and it causes a lot of distress, but the anguish tends to be a bit less drawn-out if people can just bring themselves to cooperate and answer the questions they are asked. After all, I'm not asking you to incriminate anyone, I am merely trying to get an understanding of how relationships worked at the clinic.'

Hadden was silent for a moment, head down examining his hands.

'What's the problem, Mr Hadden?' Longman asked, slapping his notebook hard against his knee. '*Do* you know of something incriminating involving Mrs Maguire?' The sharp sound startled Simon and Hadden both. Simon hoped that Longman's unhappy personal situation wasn't going to encourage him to vent his frustration on an unwitting public.

'Heavens no!' Hadden gave a nervous laugh, his head jerking up at the noise. 'Not at all. It's just, as Chief Inspector Simon says, it doesn't come naturally talking about friends to relative strangers, especially in the circumstances.'

Longman continued to give him a hard stare.

'As far as I know, Ruth and Sebastian had no problems with each other,' Hadden said. 'On the contrary, Sebastian looked out for Ruth and had helped her all he could after her husband died.'

'He knew her before she came to the clinic, then?' Simon asked.

'Yes. You may know that Sebastian was a general practitioner before he went on to train in homoeopathy — quite a lot of doctors take that route. Ruth's husband was one of

158

his patients. Ruth decided to make a career in medical herbalism and qualified not long before we opened the clinic, so Sebastian, as an old friend, offered her a place there.'

Simon wondered whether it was another of Sebastian Kingsley's apparent gestures of friendship that had behind it some different agenda.

'He no longer used the title of doctor, though?' he asked.

'I think he was unhappy with the world of general medicine and glad to dissociate himself.'

'We understand,' Simon said, 'that Mr Kingsley upset Mrs Maguire over his relationship with her daughter Cass. Can you tell us anything about that?'

Hadden gave a quick laugh.

'Who told you that story? Hannah, I expect. She watched him like a hawk and was as jealous as hell.'

She had disguised it quite well, Simon thought. Was Hadden's response more a reflection of his own attitude to Hannah Crossley than a true image?

'There was no such relationship, then?' he asked.

There was a pause. 'There might possibly have been in Cass's eyes. She might have been flattered by Sebastian's attention and read more into it than he intended. He was a bit of a flirt.'

'And that was all?'

Again Hadden hesitated. 'I hate all this. It's like gossiping.'

'It's not gossip, Mr Hadden,' Longman said abruptly. 'It's necessary information so that we get a picture of what had been happening in Mr Kingsley's life, if you have any interest in us catching his killer. This information is entirely confidential. So we'd appreciate it if you would stop treating us to a parade of your finer feelings and just answer the questions put to you.'

Hadden flushed and ran his tongue along his upper lip.

'I'm sorry. I don't mean to be obstructive. I'm upset. But there I go again, and you are not interested, as you say, in the finer feelings of people who have lost a loved friend.' He sounded bitter and defensive.

Simon thought, as he had done often before, that the mechanics of a murder investigation were comparable to the wielding of a surgeon's knife: painful, but necessary to get at the truth of the malaise.

'Was that all that the matter of Cass involved, Mr Hadden?' he repeated.

'It was nothing!' Hadden gave an irritable shrug. 'Sebastian got himself involved in talking with Cass about her future career, that's all. He said that going to university wasn't the only option open to her. As a result of which Cass said for a while that she wasn't going there, that she was going to wander the world for a bit and decide what she wanted from life.'

'A gap year is considered perfectly commendable, I thought,' Simon said mildly.

'But she refused to call it that.' Hadden made an impatient gesture. 'Look, this is all a waste of breath. Cass changed her mind, no doubt partly as her interest in Sebastian declined, or was discouraged. She went off to university in London last autumn and she'll be home soon for Christmas, apparently.'

'Mr Kingsley spent a lot of time in London I understand,' Simon said. 'Do you think it's likely that he was seeing Cass there?'

'No, I don't! Sebastian has always gone to London a lot. He likes — liked — concerts and the theatre and exhibitions and the sort of things that London has to offer rather more than Westwich. There's really no point in you following this line of thought; it's a waste of time.'

'What wouldn't be a waste of our time in your opinion, Mr Hadden?' Longman asked sharply. 'Perhaps you could make a few suggestions?'

Hadden got up, nearly knocking over the chair he had been sitting on.

'I don't know! I'm sorry, I just don't know.' He turned away and walked over to the sliding doors that gave on to the balcony. 'You're quite sure it was not some burglar who broke in?'

'Quite sure,' Simon said. 'Whoever killed Mr Kingsley was either let in by him or had their own key or access to the building.'

'Well I can't help you,' Hadden said in a low voice. 'I wish I could. But at the same time I can't believe it was anyone I know, anyone from the clinic.'

'It was a blow to the head, Mr Hadden, that killed your friend,' Longman said. 'Something that just about anyone is capable of dealing someone if they have enough provocation. The killer is not going to be sprouting little horns and developing cloven feet.'

Hadden turned back to them, his expression sad.

'I know. But I don't know how it happened.'

Simon gave a small cough. 'We need to ask you about your alibi for that night, Mr Hadden. I understand you were babysitting your son until ten-fifteen at his home in Madderley, then returned to town and came straight to your own home here.'

'*Is* that an alibi?' Hadden, still standing, asked with a half-smile. 'I've no idea what time Sebastian died.'

'It'll do for now,' Longman said abruptly.

Simon stood up, bringing the interview to an end. He had hoped that Hadden might have proved more willing to speak about relationships at the clinic but recognized that, unless they had heard of something specific that Hadden could be called to comment on, he was not likely to volunteer anything. Then he remembered Anne Stillings.

'Did Mr Kingsley speak to you about his plans to ask Anne Stillings to leave the clinic?' he asked.

'I knew he was unhappy about her,' Hadden said cautiously. 'He felt she didn't fit the image, though it may have been more to do with Anne's slightly caustic relationship with Sebastian. She isn't a person who kowtows readily to anyone and she was inclined to make the odd remark in his and others' company on the subject of his behaviour at times.'

'What aspect of his behaviour would that be?'

'Oh,' Hadden waved his hand vaguely, 'Sebastian's way of always having to make an impression on people. He could be very

163

engaging and charming when he chose.'

'As with Cass, and perhaps Mr Patel's fiancée?' Simon enquired.

Hadden hesitated. 'That sort of thing, yes. Just Sebastian flirting a bit, really.'

It was obvious that Hadden would be likely to put the best spin possible on Kingsley's behaviour, so Simon didn't press him any further, but made his way towards the door, Longman in his wake. He noticed on the wall a large black-and-white photograph of a young child. The boy was running, arms wide, towards the photographer, who had obviously positioned himself on a level with the child. It was a charming picture, the child's face full of joy and love, his little body straining to be with whoever was taking the picture.

'Your son?' he asked Hadden.

'Marcus,' Hadden agreed, his expression full of pride.

'You took the picture? It's very good.' It was indeed technically accomplished, but its real achievement had been in catching the quality of the moment.

'Thanks,' Hadden said. 'That was when he was four years old.'

'You're divorced from your wife, but you still manage regular contact with your son?' Simon imagined how hard it must be for

Hadden whose pride in and love for the boy were so obviously deeply felt.

'As much as I can,' Hadden said, his expression closing. 'Madderley is not far away.'

They thanked Hadden and made their way down the utilitarian stone staircase.

'Another poor bugger deprived of his kid,' said Longman, whose attitude to Hadden seemed to have softened.

Longman, unlike the majority of his colleagues, did not swear often. Simon was aware that the lapse was a result of the current depth of his feelings on the subject.

'The timing would be tight but Hadden could have got to the clinic in time to kill Kingsley,' Simon said.

'But why would he?' Longman asked. 'They were good friends.'

'As far as we know.'

Jonathan Hadden went to the phone as soon as the door closed.

'Jean?' he said. 'I'm free now. Can I come over and collect Marcus?'

His ex-wife's voice was distinctly cool.

'You've left it a bit late, haven't you? We've made other arrangements now.' She said consideringly: 'Perhaps you'd better come here tonight, then, so that you can babysit for us.'

165

'But why can't Marcus still come here as arranged?'

'I told you. I've made other arrangements.'

'What arrangements?'

'Nothing to do with you.'

She almost certainly had no plans to do anything but stay at home and prepare herself for her meeting with Terry tonight, but to argue the point would end with her denying him any chance to see his son this weekend, access agreement or not. She would gladly forgo an evening out with her boyfriend if she could have the pleasure of denying him Marcus's company.

'What time do you want me to come over tonight?' he asked flatly.

'Half past seven will be fine. And don't be late.'

12

Simon and Longman had a midday meal in the lounge of the Comfy Pew in the Cathedral Approach, managing to avoid being recognized by the noisy media crowd in the bar. It was only a short walk to the clinic and Jock Patterson's flat.

'We should be following up that doctor that threatened Kingsley instead,' Longman objected. 'It's the only likely lead we've got so far.'

'He'll keep,' Simon said. 'We'll catch up with him later.'

Jock Patterson answered the door promptly and showed them in to the living-room. As he did so, a young boy pushed past them muttering something about going to his room.

'Your son, Mr Patterson?' Simon asked, pausing on the threshold. 'I understood he was missing from home.'

'He came back to us,' Patterson said expressionlessly, holding out his hand gesturing for them to go ahead.

A plump grey-haired woman smiled up at them from a high invalid's chair, a wheelchair

167

parked beside her. It was cramped and stuffy in the small room, the flame gas fire burning in the Victorian fireplace making the room over-heated. Simon supposed that Valerie Patterson's enforced inertia must make her feel the cold more than others and made an effort not to show his discomfort by whipping off his overcoat, as he desperately wished to do. Longman, perspiring freely, seemed to have made the same decision.

Furniture had obviously been kept to a minimum so that Mrs Patterson could move her wheelchair around, though a wide-screen television filled one of the corners. The paucity of furniture had been made up for by the number of pictures on the walls. Many of them were prints of improbably clean and well-dressed country maidens bringing home the cattle, feeding the chickens or loitering under giant hollyhocks. The photographs on display included Jock looking bright-eyed and alert in a guardsman's uniform, a wedding photograph showing a much slimmer Valerie Patterson, her husband still in uniform, and one of their son in yet another uniform, that of the Cathedral School. In pride of place on the mantelpiece was a large colour photograph of the boy looking solemn in choirboy robes, taken perhaps a couple of years ago.

'Have you found out anything yet?' Valerie Patterson asked, her accent local, unlike her husband's which was broad Glaswegian.

'Not really, Mrs Patterson. We were hoping that you or your husband might have something you could tell us.'

Her hand went to her throat where she wore a silver crucifix. She caught hold of it and began rubbing it with twisted arthritic fingers.

'We don't know anything, do we, Jock? We would have told you if we did.'

Jock nodded supportively.

'You were both here the night that Mr Kingsley died, I understand,' Simon said. 'Did you hear anything out of the ordinary, or see anything?'

'Not a thing,' Patterson said firmly.

'Your son, Kevin, was he here too?'

'Yes, we were all here in the living-room until about eleven when we went to bed,' Valerie Patterson confirmed.

'We wouldn't expect to hear anything, y'see,' Patterson said helpfully. 'We're right at the back of the building.'

'Would you be aware if anyone used the rear door to the clinic next to your own?' Simon tried again.

They looked doubtfully at each other.

'We had the television on,' Valerie Patterson

said. 'We certainly didn't hear the door being used.'

'Do people who work in the clinic sometimes use that exit?' Longman asked. 'Or do they usually use the front door?'

'There's a narrow lane that runs up beside the back garden,' Patterson said. 'Sometimes someone might come out that way and use the lane as a short cut into the North Gate. But it's not lit and the women in particular don't use it in winter. The lane is pretty dark at the front of the building for that matter, but you're more quickly into a lighted area from there.'

'What time did you finish your rounds on Thursday night, Mr Patterson?' Simon asked.

'About nine o'clock.'

'Did you see Mr Kingsley come in to the clinic? Apparently he left his uncle the dean at around ten o'clock, saying he was coming back here.'

'No. But I saw him when he went out at about seven, when I went up to do my initial check that the place was locked up all right. He was going to choir practice.'

'Did he speak to you, say anything about his plans that evening?' Simon asked.

Jock shook his head. 'He was coming down the stairs to the ground floor as I was going up. He just put up his hand and said

170

'Evening, Jock,' and carried on out.'

'Did he often spend time in his consulting room at night?'

'I don't know about that sort of hour, around ten,' Jock said doubtfully. 'He was sometimes there when I was doing my cleaning after the clinic closed.'

'Was the light on in his room when you discovered his body?'

'No. The light was off and the curtains closed. An' of course the door was open, which was why I entered the room a bit cautiously like.'

Valerie Patterson was still fiddling endlessly with her silver crucifix.

'What sort of employer was Mr Kingsley?' Simon asked, including Valerie in his question. She responded quickly.

'He was really very good to us, wasn't he Jock? He was very kind to me over my illness and allowed me free treatment in the clinic. And he had the ramp built at the back so that I can get out into the garden in my wheelchair.'

'He was fine,' Jock confirmed. 'He liked things done properly mind you. Didn't accept any slacking, and I didn't offer any.'

'So you both liked him?'

'Aye,' Jock said, his wife nodding confirmation. 'It was an employer-employee

171

relationship of course, but he was fair.'

'It's been remarked by others that he could be abrasive and upset people. You apparently didn't experience that, but did you come across this in his relations with others?'

'I'm not around that much when people are actually working in the clinic,' Jock said.

It wasn't really an answer, but Jock's lips had set in a firm line and he obviously had nothing he wished to add on the subject of Kingsley's behaviour.

'On the other hand, you were better placed than others to see what went on in Mr Kingsley's life after hours. Did you see any visitors to his flat, for instance?'

Jock stared at the floor.

'I didn't see anyone visit much. His uncle came over a few times. Mr Hadden, of course, spent time with him discussing clinic business, but that was in Mr Kingsley's office. I got the impression he didn't socialize much. And he was away a lot — in London, so he said.'

'Did your duties include cleaning his flat?'

'No. He did for himself. I just cleaned the stairs to his flat. He seemed to like to keep himself to himself.'

Simon had the impression that some employees of the clinic were being deliberately reticent on the subject of Sebastian

Kingsley and wondered if it was because they were being careful of their jobs. Jonathan Hadden was now apparently their employer; perhaps they were anxious lest word get back to him of any indiscretions on their part. Not, perhaps, that they might have anything to say that implicated Hadden himself, but they might not want him to think they had talked too freely to the police.

Of all of them, Jock and his wife were the most vulnerable if they lost their position here: not only their income but their home depended on it, so Jock was maybe less likely than any of them to volunteer information. It was also home to their son, who had suddenly and mysteriously reappeared. He glanced at the photograph on the mantlepiece.

'I see your son was in the choir?'

'Yes, the Cathedral Choir,' Valerie Patterson said quickly, her hand gripping the crucifix. 'That's another thing we have to be grateful to Mr Kingsley for, isn't it, Jock? He helped with Kevin getting into the Cathedral School and that was really because his voice was so beautiful so he got a place in the choir. Heard our Kevin singing one day soon after we moved here when the clinic opened and he went ahead and got things organized.' She was gabbling a little, her husband not responding, except with a small nod.

173

'But he ran away, I understand,' Simon said sympathetically.

'Yes,' she agreed briefly as if she had run out of steam.

'Was he not happy at the school?'

'We think he may have been bullied,' she said in a small voice.

Jock cleared his throat. 'He's only just come home,' he said gruffly. 'We're not sure what it was all about.' He glanced across at his wife expressionlessly.

'How old is Kevin?' Simon asked.

'He's just fourteen,' his mother replied.

So he would have been nine years old when they moved here. He was small for his age: perhaps he had indeed been bullied.

'How long was he away?' Simon asked gently, aware this must be a sensitive issue, the boy's parents must have been over-whelmed with worry. And with Valerie's illness to contend with Jock had been having a very difficult time, as Anne Stillings had remarked.

'Do we have to discuss this?' Jock said sharply, getting up and going over to a small sideboard where he picked up a whisky bottle. He turned back with a half-full glass. His wife cast him an anxious look as he sat down again.

'I didn't mean to intrude,' Simon said. 'I

174

can understand that it must have been a very trying time for you when Kevin went away.'

Longman, who had been silent apart from the very occasional rustle of the pages of his notebook, suddenly spoke.

'When did your son come back, Mr and Mrs Patterson?'

'Yesterday,' Jock said, tipping back his head and swallowing a large shot of whisky. He wiped his mouth with the back of his hand. 'But I don't see what our private business has to do with what you're investigating,' he added firmly. Longman was not put off.

'But did the boy go out again? Might he have seen anyone around the clinic last night? Young boys usually do go out in the evenings.'

'Oh, no. He didn't go out,' Valerie Patterson said earnestly. 'We had such a lot to talk about and Kev was so tired.'

Longman glanced at Simon. They should really speak to the boy himself, but Simon was reluctant to upset the Pattersons any further on the subject. Kevin could be interviewed at a later date if need be, when the Pattersons had got used to the possibility.

'You'll be finished with us, then?' Jock said, standing up.

'We didn't offer you a cup of tea,' Valerie lamented. 'I'm so sorry.'

Simon smiled down at her as he rose to his feet.

'It's a kind thought, but we've just had lunch anyway.'

She returned his smile. It was a sad sort of effort, Simon thought, full of uncertainty and anxiety. He felt impelled to offer her some sympathy.

'You've both been very helpful, and we are sorry to have intruded on you. You've obviously been having a difficult time privately and the murder of Mr Kingsley must have distressed you further.'

She looked away, her face crumpling. 'Thank you,' she said quietly.

Jock saw them to the door and let them out without another word.

When he returned to the living room his wife was trying to manoeuvre her way towards the kitchen.

'I could do with a cup of tea,' she said.

'Go back,' he said. 'I'll see to it.'

She complied reluctantly: she would really have preferred the chance to make herself busy with something, and she needed to assert her independence as much as she possibly could. It was ironical, she thought, that when you could carry out a simple domestic task without even thinking about it, you were only too pleased to let someone else do it for you, but once you began to lose the ability then you longed simply to be able to do it yourself. Jock already took on too much. Perhaps now that Kevin was back he would be able to help out again. The thought of her son, never far from her mind, filled her again with anxiety. She hoped he would emerge from his room soon without being called.

Jock came in and handed her her cup of tea.

'You talk too much,' he said, not unkindly, lightly touching her shoulder. She had to use both hands to steady the saucer or she would have grasped his hand in return.

'I'm sorry,' she said. 'I was nervous. You're a good man, Jock.'

'Let's hope they think so, eh?' he said with a smile, jerking his head in the direction the two policemen had taken and sitting down opposite her.

'Do you think they'll question Kevin?' she asked.

'We were all together, weren't we,' her husband said. 'There's nothing for them to find out.'

She placed the cup and saucer on the small table next to her and spoke in a small voice.

'I know I shouldn't say it but I could almost wish Kevin hadn't come home. I'm so afraid.' She put her hands over her face and Jock again reached out to her.

13

The scene of crime officers were still at work in Kingsley's consulting-room and his flat. Longman went to stare moodily out of the window while Simon found Richards, the longest serving SCO, under the desk.

Richards indicated the blood spatter, carefully outlined in chalk, which radiated from the desk where Kingsley must have died. Some marks had been tagged on the curtains, some on the wall next to them and the rest were splayed across the expensive carpet.

'Those wouldn't have been so obvious to you at the time you first saw the body,' he said slowly, his speech always seeming to reflect the careful methodical movements of his work, 'but they're clear enough now.'

'The killer would have blood on him or her.' Simon said.

'They would,' Richards confirmed, 'though it wouldn't necessarily be a vast amount.'

On such a cold night, Simon thought, the murderer was likely to have been wearing an overcoat of some sort, a garment easily shed and folded to hide such evidence.

'Have you found anything of interest?' he asked.

Richards shook his head. 'There's a variety of fingerprints about the room,' he gestured to the armchairs near the fireplace and the bookcases, 'but the area around the desk and the murder weapon were wiped clean of prints, as was the door. It would have taken the killer only a few minutes.'

'No obviously fresh prints?'

'A few which appear to be those of the victim, that's all. You already know that the carved head had been wiped, but there was enough blood in the crevices to leave no doubt that it's the murder weapon.' Richards stood up fully from where he had been kneeling by the desk. 'We'll soon be finished in here, sir.'

Simon had not really been expecting that the killer would leave his or her signature in the room. The fibres being collected and bagged for forensic examination would at best be of use for the purposes of confirming evidence only after the killer was caught. Though if the killer were one of the members of staff such evidence would be worthless since they could argue that they had been in the room previously.

In Kingsley's flat Simon asked Price if they had turned up anything of interest.

'Negatively, I suppose,' Price, an unusually large young Welshman answered. 'The door to the flat and the bedroom and bathroom have been rendered sterile, as have certain other areas of the premises.'

Simon wondered whether the usual teases that the Welsh suffered in these border areas had encouraged Price to weight his language with some of the more ponderous elements of the English language.

'Where's that?' he prompted.

'The furniture in the living-room.' Price pointed to the dark-brown leather sofa and chairs, dusted with powder and innocent of the smallest smudge.

Simon walked into the bedroom where a double bed with a mahogany headboard, also dusted and free of any evidence of earlier human contact, stood in the centre of the room. Behind it was the door to the ensuite bathroom, equally clear.

'The kitchen?' he asked Price who had followed him.

'We found plenty of Kingsley's prints.' Price guided him back to the living-room and into the small kitchen. 'Actually, he does seem to have been a very tidy housekeeper, the place is generally clean and well kept. I suppose,' he said doubtfully, rubbing his nose, 'Kingsley himself may

180

have wiped all those surfaces.'

'Even to wiping the doors and the headboard?'

'What I mean is,' Price said slowly, 'the cleaning might not have been done by the killer. We may not have to attach particular significance to the fact that the headboard is clear, for instance. It may be that the killer was not his mistress, I mean,' he ended less confidently.

Simon thought he saw what he was getting at. They had no way of knowing whether Kingsley had a fetish for cleanliness to the point of sterility in the bedroom area and the bathroom. But to Simon it seemed more likely that as the areas that had been wiped were those likely to be used by a close intimate it suggested that the killer was exactly that.

Hannah Crossley would have had no reason to try to destroy evidence of her presence in his flat, and anyway she had volunteered the fact that they had not been in the habit of spending time there together. So perhaps Kingsley had been in a relationship with someone else — and that person had killed him.

It did mean, though, that the killer would have been in the building for longer than they had thought. If he or she had spent what must have been at least half an hour wiping evidence of their presence in Kingsley's flat, then that changed the time period of alibis required.

'Anything else of interest?' Simon asked as they rejoined Longman in the living-room.

'Find anything on the computer?' Longman added, pointing to the modern beech desk in a corner of the room.

'Nice one, as well, with all the latest bits and pieces. It's gone to HQ for checking,' Price said, 'to see if there's anything on the hard drive that wasn't apparent to us. But I know Grantham is overwhelmed with work at the moment. Something to do with the big fraud investigation.'

Simon knew about it. It was absorbing most of the manpower at headquarters for the duration.

'What about the camera?' Longman pointed to a silver digital camcorder on a shelf above the desk.

'Nothing in it. And we haven't found any photographs. Nor have we found any discs — they must have been removed by whoever cleaned the place up.'

Simon took a last glance around the room. There were no family pictures giving some clue to Kingsley's background, the only photograph on view, near the desk, was a

182

copy of the one Simon had noticed in his uncle's study, the one of the choir. Otherwise the wall hangings were of modem art, brighter than Hannah Crossley's, and originals.

Something significant might yet turn up, Simon thought as he and Longman made their way down the stairs and out into the foggy day. There might be something on the computer, and Kingsley's phone calls were still being checked.

'Are we going to see the irate doctor now?' Longman asked.

Simon had obtained Dr Woolbridge's address while they were in the Comfy Pew.

'It's just a walk from here to Frances Fulton's place,' he said. 'The people from the clinic have been asked to be at home today,' he reminded Longman, 'and I don't want to miss them,' he added at Longman's stifled irritation.

They followed Candlemaker Lane to the West Gate, after being let through by the official on duty at the ancient barred gate.

'Bit of a luxury, this,' Longman said, obviously making an effort to be cheerful. 'Freedom from the mad media crowd makes a pleasant change.' He added: 'Have you got any ideas yet about who the murderer might be?'

'Not really. I think it's a bit soon yet to form any opinion,' Simon said.

'The business about the fingerprints in his flat might be suggestive,' Longman pursued brightly.

'Kingsley might just have been a cleanliness freak.'

'I can imagine Hannah Crossley knocking someone on the head.'

'So you said last night.'

They entered the West Gate where Christmas crowds jostled them and made conversation difficult.

'But don't you agree?' Longman skipped around a woman heavily laden with shiny bags of shopping.

'Maybe, but the fact that she's got no alibi to speak of might be a point in her favour.'

'True, she looks the efficient type, so she'd probably have managed to arrange one if she needed it.'

They had reached the narrow lane that led to Frances Fulton's flat. Simon turned into it abruptly, leaving Longman stranded in the crowds for a moment. The fog was swirling thickly and the garish Christmas lights glowed eerily on people's faces as Simon turned back to search for him. Seeing him looking lost, Simon felt a rush of compassion that we sometimes most readily feel when we observe those we know well standing unconscious of our observation. He called Longman over the heads of the crowd and saw his face relax.

'This used to be the old *Courier* printing works,' remarked Longman, who knew rather more about the city's history than Simon, as they paused at a row of intercom buttons. The *Courier* was the Westwich city news-paper.

'Yet another conversion, then,' Simon responded, pressing the appropriate button.

'Better than building on all those green fields.'

'Brown sites are very green,' Simon agreed, who knew all about it from Jessie.

'Hallooooeee!' a voice sang over the intercom.

Simon and Longman looked at one another. Simon explained who they were.

'Come on up!' sang the voice, equally enthusiastically. Such a welcome was unusual.

The door clicked and let them into a stone-flagged entrance hall with an old wrought iron staircase leading to the first floor and upwards. A lovely young Asian woman met them at the door of the flat and held it open with a flourish.

'I'm Aisha!' she announced. 'Franny and I share.' She looked them both up and down before deciding to fix her attentions on Simon as the younger and more obviously good-looking of the pair. 'Franny is in the sitting-room.'

She turned and led them onwards, a colourful figure in a creative blend of colour and texture, a mix of East and West, and plumped herself down on a sofa beside Frances Fulton who was flicking through a magazine. The two made a contrast unflattering to Frances who wore a navy-blue tracksuit and whose hair hung lankly to her shoulders.

The room itself was as colourful and eclectic in style as Aisha with a great number of artefacts spread about. Minimalist it was not.

'Oh!' said Aisha, who seemed to speak mostly in exclamations. 'Would you both like some refreshments? A cup of coffee, perhaps?'

She was behaving as if this were a favoured social call and it seemed a pity not to respond in kind.

'Thank you,' Simon said, amused. Longman, transfixed, nodded his agreement.

She sprang to her feet and went out of the room. Frances Fulton laid aside her magazine.

'You've come to ask me about my alibi for the night that Sebastian Kingsley died?' she said, her face and voice expressionless.

'That among other things,' Simon agreed.

'Oh? Well as you're aware, I've already given my alibi to your officers. I was here that night with Aisha. Anil was here as well, he called in and joined us for a meal and we spent the time talking and listening to music. Anil left us at about eleven.' She seemed defiant, or perhaps it was just the contrast with Aisha's sunny enthusiasm.

'So you and Mr Patel are each other's alibi,' Simon observed, looking through his file of papers at the statement Anil had given. He wondered quite what were the relationships here, and whether they conflicted with Patel's relationship with his fiancée. Perhaps he believed that sauce was reserved exclusively for the gander.

'If it is an alibi,' she pointed out. 'After all, we don't know when Sebastian Kingsley died, do we?' Her smile was more of a smirk.

'You've worked for the clinic for about six months I understand,' Simon said. 'So you've had a chance to get to know the people there quite well by now. Can you tell me anything about them that might be relevant to our inquiry, particularly Mr Kingsley?'

Her sullen look returned. 'He was a control freak,' she said. 'I can't say I liked him. He had a way of picking on underlings like

187

myself, trying to show me up in front of others. He would always do it in front of an audience.' She lifted her legs and hugged her knees, wiggling her bare toes.

'When you say 'underlings', do you mean anyone who was not a therapist at the clinic? So was he unpleasant to Jock Patterson?'

'He was unpleasant to everyone at one time or another. But it was me he picked on most. He was an élitist.'

'Are you talking about Sebastian?' Aisha sang, returning to the room with a loaded tray and placing it on the low carved table between them. 'He was not so bad,' she scolded Frances. 'You just did not know how to handle him.' She sat down and began to pour their drinks.

'You think you only have to flirt with a man and he'll fall at your feet,' Frances said scathingly.

'And I am right, am I not?' Aisha smiled dazzlingly at them. Longman leapt forward to take a mug of coffee from her and hand it to Simon.

'Isn't it true, you just have to be nice to men and they will be nice to you?' Aisha persisted, giving Longman his own mug.

'It can help,' Longman agreed abjectly.

'It's not being nice, it's being sycophantic.' Frances took her own mug of coffee and poured cream into it.

'You met Mr Kingsley then?' Simon said to Aisha.

'Yes!' she said with enthusiasm. 'He was a very nice-looking man. Franny took me to an open day at the clinic and I flirted with him, which I found very enjoyable,' she said sternly turning to Frances. Frances made a derisive sound.

'He flirted with anyone who'd let him, couldn't let pass an opportunity to dazzle.'

'He didn't try it with you,' Aisha retorted. 'Perhaps if you had let him you would have got on better with him. Men love flattery. And what's wrong with that?' Aisha asked. 'It can bring a little happiness into the world, can't it? You are so serious Franny!' Aisha settled back comfortably on the sofa holding her mug in small brown hands adorned with gold rings.

'Do you confirm Miss Fulton's alibi that she was here with you and Mr Patel last Thursday night, until eleven?' asked Simon.

Aisha nodded vigorously.

'Of course. We had a very good evening, didn't we, Franny? Anil went home around then, but when did Sebastian die?' She opened her eyes wide, appealing to Simon and Longman both.

'That's yet to be established,' Simon said.

189

Aisha pouted.

Simon wondered how regularly Anil Patel called here at their flat. It seemed unlikely that Frances Fulton was the attraction. He said, addressing her:

'What do you know of Mr Kingsley's relationship with other members of staff? Was he to your knowledge at odds with any of them?'

But she had nothing to add to anything they had heard before.

'I understand the so-called clinic gremlin has been causing trouble since you began working at the clinic. As the receptionist, who sees everyone come and go at the clinic, have you formed any ideas about who might be responsible, Miss Fulton?'

'It's Mrs Fulton, actually,' Frances said. She shrugged. 'I was thinking of reverting to my maiden name anyway as I'm no longer married. And the only opinion I have formed is that the gremlin is a malicious nuisance.'

Aisha, who had been uncharacteristically silent for a few minutes, said:

'This gremlin is upsetting everyone at the clinic. Poor Anil had his needles, his sterile needles, thrown about his room and then,' her eyes widened, 'they stuck into one of Miss Crossley's clients! Don't you think, Chief Inspector, that the gremlin might be the person who murdered Sebastian? It's obviously someone who wants to do damage to the clinic. It will put people off going there now that things like that are happening. And now, there has been a murder! Which is even worse.' She sat back and looked from Simon to Longman enquiringly.

'We're certainly keen to find out who this person is,' Simon said.

'I assume you'll be checking the people who are attending evening classes?' Frances Fulton asked.

'We shall be doing so.' Longman replaced his coffee-mug on the tray.

'Where were you working before you came to the clinic, Mrs Fulton?' Simon asked.

She looked irritated at the question.

'I had been travelling in Australia for almost a year. I decided to go after my marriage broke up.' She shrugged. 'I applied for the job at the clinic soon after I got back.'

'Poor Franny!' Aisha sympathised. 'She has had such a hard time, you know, she — '

'Thank you, Aisha, but I don't think they want to know about any personal problems I may have experienced,' Frances said quickly.

Aisha looked hurt and wrapped her arms around herself.

Simon stood up, towering over the three of them. Aisha appeared to have cheered

Longman, but this was not achieving much otherwise. Frances Fulton escorted him and Longman to the top of the staircase, Aisha waving 'Goodbyee!' from the doorway.

'You're very good at it,' Frances commented as she returned to the living-room.

'What? Flirting with men and making them like me?' Aisha raised her pointed chin.

'No, telling lies.'

14

Walmcot, formerly a village on the main road east from Westwich, was now a commuter town, its old houses and cottages crammed between endless modern estate developments. Dr Woolbridge lived in a large Victorian house in a lane that had managed to retain its identity amidst the ugly sprawl that surrounded it. Trees in his unkempt front garden dripped moisture as the fog from earlier in the day turned to mizzle and early darkness. A lamp lit in a front room of the house served only to emphasize the gloom of the day.

He answered the door promptly enough, a middle-aged man, unshaven and unkempt, thinning dark hair falling forward on his forehead, eyes peering at them in the dim light. After Simon and Longman showed their identification he invited them in to the room from where the light had shown and sat down by the empty fireplace, not bothering to suggest they do likewise. He seemed incurious about their presence.

Simon decided to sit down anyway and chose a hard little brown-leather sofa, where

Longman joined him. The room was cold and comfortless with neglect, a layer of dust seeming to have settled on every surface, lacking any appearance of being lived in in any real meaning of the word.

'Do you have any idea why we are here, Dr Woolbridge?' Simon asked.

The doctor lifted his thin shoulders in an indifferent shrug.

'No doubt you are about to tell me,' he said, his voice patrician and stronger than his appearance suggested.

'You may have heard of the murder of Sebastian Kingsley at the Cathedral Clinic?' Simon said.

Longman brought out his notebook and Woolbridge cast him a look of vague surprise.

'Yes,' he said.

'I understand that you were at odds with Mr Kingsley, that you made threats against him?'

'Did I?' Woolbridge's eyebrows rose slightly and he pursed his thin lips. 'If you say so.'

'You were angry about the treatment that the clinic had offered your wife before she died.'

There was a spark of response in the doctor's eyes.

'Yes, I was very angry. Kingsley should never have accepted my wife for treatment.

The only hope she had was with chemo-therapy and radiotherapy and he took that chance away from her.' He looked with pale-blue eyes at Simon. 'As far as I'm concerned he murdered my wife.'

They need be in no doubt then of the strength of Woolbridge's feelings about Kingsley, Simon thought. Had he made a judgement of an eye for an eye, though?

'I understand that it was your wife's choice to seek alternative treatment,' Simon said, realizing as he did so that it was probably unwise to offer what suggested an opinion about what had happened.

Unwise or not, it prompted a stronger response.

'My poor wife was not in any position to judge what was right for her at the time.' Woolbridge snapped. 'She was frightened and vulnerable and that criminal exploited her vulnerability.' His skin tightened over the harsh planes of his face and some spittle appeared at the corner of his mouth.

'Did you kill Sebastian Kingsley, Dr Woolbridge?' Simon asked.

Woolbridge gave a harsh laugh.

'Do you know, when I heard about it, I truly regretted that I wasn't the one who did.' He looked away, his voice subsiding, as if he were talking to himself. 'I think I would feel better if I had. It would be a kind of solace. It is a relief, though, to know that he is dead.'

Simon wondered whether Woolbridge lived entirely alone, whether he had any family close by, because he seemed singularly in need of company, showing every indication that he was suffering from depression. He looked about the room as usual for some evidence of family portraits and saw a couple of framed photographs on an oak chest in the gloom of an alcove but could distinguish no detail from where he was sitting.

There was no way of evading the questions they had come to ask, but Simon was tentative, concerned about putting unnecessary pressure on the man.

'All the same, Dr Woolbridge, we need to ask you to account for where you were on the night of Thursday last,' he said.

Woolbridge pushed out his lower lip.

'I was here and I was alone,' he said after a moment. 'I'm afraid that if you want to make me responsible for Kingsley's murder you will have to find further supporting evidence. I suppose,' he went on conversationally, 'it would give me what they call 'my day in court'. It would give me a chance to damn in public all these quacks that prey on vulnerable sick people.'

His hunched posture straightened. 'So, do

go ahead, Chief Inspector, arrest me and try and 'pin it on me' as they say in modern vernacular. It will give me something to do that might be useful. And, after all, I have some sympathy with the real murderer.'

Simon had never had anyone positively invite him to arrest them for murder before.

'I'm afraid we won't be able to oblige you just yet, Dr Woolbridge,' Longman said cheerfully. 'We'll have to do some more investigations first. You do have a car, I take it?'

'Yes, I do,' Woolbridge said, holding out his hand as if gesturing to lead them to it. 'Would you like to check it over?' It was obvious that the situation was beginning to amuse the doctor. 'Perhaps you'd like to look for some evidence of blood?'

'Thank you,' Simon said. 'We'll certainly do that. We'll send some people to collect it.'

Woolbridge gave them both a condescending and cynical smile.

'Alas, I'm afraid it won't help you.'

'You have no one at all who can confirm you were here that night? No one called on you, or telephoned?' asked Simon.

'I'm afraid not, Chief Inspector.' Woodridge sounded almost sympathetic.

Simon pushed himself to his feet, the leather of the sofa creaking in protest, and walked over to the portraits on the oak chest. One showed the doctor sitting on a garden seat with a woman, presumably his late wife. He looked fuller of face, with more abundant hair, his arm around the woman at his side. She was a slight figure, dark-haired as her husband and attractive. The other picture showed the pair of them with a young woman in graduation robes, a wide and happy smile showing in place of her usual sullen expression. It was Frances Fulton.

Woolbridge had come silently to stand beside him.

'My wife,' he pointed, 'and my daughter Frances.'

'She works at the Cathedral Clinic,' Simon said, surprise making it something of an exclamation.

'Of course, she doesn't have my opinion of alternative therapies, quackeries,' Woolbridge said quickly as Longman came to stand beside them and examine the pictures. 'She approved of her mother's choice, I'm afraid.'

Simon frowned. 'She would have been away in Australia at the time her mother was being treated there,' he said.

'But they were in touch with each other,' the doctor said firmly, taking the picture of his daughter from Simon and replacing it carefully on the chest. He said sadly: 'It caused something of a breach with Frances and myself, the fact that she encouraged Patricia. She doesn't come to see me very often.' His eyes were watchful, turned to Simon's face.

'Your daughter didn't come home then, when she knew her mother was dangerously ill?' Longman asked.

'Patricia played it down, she didn't want to spoil our daughter's stay in Australia; Frances was trying to get over the break-up of her marriage. And when Frances did get home she could hardly have opposed me more than by going to work in that damnable clinic.' Woolbridge turned away and resumed his seat by the empty fireplace. 'Now, if you are not going to arrest me, gentlemen, I should prefer it if you would go.'

They let themselves out into the thin sunshine that was struggling through misty rain, Simon feeling depressed and uneasy after the encounter.

Longman, though, still seemed thoroughly restored after his apparently therapeutic encounter with the lively Aisha.

'That's a turn up, Frances Fulton being his daughter. She could have let him in to the clinic, she's got a key.'

'In that case Aisha Markandya would have to be lying about Mrs Fulton's alibi that

199

night,' Simon said, starting the car.

That silenced Longman for a moment. Then he said:

'What did you make of him? I didn't know how much he was bluffing about everything. He might just have been being clever, pretending he wished he'd killed Kingsley. And he had plenty of motive and he had opportunity what with having no alibi and his daughter working there.'

'It would mean that Anil Patel as well as Aisha was lying,' Simon said, 'if he relied on his daughter letting him in to the clinic.' He turned left on to the main road in to the city. 'And according to Woolbridge Frances is in favour of alternative medicine.'

'He wasn't very convincing. He might have said that to deflect our suspicions from her.'

'But you're back to Aisha and Anil lying if Frances was involved.'

'Aisha might have lied,' Longman said doubtfully. 'But why should she?'

'Oh, come on, Geoff! People do it all the time, lie about things to give their friends an alibi when they're asked to. Frances might have said she'd just been out for a walk and asked them both to cover for her.'

'Frances Fulton might have done it herself without any help from her father. She might have got a job there to give herself a chance for revenge of some kind.'

'Like murdering Kingsley.' It was perfectly possible. Woolbridge *had* been quick to point out to them that Frances had not shared his views, uncharacteristically informative given the way he had behaved until then. That could have been simple protectiveness on his part in case they should suspect her of having her own agenda where Kingsley was concerned. And what if the agenda had been somewhat less extreme? Could Frances Fulton be the gremlin? Suppose she had decided to work at the clinic in order to undermine it from within? And if so, was it possible that that had not satisfied and she had graduated to a far greater revenge for the death of her mother?

'What about Anil Patel's involvement in the alibi? How do we know who's covering for someone else?' said Longman.

'They're all part of each other's' Simon said cynically. 'And I don't find it wholly believable.'

'Why?' Longman sounded as if he was still reluctant to allow that the delightful Aisha might have been telling a blatant lie.

'Think about it,' Simon said. 'It strikes me that Frances Fulton had the means of putting a little pressure on Aisha and on Anil when it came to a need for an alibi.'

'Why?' Longman repeated. 'What are you getting at?'

'It seems fairly obvious to me. I don't think Anil Patel is visiting their flat for the pleasure of Frances's company, do you? And when he is there, I can't see Frances playing an unwanted third. She'd have gone off to her room, or gone out. And if she was out that night she need only suggest to the others that she would tell Anil's fiancée about Anil's visits to Aisha to persuade them to keep quiet about her absence. Added to which, she gave Anil an alibi at the same time, with the added advantage of appearing as chaperon to any possible goings on.'

'Or the two women could be giving Patel an alibi,' Longman suggested again, jutting out his chin. 'It cuts both ways.'

'Except that we don't have much of a motive for Patel. The fact that Kingsley made a pass at Patel's fiancée is hardly grounds for motive in this day and age. But we'll question them more closely and separately,' Simon added.

Longman was silent as they drove into the busy centre of town, the traffic almost at gridlock so close to Christmas. The sun's appearance had been brief and the gaudy seasonal lights created a lurid aura in the foggy gloom.

Christmas was now only ten days away and Simon had given no thought to what he was going to buy Jessie as a gift. Longman suddenly spoke again.

'We didn't say anything to the media about blood, did we?'

'Kingsley's?' Simon said. 'No, we haven't yet said how he was killed. Why?'

'Dr Woolbridge asked if we would be looking for evidence of blood in his car. So how would he know that the killer would have blood on him, or her?'

'It's an assumption people make when someone's been murdered. Perhaps it was just that.'

'Or perhaps he knew there'd be blood,' Longman said stubbornly.

'His daughter might have told him,' Simon suggested, aware that his usual role of shooting down Longman's ideas was meeting with more resistance and resentment than usual. It had been too much to hope that the sergeant would retain his measure of good humour for too long. Leaving him with silence allowed him to brood too much.

'We didn't tell them at the clinic how he had been killed, nor when. We've kept it quiet for now.'

But the chances were that word had got around all the same, Simon thought. Jock

Patterson had found the body and the others would have been bound to ask him about it and what he had seen. He said so to Longman.

'You don't rate Woolbridge as a suspect, then.' Longman sounded accusing.

'He'll get the same treatment as everyone else, Geoff.'

Simon, with some relief, pulled into the carpark at headquarters. He could see the lights on in Detective Superintendent Munro's room on one of the floors above. But he was not planning to call in on her: it was Saturday night and he and Jessie were going to an Arts Club exhibition at the university. He would write up his reports and be away as quickly as possible.

15

If you were looking for relief from Christmas jollity, Simon thought as he looked around the exhibition at the university, this was the right place to come for therapy. The canvases were mostly monochrome shades of grey and black with the occasional uplifting touch of sludgy brown; the subjects death and disaster in about equal measure. He felt a strong desire to drive to the city centre and take in the tacky Christmas lights.

'Good evening, Detective Chief Inspector Simon,' a low voice said.

He looked round to see Hannah Crossley smiling at him, wineglass in hand and dressed in white with a silver shawl of some sort draped over her bare shoulders, a vision of light with her blond hair dressed and waved. She was obviously not in mourning, then.

'Hello,' Simon said, startled.

'What do you think of the exhibition?' she asked, waving her glass at the nearest paintings.

'Very life-enhancing,' he said solemnly. She looked at him searchingly.

'Ah, I see you're joking. You had me

worried for a minute.'

They made pleasant small-talk for a while, she explaining that she had joined the Arts Society only six months ago. Jessie and he had not been to recent exhibitions, which was why he had not seen her there on previous occasions. Jessie abruptly appeared at his side, the artist in tow.

'This is Dan Turner,' she announced. Simon thought he discerned a note of desperation in her voice.

Introductions were made all round.

'You're a policeman,' Turner said to Simon, thrusting a hairy chin at him. 'Are you investigating this murder at the Cathedral Clinic?'

Simon almost replied: 'Are you investigating the possibility of being an artist?' Instead he said that he didn't discuss his work in his time off.

Turner laughed and moved even closer.

'I do, all the time.' He turned his attention to Hannah. 'I've seen you at Arts Society dos before, haven't I?' He scrutinized her more closely. 'You were with him! The bloke that's just been murdered — Kingsley. Who d'you reckon did it, then?' Turner asked, looking from Hannah to Simon and back.

'You're neglecting your other guests,' Jessie said to him.

'Yes, do run along.' Hannah said, smiling insincerely. Turner moved away, looking bemused, and approached a different group of erstwhile happy people.

Simon knew that the two women had met previously only in passing since Hannah had begun working at the clinic, so he left them to it. He was quickly pounced on by Hermione, a colleague of Jessie's in the psychology department. Her red hair was piled on top of her head with a diamante comb and she was wearing an emerald-green lamé dress that hugged her voluptuous figure.

'Chris!' she exclaimed, planting a red-lipsticked kiss full on his lips. She stood back and surveyed him theatrically. 'I see poor Dan didn't do too well with you. And he looked as if he was trying so hard!'

Simon carefully wiped his mouth with a handkerchief and looked at her mystified.

'You think he was trying to sell me a painting?'

Hermione spluttered into her wine.

'He obviously fancied you,' she said, recovering her breath. His expression made her laugh. 'He's *gay*, didn't you realize?' She looked around. 'There's a lot of eroticism of a murky sort lurking in Dan's stuff.'

'Is there?'

'Death and sex.' Hermione nodded.

'You talk a lot of nonsense,' he said amiably.

She grinned at him and took another mouthful of wine.

'Who was that blonde woman who's been monopolizing you?'

Simon explained.

'So she's the woman who took over Jessie's job at the clinic. Where Seb Kingsley was murdered.' She fixed him with a look, eyebrows raised.

Simon noted her familiar use of Kingsley's first name, as he was no doubt meant to do.

'You knew him?' he asked.

'I went out with him a few times,' she said airily, looking about her and knowing that he would pursue the subject.

'So you knew him quite well?'

She looked back at him with an amused smile.

'Not in the Biblical sense,' she said.

That was perhaps surprising, Hermione being an enthusiastically promiscuous woman.

'Do you want to know all about him?' Hermione teased. 'Well,' she said, drawing out the word. 'He was a dark horse, our Sebastian, didn't talk about himself much, which is rare in men.' She reached and touched Simon's arm with a red-taloned hand, 'In fact you're about the only other man I've known who doesn't require constant attention to his ego.'

Simon frowned. 'I've been told he was a control freak, which doesn't seem to fit with your image of him. I'd have thought control freaks were monstrous egos.'

She laughed. 'His ego was big enough not to *need* constant attention, dear heart. No, he didn't like invasion of his privacy, which is a part of control, isn't it? *But* he loved to gossip about other people, wanted to know as much as he could about their lives and any dark little secrets they might have.'

Simon, much of whose life was spent reluctantly trying to reveal other people's dark little secrets, felt distaste. The idea that Kingsley might have gossiped about Jessie, for instance, was abhorrent to him.

'When were you going out with him?'

'A couple of years ago now. And it wasn't very often. Apart from the issue of Biblical knowledge, I didn't really like him much. He was a sensationalist,' she said. 'He had a taste for the lurid. And yet, when it came to it, he wasn't in business.'

'You mean sexually?'

'I think he was gay,' she said. 'Or at least bisexual.'

'Because he didn't sleep with you?' Simon smiled, doubting her assessment.

'Yes,' she said, still serious. 'Not many males refuse an opportunity, I can tell you. But it wasn't just that. There was a definitely camp edge to him. But because he was so careful about his private life I could never be quite sure.'

'But why should he care?' Simon said. 'In this day and age? It's really not an issue any more, is it?'

'You think so?' Hermione raised her finely plucked eyebrows. 'Don't be naïve, Chris. Laws may change, but it takes a little longer for people's prejudices to evolve to match them. He may have thought his practice might be affected perhaps.'

It might well explain Kingsley's frequent trips to London, Simon thought, and wondered how much bearing his sexuality might have on the case, if any.

'But Kingsley was a known flirt,' he said. 'I've been told he had to impress any woman he came across.'

She shrugged. 'Bisexual then? Anyway, gay men love women, strong women anyway.'

'He had a gay member of staff, whom he wasn't fond of,' Simon remarked.

'Anne Stillings?' Hermione suggested. 'Male and female gays don't necessarily have some kind of sympathetic understanding, you know. Sometimes it's quite the opposite.' She planted a kiss on his ear and moved away as Hannah Crossley approached him again.

'I should have mentioned it before,' she said, looking anxious 'when you came to my apartment. But,' she scanned his face, 'it's not an easy thing discussing one's colleagues with strangers. You remember I told you about Sebastian's argument with Ruth?' She tipped back her head and looked at him along her aquiline nose, waiting for his nod of response. 'Well there was more to it. Ruth accused Sebastian of trying to blackmail her.'

'Over what?' he asked.

'I don't know. But it was because he wanted her support for firing Anne.'

'And you didn't hear what was the basis of his threats?'

'I'm sorry, no.' She shook her head.

'Thank you for telling me,' he said. 'You're sure there's nothing more you overheard?'

'No, nothing else.' She quickly turned away.

Simon looked speculatively after her distinctive figure weaving through the still busy room, wondering whether she had some motive of her own for expanding on Ruth Maguire's interview with Kingsley. It was possible that the word *blackmail* had been misinterpreted, deliberately or otherwise. It was not uncommon, after all, for people to accuse each other of *emotional* blackmail, or even straight blackmail in a lighter sense of the word.

'You're looking very thoughtful.' Jessie appeared, the remains of a samosa in her hand. 'Indigestion?'

'The mental form,' he said. 'Shall we go?'

'So did Hermione offer you one of her psychics to solve the case?' Jessie asked as they went through the double doors on to one of the wide terraces at the centre of the university campus.

'No, she didn't,' he said, surprised that she hadn't. Hermione's specialism was in parapsychology and she frequently encouraged him to employ one of her 'sensitives' as she preferred to call them. 'She was talking about Sebastian Kingsley. She used to go out with him,' he said pointedly.

'Only casually,' Jessie said over her shoulder, her breath drifting in a mist. 'He wasn't one of her *grandes affaires*.'

'She thinks he might have been gay.'

'Mmm. It's possible.' Jessie turned back to him, laughing. 'Though Hermione would think that of any man who didn't take her to bed, or demand to, on a first date.'

'The thought had occurred to me. But what do *you* think?'

'About Sebastian Kingsley?' She shrugged.

'He might well have been, or more likely bisexual.'

They were quiet for a while as Simon drove south to the bypass and on westwards towards Oxton. Conscious that he had Jessie as a captive audience, he asked:

'How well do you know Ruth Maguire?'

Jessie had been on the point of nodding off.

'Oh please, Chris. Do you have to give me the third degree at this time of night?'

'I haven't noticed any thumbscrews.'

She wriggled more upright in her seat.

'A slight over-exaggeration due to fatigue.'

'What do you know of her personal life?' he asked. 'She's a widow, isn't she?'

'Yes. Her husband died a few years ago from a reaction to a drug her doctor prescribed for high blood pressure. He was in renal failure for quite a while and they couldn't get a match for a transplant. Poor Ruth was looking after him for a long time.'

With something of a shock, Simon recalled what Jonathan Hadden had said.

'But Sebastian Kingsley was their doctor. So he must have prescribed the drug! I was told he had given her a job at the clinic after she retrained because he knew her from when he was the family GP. It looks more like a guilty conscience.'

'Yes,' Jessie said in a small voice. 'I suppose

that now you are going to suspect that Ruth has murdered Sebastian in a delayed act of revenge.'

'Your high opinion of my reasoning capacity is so reassuring,' he said.

But all the same he wondered whether such a background to their relationship might not make Ruth's reaction all the stronger if Kingsley was indeed blackmailing her. He told Jessie what Hannah Crossley had reported to him.

'I can't imagine doing that to a friend, or even colleague,' Jessie said.

Seeing it from Jessie's perspective made Simon question Hannah Crossley's motives again.

'So you can't think of any grounds for blackmail in Ruth's life?' he asked.

'I wouldn't tell you even if I could,' Jessie said coolly.

And there the subject, and all other issues, was left until they got to bed and less controversial personal matters.

16

The preliminary report on Sebastian Kingsley's post mortem was on Simon's desk on Monday morning. There was nothing of interest to add to what was already known — except that Evelyn Starkey noted that he had been an active homosexual. He passed the report to Longman, repeating what he had learned at the Arts Society exhibition.

'Is this likely to be relevant, d'you think?' Longman asked.

'Not necessarily,' Simon shrugged. 'It may explain his time spent in London and his general secretiveness. But whether it has any other bearing on the case, time, and evidence, may tell.'

They went to the incident room where the team looked bright and keen for a Monday morning. Simon told them he had allowed the clinic to reopen today and brought them up to date with what he had been told. Everyone seemed to have something to say on the subject of alibis.

Anne Stillings had, according to the door attendant, left the Corn Exchange during the showing of the second film at around ten fifteen, saying that she was going outside for a cigarette. 'She doesn't smoke, of course,' DC Rhiannon Jones said. 'I checked.'

'When did she come back, if at all?' Simon asked.

'About half an hour later, he thought, around the time the second film ended. I've checked the time needed to walk from the Corn Exchange in the East Gate to the clinic and it's ten minutes. Possibly less at night without the crowds in the streets.'

Simon stated the obvious: 'So she had the time and opportunity to kill Kingsley and she also had a motive — the fact that he was intending to get rid of her from the staff of the clinic. Her motive may have been all the more urgent in view of the fact that she and her partner are planning to buy a house, which would increase her financial burden. See what more you can find out about the pair of them, Rhiannon, then speak to Mrs Stillings about what she was doing during that half-hour or so.

'However,' he added, 'the fact that the killer seems to have been to Kingsley's flat to wipe away fingerprint evidence, means that we're probably looking at a longer amount of time than she had available. The effort in his flat might have taken as long as half an hour in itself.'

DCs Savage and Tremaine had followed up the house-to-house inquiries and extended the search to the Cathedral School. The headmaster had proved co-operative, requiring the staff to report to his study if any one of them had seen any activity near or at the clinic on last Thursday night.

'And we were told by a housemaster, who was returning from having a drink in the Comfy Pew, that he saw Jonathan Hadden approaching the clinic at about quarter past ten. He knows him quite well, he's even been treated by him for sports injuries,' Savage said.

'Did he speak to him?'

'No, sir. He was a bit ahead of him.'

'That area, the lane and the clinic, is not very well lit at night,' Simon said. 'Was he quite sure it was Hadden?' He was aware of a familiar feeling of disappointment, even betrayal, at having been lied to yet again. It happened constantly of course, but he liked Hadden and was still grateful to him for his relief from intense pain. Perhaps it had not been precisely a lie, just economy with the truth, and an understandable one. Most people would omit telling the police anything that might implicate them, quite innocently perhaps, in a crime. Hadden might even have made a genuine mistake over the time. There was only a difference of fifteen minutes between what he had claimed and the actuality.

'We pointed out the bad lighting, sir,' Tremaine said. 'But he first noticed him passing under the light near the precinct gates. He seemed quite sure. Hadden wears a distinctive long camel overcoat.'

'Shall we question him?' Savage asked eagerly.

But Simon preferred to do that himself; he had other questions for Jonathan Hadden.

'If he was seen at that time,' Detective Inspector Stone said, 'it would tie in with when his ex-wife said he left Madderley — at just after ten.'

'What did you think of the ex Mrs Hadden?' Simon asked her. She looked blank.

'She didn't make any difficulty about telling us when her ex-husband left,' she said.

'Did she say anything else?'

'Like what, sir?'

'On the subject of her ex-husband, for instance. On the fact that Sebastian Kingsley had been murdered?'

'She was hostile, I suppose, to her husband I mean. She seemed bitter, I thought. And she didn't seem the least upset about Kingsley.' She faltered to a stop.

'That's right, sir,' DC Williams said, with a

glance at DI Stone. 'Like the inspector said, she was sarcastic about Kingsley and the clinic and she was nasty about her husband. She did say though that he wouldn't have the balls to murder anyone and that he wouldn't have done it anyway because Kingsley and the clinic always came first with him. She went on about Hadden being an unfit father and how he'd left them, but the unfitness didn't seem to amount to any more than that fact. She really didn't have anything of substance to say against him, it was all a lot of bitching as far as I could tell.'

'Explaining, perhaps, why he left,' Simon said drily. 'Hadden does have a motive of sorts, since he benefits from Kingsley's death by taking over as head of the clinic. But it's not a very convincing one since Kingsley's murder only damages the value of that inheritance.' He paused. 'Did anyone get the information about Kingsley's will?'

'I did that,' DI Stone said. 'It seems that most of his money went to his uncle, the dean. He left Jonathan Hadden the sum of ten thousand pounds and Jock Patterson and his family five thousand.'

It was another instance of a more generous side to Kingsley's nature, to include the Pattersons in his will.

'I don't think it's enough to provoke Jock to murder, and the ten thousand is not really a motive for Hadden, who is independently quite well off,' Simon said.

'Perhaps we should check that, sir?' DI Stone said.

He nodded agreement.

'What about the dean?' someone said. 'How's his alibi?'

There was a murmur of amusement in the room.

'Anything else?' Simon asked. Rhiannon lifted her head.

'Ruth Maguire's telephone calls, sir. She did receive them but they were earlier than she claimed. It means that she could have got to the clinic in time that night. And we know now that she had a motive, if Kingsley was blackmailing her over something.'

'I'm not sure I attach too much weight to that idea. It may have been the kind of thing that any of us might say over a slight issue — accusing someone of emotional blackmail, for instance, but we'll bear it in mind.' Simon glanced over to the others. 'Anything else to report?'

Rhiannon persisted.

'There's the matter of Kingsley being responsible for giving her husband the drug that killed him, sir.'

Simon's eyes went back to her. It always cost Rhiannon to challenge him, particularly in company, and colour stained her cheeks.

'It's a bit late in the day for Ruth to be getting revenge for her husband's death, don't you think? She's been working at the clinic for a few years with plenty of access to Kingsley before now. On the other hand, there's always the possibility that Kingsley's offences accumulated — he apparently involved himself in some way with her daughter Cass, for instance — and, if he really was blackmailing her it may have been the final provocation. We'll certainly keep her on our list, Rhiannon. What was the actual time of the calls she received?' Simon asked her.

'The one from her daughter was at nine fourteen and the one from James Flamborough was at nine thirty-three.'

'Do we know anything about him?'

'He's a prospective parliamentary candidate for the city,' Detective Inspector Stone said.

There was a murmur of speculation.

'Mrs Maguire is involved in some committee work that he is taking an interest in,' Simon said.

'And he may be taking an interest in her as well,' DI Stone said. 'Perhaps that was the subject of Kingsley's blackmail. Flamborough's married and he wouldn't want a scandal at this stage in the run up to the by-election.'

'You're well informed, DI Stone,' Simon remarked. 'Are you interested in politics?'

'Just politicians, sir. We should all be interested in Flamborough. He never has a good word to say about the police.'

'We'll try not to let that prejudice us against Ruth Maguire by association, then,' Simon said, amid general laughter. 'But I shall ask her about the blackmail when I speak to her. Any other reports?'

'The checks on Kingsley's phone didn't show up anything that looked interesting,' Stone answered. 'There were no recent calls to employees at the clinic and just a couple of calls received from Hannah Crossley, the last being the one she mentioned she made when Kingsley was with the dean.'

Simon was reminded that he was due to make another courtesy call on the man. But this time he had some particular questions to ask him.

'Those cards that were found in Kingsley's flat for clubs in London,' said Savage. 'It looks as if they might be gay clubs. Should we check them out and see if he had any regular companion?'

'Clear it with the Met first,' Simon agreed.

He looked from one to the other of them. It was early days in the investigation, too soon for frustration to have set in, and they all, apart perhaps from DI Stone, who had not yet had sufficient material to administer, looked keen to be on their way.

'Have you arranged for Dr Woolbridge's car to be collected yet?' DI Stone asked.

'It's already been done. The fact that his daughter, Frances Fulton, works at the clinic is interesting, though at the moment her alibi seems to hold, supported by Anil Patel and her flatmate. Was anything seen of Patel by his neighbours that night?' Simon had not yet got round to speaking to him.

'Nothing so far,' Tremaine said.

'We need to bear in mind that the killer would have been there at the clinic that night for a longer period than we thought. The time of death can't be exact but it suggests that the killer was most likely to have been at the clinic between, say, ten-fifteen and eleven forty-five.'

'He could have come back later,' Savage interjected. 'To clean the flat, I mean.'

'He, or she, could,' Simon agreed. 'But that would increase the risk of discovery rather than reduce it.'

'It's a bit suggestive, that,' Rhiannon said,

her Welsh vowels drawing out her words. There was more laughter, making her colour up again. 'I mean the way the flat was wiped clean of prints.'

'In what way suggestive, Rhiannon?' Simon asked. She was over-sensitive for a police officer, but she did stand her ground.

'Well,' she took her time answering, 'if the killer needed to cover up his or her presence in Kingsley's flat then it makes it less likely that it was someone like Anne Stillings or even Ruth Maguire. It was probably someone with whom he had a sexual relationship.'

'And that would also seem to let out Hannah Crossley as well,' Simon agreed, 'since she had no need to hide the fact that she was in a relationship with Kingsley and she said she never visited him there.'

'It doesn't necessarily follow, though,' DI Stone's dry tone was repressive. 'Whoever killed him might have gone up to his flat before they both went down to his consulting-room for some reason afterwards. Then returned to the flat to try to get rid of any evidence of their presence. The keys to his flat were in his pocket, I believe?'

'They were,' Longman said, joining the meeting in spirit as well as in the flesh. 'But DC Jones did use the word 'suggestive'. I think she's right and that what she said is

224

worth bearing in mind. Remember that the areas wiped clear of prints included the bedroom.'

Rhiannon flashed Longman a smile: DI Stone had a habit of putting down her contributions to meetings.

Stone persisted. 'Maybe someone gave him some therapeutic treatment on his bed.'

This time the amusement in the room was directed at Stone.

'Why, when there are any number of proper couches in the consulting-rooms?' Longman asked.

Stone ignored him. 'Kingsley may have been active homosexually but all the evidence seems to suggest he was likely to be bisexual. He was involved with Hannah Crossley and we don't know exactly what his relationship was with Ruth Maguire's daughter. It's possible that the killer was not just hiding evidence of their own presence in Kingsley's flat. It might have been someone else's.'

'It's possible,' Simon agreed.

'To sum up on alibis,' he said, anxious to get away, 'they all seem to have covered, or attempted to cover themselves for a time slightly later than seems to have been crucial. Which suggests they had some idea of the likely time of Kingsley's death.' He saw Stone open her mouth to interrupt and hurried on.

'Since I can't believe that they were all in it together I can only imagine that they were all aware of Kingsley's regular attendance at choir practice on Thursday nights and that he sometimes had a drink with the dean afterwards and so had a fairly good idea of when Kingsley might be back at the clinic. They probably tried to cover themselves for the time-period after that.'

'So you're suggesting that if they are caught out in lying about their alibis, like Hadden and Maguire, it is not necessarily indicative of guilt?' Stone sounded offended.

'Exactly,' Simon said, smiling at her and failing to get a like response. 'But with the likely additional time for cleaning the flat, none of them has a really satisfactory alibi. In fact the only ones with any alibi now are the combined one of Anil and Frances and the one the Pattersons share.

'As for the question of the motive of who benefits from Kingsley's death, I don't think the motive is a material one.'

'It's possible,' Stone said tightly. 'And the dean should be checked out.'

'Please do that then,' Simon said agreeably. 'But I believe the death of Kingsley was a result of uncontrolled anger on the killer's part. It doesn't look planned, and it suggests that the motive was something more visceral than Kingsley's money.'

Nobody argued the point this time so he hurried on. 'Members of the evening classes need checking on. It's always possible that there is someone among them who is the clinic gremlin and their beef with Kingsley or the clinic got carried too far that night. Continue looking into the backgrounds of the clinic employees and I'll speak to Hadden and Ruth Maguire myself.'

17

When Simon and Longman let themselves into the clinic later that afternoon they found Frances Fulton looking baleful and harassed.

'What do you want?' she asked.

'We've come to see Mr Patel.'

'Well you can't. He's gone home early like most of the others. There have been so many cancellations there hasn't been much for anyone to do today, except me, trying to sort it all out.' She looked at Simon accusingly as if it were his fault.

'Murder isn't good for business,' Longman said, nodding knowingly.

'I had noticed!' she snapped.

'Is Mrs Maguire here?' Simon asked.

'No,' Frances said irritably, turning back again from the computer. 'And before you ask for anyone else, no one is here except Hannah Crossley, who is with a client. Perhaps they think psychotherapy is less threatening than some of the other treatments on offer here. Maybe they think they might be poisoned with herbal remedies or jabbed with tainted acupuncture needles or something.'

'You've had some clients in today, though?' Simon asked.

'Some,' she said grudgingly. 'I had to rejuggle appointments where I could so that the therapists weren't all hanging around between appointments for too long. And at the moment I am trying to do the same for tomorrow and to find out which clients will still be keeping their appointments at all. So, if you don't mind . . .'

They left her to it, Simon wondering how much her irascible manner would add to the general exodus.

Anil Patel lived in a mews cottage in a narrow street near the South Gate. What had been the stables for the Victorian crescent backing on to the mews, were now garages with modernized flats above. There was a light on in an upstairs window. Simon rang the bell.

They heard the sound of footsteps running down the stairs and the door was flung open by Patel with a wide smile on his face. It faded as he saw who it was, his eyes lifting to the level of Simon's. He was several inches shorter, a neat slim figure built on a smaller scale.

'We've obviously disappointed you,' Simon remarked.

Patel invited them in, leading them up the

stairs. As soon as they reached the living-room he excused himself and they heard him speaking to someone in a low voice in an adjoining room. It was a moment before Simon realized he was making a phone call — possibly to warn his expected visitor to delay for a while.

His countenance restored to a semblance of welcome, Patel reentered the living-room, inviting them to sit down and offering them coffee. They accepted and Simon did his usual tour of the living-quarters while the owner was busy. However, the room was only sparsely furnished and looked barely lived in. There were a few attractive pieces of Indian carvings and a happy-looking Buddha on its own carved stand, but no personal mementoes or photographs. Some rich Indian hangings served as curtains for the window which overlooked the mews but otherwise the furnishings were simple and modern.

Seeing Simon still looking around when he returned to the room, Anil said:

'I am waiting for my future wife to put her own imprint here. I'm afraid it is not yet any kind of proper home, I have been here only a couple of months.'

'You're to be married soon?' Simon asked.

'In India in March. It will be a wonderful

occasion,' Anil said, without obvious enthusiasm. He placed the tray on the coffee-table and straightened up.

Simon wondered just how long Anil Patel's relationship with Aisha Markandya had been going on and how much it was limiting the acupuncturist's joy in his imminent union.

'You were born in England, I understand?' Simon said, accepting the cup of coffee he was handed.

'I was.' Patel handed Longman a cup and turned to Simon. 'But it is quite usual for us to marry wives from our country of origin. We maintain contact with our relations and so on.'

'Your fiancée is here now, isn't she?'

'She has returned to India to prepare for our marriage ceremony.' Patel sat down.

'But you seem very close to Miss Markandya,' Simon remarked, sitting facing him.

'We are good friends.' Patel's face took on a closed look as he sipped from his cup.

'Just friends?' Longman asked.

'What is it to you? It is my own private business.' Anil Patel's liquid brown eyes seemed to glitter in the light from the lamp at his side.

'It is of some interest since she has provided you with an alibi for the night that

Sebastian Kingsley died,' Simon said mildly.

'A friend would naturally do so if it is true.'

'Someone who is more than a friend would naturally do it if it were *untrue*,' Simon pointed out. Anil gave a brief smile.

'But don't forget that Franny was there too.'

'So we've been told. You were all together until around eleven that night, is that correct?' Simon asked.

'That's right. We were all together.'

Again Simon doubted that Frances Fulton would have tolerated the role of chaperon, nor could he imagine Aisha requiring it. He suggested as much to Patel. Patel shrugged.

'You will just have to believe us.'

'Not necessarily, Mr Patel,' Longman said.

Patel swallowed, the Adam's apple convulsing in his throat.

'Aisha appears to be a terrible flirt but she is very respectable really.'

He studied his coffee for a moment then looked up suddenly. 'What are you saying, anyway? That you think that we are somehow covering for Franny? I assure you we are not.' He was giving every appearance of having taken real offence at what they were suggesting.

'We don't know who might be covering for whom,' Simon said. 'Did you have reason to feel any enmity towards Mr Kingsley?'

'Of course not!'

'We understand he behaved badly towards your fiancée when she was at an open day at the clinic.' Simon made the comment in the mildest of tones but Patel reacted quickly and angrily.

'Whoever told you that nonsense? Salena would never allow herself to get into a situation that compromised her in any way. What are you suggesting?'

Simon thought that the idea had certainly hit a nerve, whatever the truth behind it or otherwise.

'Mr Kingsley was known to be attentive to any attractive woman who crossed his path and he was particularly so on that occasion, I was told. I was also informed that you were very angry with Kingsley and threatened him about his behaviour.'

Patel's eyes half-closed, as if he were taking time to think. His shoulders relaxed after a few moments.

'Yes,' he said. 'I do remember what happened. I can't really believe that anyone should think it so important that they should tell you all about it. As if it means I would take my revenge in such an appalling way!' He looked reproachful.

'That wasn't how the story emerged,'

Simon said. 'It was mentioned only as part of a catalogue of examples of Kingsley's behaviour. But is it possible that he followed up his interest in Salena, your fiancée?'

Anil relaxed, leaning back on the sofa.

'There was no chance of that! Salena was here with her parents and was well chaperoned, I can tell you. It's true, I did speak sharply to Sebastian — Salena has led a sheltered sort of life and his attentions upset her. But I assure you I have not murdered him in revenge, or any nonsense like that.'

Simon thought he was likely to be telling the truth, on this issue anyway.

'Do you have any idea yourself then, Mr Patel, how Kingsley came to be killed?' he asked.

'None at all. I have no idea who might have done it. I know Sebastian could be a bit insensitive about other people's feelings at times, but that's not a cause for murdering him.'

'That would depend on the source of the upset, though, wouldn't it?' Longman said. 'How well did you know Mr Kingsley?'

'Socially? Hardly at all.'

'And what did you know of him?' Simon asked.

'Not much. I know he was in the cathedral choir and that he used to go to London a lot.

He was a good homoeopath and he believed in the principles of holistic treatment and the dangers of modern drugs. And that's about it.'

'Did you know he was gay?'

Anil blinked. 'I had no idea,' he said. 'Was he really?'

'Or bisexual,' Simon added.

'Yes, of course, he was going out with Hannah. He must have been. Are you sure about this?' Anil turned a puzzled gaze on Simon.

Simon wondered whether Patel was trying a little hard to convince them of his ignorance of Kingsley's sexual proclivities. He was a very good-looking young man with a boyish height and figure. Simon wondered whether Kingsley might have propositioned Patel.

'Yes, we are quite sure,' Simon said. He abruptly changed the subject. 'Do you know anything about the doctor who made threats to Kingsley after the man's wife died after being treated at the clinic?'

'No I don't. I wasn't involved in the woman's treatment.' Patel pushed his cup on to the tray and sat back again.

'Did you know that Dr Woolbridge is the father of Frances Fulton?'

Patel's eyebrows rose. 'No, she has never mentioned it.' He did seem genuinely

235

surprised, but the idea didn't seem to trouble him.

'You've talked to Frances at home as well as at work,' Simon said. 'What is her attitude to the clinic, its ethos and so on?'

'Actually, she doesn't say a lot.'

'She doesn't mention work?' Simon sounded surprised.

'Well, a bit, I suppose, as we all do.' Patel made more effort. 'She didn't like Sebastian, it's true, Not surprisingly, because he treated her like an underling. And it did affect her work and made her nervous when he was around, but it was hardly grounds for murderous rage, if that's what you are getting at.'

'How committed is she to the work that goes on at the clinic? Does she ever talk about the treatments and their effects?' Simon asked again.

'Not really.' Patel looked away, refusing to be drawn further on the subject of Frances.

'I understand you have been affected by the so-called gremlin at the clinic. Do you have any idea who may be behind it?'

'If I had, I would have said so by now.'

'You don't seem to be too concerned about it, Mr Patel,' Simon said.

'You policemen really are amazing!' Patel suddenly sat upright, his eyes fixed brightly on Simon's own. 'We have just had a murder at the clinic. Not just any old murder but the murder of the head of the clinic. That is unpleasant enough, but the effect of his death may well turn out to be the death of the clinic. That will mean that all our jobs and futures are compromised. For a man who is about to embark on married life, this is not the happiest of situations. And as for the gremlin, its activities rather pale in the light of what happened last Thursday night, don't you think?'

'But that's exactly why we are trying to find out who killed Mr Kingsley, so that you can all get back into some sort of routine, with it all cleared out of the way,' Longman said, soothingly. 'Detective Chief Inspector Simon here isn't asking questions for the sake of it, you know. The reason we are asking about the clinic gremlin is because there may perhaps be a connection between it and the person who killed Sebastian Kingsley.' His voice hardened a little. 'So, if you have any idea about any of the things you have been asked, it's in your own interests to help us as much as you can. Do you have any idea who is behind the prior events at the clinic Mr Patel?'

'As I said, no I don't.'

Longman's effort had come to nought and

Simon decided that an increasingly hostile Anil Patel was unlikely to become more communicative. He thanked the man, not without irony, and they left.

'He's definitely cagey about something,' Longman said, not bothering to lower his voice as they went down the stairs.

'But what about? I think it's the alibi.'

As he heard the front door slam behind them, and their voices fade, Anil Patel went back into his bedroom and picked up the phone.

'They've gone,' he said.

'Was it difficult?' Aisha asked, her voice soothingly sympathetic.

'I thought so. But then I'm not used to dissimulation.'

He heard a soft laugh. 'But you are getting used to it. Shall I come over now?'

18

Jock Patterson pushed Valerie in her wheel-chair along the path dividing the green towards the south door of the cathedral. Although only four o'clock it was quite dark, the huge building already lit up. It had been Valerie who had suggested they both come here. Jock was used to his solitary visits and it felt strange to be in company. It was a departure from the norm and only added to his overwhelming feeling that his life was spinning out of control. He felt troubled, too, at leaving Kevin alone in the basement flat.

'He'll be all right,' Valerie said, as if picking up his thoughts. 'He was listening to some music. I think he'll start to settle down now.' Her voice was weak, seeming to crack in the cold evening air.

'So long as the police don't come round questioning again,' Jock said, unable to make the effort required of him. 'And I'm afraid they're likely to.'

Valerie twisted painfully in her wheelchair and looked up at him, her face yellow in the reflected light.

'If they do, it will be nothing to worry

239

about. They have no reason to question Kevin.'

'They make their own reasons,' Jock said gruffly.

Her head bowed and she turned back.

'We'll just have to do our best,' he said, trying to inject a note of heartiness. 'There's nothing for them to find.'

They had reached the porch and could hear the choir practising as soon as they were through the door, a sound redolent of the many proud, happy memories of when Kevin had been a member of the choir, memories now shrouded in darker, more recent recollections.

Jock pushed the wheelchair down the central nave and close to the intricately carved rood-screen where she asked him to leave her for a little while. He watched her head bow in prayer and wished he could find the necessary submission to fate, submission to a deity that allowed so many bad things to happen in the world, even in his own home. He was at a loss what to do now that he was here, but the power of the lovely building, its sheer scale and beauty, began to have its accustomed healing effect on him as he wandered off, looking up at the magnificent fan-vaulted ceiling, the immense pillars that held the structure together. The sight of the prayer candles though, lit by so many for others who were in pain or need, moved him almost to tears. He dropped some coins in a slot and lit candles for the three of them, offering up a prayer that all would be well after all.

The individual flames from the candles blurred through his tears into a whole and he was blinded and lost. Shaking, wiping his face with a handkerchief, he stumbled to the nearest seat and sat there, head in hands. He could see only blackness and felt only the burning hatred in his heart that he thought nothing could assuage.

He had no idea how long he had been sitting there in that quiet corner of the cathedral when he felt a hand on his shoulder and a body seat itself beside him.

'Can I help in any way?' It was gently spoken, a man's voice.

Jock straightened, feeling stiff and old, drained of emotion. He opened his eyes, hot from the tears he had shed, and saw Dean Kingsley.

'It's Jock, Jock Patterson, isn't it?' The dean's voice seemed unsteady.

'Aye, it's Jock,' he said, shaking his head as if to clear it. He saw that the dean looked pale in the half-light in which they sat, older than he remembered him.

'Is there anything I can do to help, Jock?' the dean repeated.

Jock examined the man's face, saw his own sorrow and let go of some of the anger in his heart. 'There might have been, but it's too late now.'

He stood up, feeling shaky, dizzy from all the emotion that he had tried to hold at bay for so long. He placed his hand on the dean's shoulder in turn.

'Thank you anyway,' he said, moving away.

He became conscious of having abandoned Valerie, unsure how long it had been since he had left her.

She was still there, staring up at the rood-screen, looking more peaceful with the lines on her face relaxed.

'I think that all the prayers prayed here over hundreds of years must be absorbed somehow by the building,' she said, as he joined her. 'It makes me feel peaceful, feeling the faith of all those ages of time.'

It had once been something Jock had readily experienced, and he had perhaps recovered a little of it today. But all he could really think of was the anguish with which so many of those prayers, like his own, had been uttered.

As he wheeled her slowly back to the main body of the cathedral, Valerie said:

'I've hardly been here since Kev was in the choir. I should like to come more often, if you'll bring me.'

'Of course I will,' he said, knowing that he would still want his own solitary visits here. Would it be faith that brought him, though, or recollected faith?

'We'd better get back,' she said. 'Kev will be wanting his tea. At least I hope he will, he hasn't eaten much since he got home.'

There was a determined normality in her voice. They had no choice now but to put things behind them and carry on, hoping that they would be allowed that option.

They reached the outer door and paused in the icy air that confronted them. The lights in Precinct Row shone brightly in the sharp air. The lane in which the clinic stood was by contrast murky and dark with only a faint rim of light showing in one of the upper windows of the clinic building.

'I wish they'd get on and put some lights in the lane,' Valerie said. 'With it being cobbled it's dangerous underfoot, especially in this weather. I'd have thought the clinic would have had a light put at the front, too. It's not very welcoming at this time of year especially, with only the glow from the fanlight.'

Jock pushed her along the path, careful of his own footing and thinking that a smooth surface was surely more slippery and dangerous than the cobbled lane. He marvelled momentarily at the sheer banality of their thoughts in the circumstances. It must have been such attention to the trivial that kept the British spirit triumphant during the blitz, he thought.

'We shall have to speak to the school about Kevin,' Valerie said. 'Do you think they'll take him back? I mean, now his voice is just broken he's no use to the choir any more and with him being away for so long he'd have to repeat a year, wouldn't he?'

'He's young for his school year, with his birthday being when it is, so a repeat year wouldn't be too difficult, I'd have thought,' Jock said, doubting that the school would really be keen to have him back. Kevin was not particularly distinguished academically, and his underdeveloped body had not been much of a help on the sports field. 'We can speak to the head about him going back next term. After all they're about to break up for the Christmas holidays now. Maybe the dean could put in a word for him.' Maybe he should and all, he thought. And the dean had asked if he could help.

'It wouldn't hurt,' Valerie said neutrally.

'Maybe he'd prefer to go to another school,' Jock suggested.

'Maybe he would,' she agreed.

Jock turned the wheelchair on to the uncomfortable surface of the lane.

'I think we should get him to see someone,' she said, her voice shaking with the vibration of the wheels on the cobbles.

'How d'ye mean?'

'You know,' her voice lowered unnecessarily as they approached the clinic. 'A kind of therapist, maybe.'

'Like Miss Crossley d'ye mean?'

'Well, not her, but someone . . . '

'We'll see, eh? We'll see how things go. The main thing is to get him comfortable again, try and build him up a bit.'

They had already spoken quietly and fearfully about the necessity for Kevin to see a doctor. Their great worry was that he might have been infected with some disease through sexual contact with a man who was probably promiscuous. It was not a subject they knew anything of, and they were delicate about raising the issue with their son.

Valerie said no more as Jock wheeled her around the side of the building to their own quarters, her mind on her damaged son, worrying again whether he would still be there when they came home.

19

Ruth Maguire lived in a terrace of large Victorian houses beyond the North Gate, not far from where Simon's flat was. She seemed philosophic at their appearance, showing them into a richly furnished sitting-room. This was the most homely of the places they had visited so far, with lots of books in evidence and plenty of family photographs. A CD of Brahms was playing, the lighting was diffused and a real fire was burning in the original Victorian fireplace. Simon sank into the comfortable old sofa and was willing to forgo all duty and fall asleep. Longman joined him and seemed similarly inclined. Despite their recent caffeine intake at Anil Patel's, they both felt soporific enough to agree to the offer of yet more.

Ruth Maguire picked up the tray that showed the remains of her own recent snack and left the room. Simon dutifully struggled to his feet to take the opportunity of examining the room more closely. The photographs on the mantelpiece included a younger Ruth leaning on the arm of a big, tall man with a stiff mane of hair, presumably the deceased husband. Both were dressed for serious walking in open country that might have been the Lake District. Another picture showed an attractive young blond-haired girl smiling over her shoulder at the camera, beside it a photograph that looked as if it had been taken at the same time and place of a boy, hair not unlike his father's, striding towards the camera. Other more recent pictures were of the boy and girl, the girl's hair short, spiky and more blond, the boy's as untamed as before.

'Our last holiday together,' Ruth said, coming quietly into the room bearing a large tray. She put it down and joined Simon, indicating the first picture he had looked at. 'We used to go walking in the Lakes every summer. We haven't been since Brendan died, but that last time was perfect.'

'You can never go back,' Simon agreed, giving her a sympathetic smile. 'Perfect memories are exactly that.'

She moved to pour their coffee. The tray was weighed with a large plate of toasted tea-cakes, manna to the two detectives who had grabbed only a sandwich lunch several hours before. They did justice to the food before settling back with their coffee.

'What did you want to see me about?' she

247

asked as Simon swallowed his last buttery crumb.

'A few things we want to clarify,' Simon said, thinking how much softer her image was in this light, her sleek hair shining, reflecting the fire.

She waited, eyebrows raised, and sipped from her mug.

'You told us you received two phone calls the night Mr Kingsley died,' Simon began.

'And I got it wrong, didn't I,' she said, looking rueful. 'Please understand that it can be difficult to think straight in circumstances like those that met us when we came into work on Friday morning. I really did think at the time that the calls I received came later than they did.'

Simon nodded, willing to let the point go.

'The first call was from your daughter in London, and the second was from a man called James Flamborough. Can you tell me what the second call was about? You said something previously about some committee work.'

'Of course. I am involved in a pressure group concerning the use of herbicides in drainage ditches in the county. The poison is getting into the water supply, and, in particular, concentrating in local natural sources, causing a problem for wildlife. James

Flamborough, who you may possibly know is a prospective parliamentary candidate for the city in the by-election, has involved himself in the campaign and was ringing that night to clarify when our next meeting is going to be.'

Simon took another mouthful of coffee.

'You were speaking to him for about fifteen minutes, which gives you an alibi until about 9.55 pm. Do you have anyone who can tell us where you were for the rest of the night?'

'I'm afraid I don't, Chief Inspector. Do I *need* an alibi?' She sounded as if she thought the idea entirely unreasonable.

'It does help, Mrs Maguire,' Longman said kindly, replete with toasted tea-cakes, of which he had eaten three. 'If only for the purpose of elimination.' Ruth Maguire visibly softened.

Simon's next words, though, made her stiffen.

'Can you tell us why Sebastian Kingsley was threatening you with blackmail?'

'Wherever did you get that from?' she asked with some indignation.

'It's true, though?'

'No, it's not true. I told you that he and I had an argument over Anne, but that was all. Why on earth would he want to blackmail me?'

'To gain your support perhaps in getting

rid of her?' Simon said. 'But you're the only person who can answer that question.'

'There's nothing for him to blackmail me over,' she said sharply.

Simon wondered for a moment if Hannah Crossley had made the claim merely out of malice, but there was something in Ruth Maguire's manner, a wariness, that made him think otherwise.

'It wasn't anything to do with your relationship with James Flamborough? He would want to avoid scandal in the run up to the by-election.'

She gave a short laugh. 'What relationship? Anyway, I doubt if Sebastian was even aware that I know James.'

She looked uneasy, though, and her voice was strained. Kingsley had been a man with a nose for gossip — he might well have found out anything, if there were anything to find. But there was little Simon could do for the moment in the face of her complete denial.

'You had quite a long association with Sebastian Kingsley, Mrs Maguire. He was your family doctor and was responsible for administering a drug to your husband which subsequently killed him, I understand.'

'You've certainly been doing your research,' she said drily. 'I hope you haven't been prevailing on Jessie to tell tales about her

250

erstwhile colleagues.'

Remembering Jessie's inadvertent admission that had made the connection between Kingsley and the guilty doctor made Simon pause self-consciously. He would be sorry to be the cause of any strain between Jessie and Ruth Maguire: he knew Jessie was fond of her, so, perhaps unwisely, he felt he had to offer some explanation.

'Jessie has been totally opposed to 'telling tales' as you put it, as she always is in such circumstances. She did make a sympathetic remark about the death of your husband and the hard time you had of it with him on dialysis. It was someone else who told me that Kingsley had been your family doctor, and that it was that connection with him which led to you to working in the clinic.'

Ruth seemed only in part mollified.

'And I suppose you wonder if I might have murdered him in some kind of delayed reaction to his treatment of my husband?'

'It's possible there might be some cumulative effect of his sins, especially if he were blackmailing you,' Simon said mildly.

'Well, since he wasn't blackmailing me, and since all the emotion over my husband is well in the past and Sebastian did his best to help me out after I qualified as a medical herbalist,

I really had no grounds to wish Sebastian dead.'

She crossed her legs and her arms defensively, glaring at Simon, her lips compressed.

Simon was finding this a particularly uncomfortable interview. Ruth Maguire had had a difficult enough life, losing a husband and being left to raise two children alone, and he felt unpleasantly intrusive in the circumstances. He felt obliged to admit to this.

'Believe me, Mrs Maguire, I would avoid this interview if I could, but I am required to ask you these questions, or I would not be doing my job as I should. I'm sorry but I have some more to ask you.'

She tilted her chin at him, unappeased.

'Tell me,' he said. 'Did you know that Sebastian Kingsley was gay, or perhaps bisexual?'

Perhaps it was relief that the question did not involve her directly, but she gave a questioning smile.

'Really?' she said. 'No I didn't know. But it does make a kind of sense. I used to wonder why he had never married and thought it was because he so obviously liked to play the field. He was forever flirting with any remotely attractive woman who crossed his path. So he probably was bisexual rather than totally gay, I would think.'

'He paid attention to your daughter Cass, I understand?' Simon said.

She paused, her face shuttered.

'He interfered with our ideas about her future, that was all.'

'But it's all resolved and Cass is at university in London, I believe?'

'That's right.' She took an audible breath.

'So no lasting damage, Mrs Maguire?' Longman asked cheerfully.

'No lasting damage, Sergeant Longman,' she agreed. 'I'd offer you some more coffee but I'd hate to prolong your stay.'

'We'll be finished with our questions very soon,' Simon said. 'I wondered whether you have had any thoughts about Mr Kingsley's death since I last spoke to you. It was so soon after you had learned about the murder at the time and everyone was in a state of shock.'

'I'm afraid it is still as much of a mystery to me now as it was then. I suppose, in view of what you said about him being gay, and obviously leading a rather secret life that we weren't allowed to know about, your answer might lie in that direction. Anyone who keeps secrets is vulnerable, aren't they?'

'Indeed they are, Mrs Maguire,' Simon agreed, hauling himself from the comfortable sofa. 'And I'm sure you are properly aware of the fact.'

She said nothing to that barb, silently seeing them into the hall and holding open the front door for them.

It was bitterly cold, the stars sparkling, the crescent moon sharp against the fathomless sky. Longman shivered and stamped his feet.

'She's definitely covering up something,' he said. 'There's something she doesn't want us to know about.'

Simon shrugged, pulling up his overcoat collar.

'People do have things they would rather not discuss with strangers. It isn't necessarily suspicious.'

'But she denied the blackmail. Do you think Hannah Crossley was lying?'

After a moment's thought, Simon said: 'No, I don't.' His meeting with her at the art exhibition had shown him a more humourous, less brittle woman than the one they had interviewed in her apartment. His gut feeling was that she had not been trying to implicate Ruth Maguire in some way in Kingsley's death, merely trying to help him out. If she were trying to point suspicion away from herself, there were more likely candidates than Ruth. And if Hannah had some particular enmity towards her, they had seen no evidence for it.

20

There was a little more sign of life the following morning at the Cathedral Clinic.

'Jonathan is in this morning if you want to speak to him,' Frances Fulton said, surprisingly helpfully. 'He's just finishing with a client.'

Voices came from the direction of Hadden's consulting-room as the door opened and he appeared, accompanied by a middle-aged woman who was hanging on his every word. He looked tired, as if his attentions to the woman were an unwanted effort, and seemed almost relieved to see Simon and Longman.

'I'm free now for half an hour or so if you're looking to speak to me.'

They went into his room where soft music was playing, a combination that sounded like piano accompanied by trees afflicted by a gale-force wind and possible trouble at sea. Hadden went to stand by the window, looking out over the frost-rimed shrubs.

'Are there any developments in the investigation?' he asked, his back still turned to them.

'Do you mind if we sit down, Mr Hadden?'

'Not at all, Detective Chief Inspector Simon and Detective Sergeant Longman,' Hadden said ironically, gesturing to the easy-chairs nearby. He sat down in one himself, slumping to one side, a hand propping his head. He looked at them with dull eyes.

'Any useful developments?' he repeated, though the question sounded more a formality than genuine interest.

'Too early yet to say.' Simon uttered the usual platitude, taking a seat.

'So why do you want to see me?'

'One matter is the issue of your alibi for the night Mr Kingsley died,' Simon said.

'Oh? What's wrong with it?' Hadden seemed unperturbed.

'You were seen approaching the clinic last Thursday night at ten-fifteen. You told us that you were leaving Madderley at that time and went home without going out again. So you lied to us. Would you explain why, and what you were doing at the clinic that night?'

Hadden crossed his legs and clasped his hands over his stomach.

'I should have thought it was obvious why I was economical with the truth, rather than really lied,' he said.

'Oh come on, Mr Hadden!' Longman

exclaimed, sitting forward. 'Let's not beat about the bush. You did lie to us and that is a very serious matter. So get on and explain just what you were up to, arriving at the clinic around the time Kingsley was murdered.'

Simon was unsurprised at the outburst from Longman. He had been quiet and moody again this morning and Simon had been too preoccupied to give him the attention he was probably in need of.

Longman's words and manner seemed to have unnerved Hadden a little. His colour heightened and he began to knead his fingers.

'I'm very sorry,' he said awkwardly. 'But since I don't know what time Sebastian was killed I can't really know what *is* an appropriate alibi, can I?'

'So why did you make it later than it really was?' Longman asked sharply.

'I was just mistaken over the time. But surely it's not enough to make any difference in the issue of time of death. It's not an exact science.'

'And don't try and be clever with us, either! Explain yourself, if you would.' Longman sat back in his chair, frowning balefully at Hadden from under his menacing eyebrows.

Hadden sighed. 'I didn't tell you I had come back to the clinic for the obvious reason that I didn't want to be considered a suspect. It was stupid of me and I am sorry, as I said, but it is the kind of thing that anyone might do, even though they are innocent of any wrongdoing.'

It was, of course, a familiar story. People lied over such things all the time, but Simon had hoped that it would not be true of Hadden, whom he had liked.

'Why did you return to the clinic that night?' he asked.

'I realized I had left my wallet here,' Hadden said, turning slightly to face Simon more fully, as if trying to delete Longman from his field of vision. 'I always put my wallet in my desk drawer when I change into my tunic.'

Simon could recall him retrieving his wallet from the desk after he had put on his jacket on the day Simon had had treatment here.

Hadden fingered the white fabric of his professional uniform.

'I'd left in a rush that evening because I didn't want to be late babysitting my son. My ex-wife can be difficult about these things.' He shrugged, 'As it was, her policeman friend was late and they didn't go out after all, but I hadn't had a chance to get anything to eat since lunchtime and I was pretty hungry by ten o'clock that night. I planned to get a take-away when I got back to Westwich and I realized that I must have forgotten to take my wallet out of the drawer, so I came to collect it.' He opened his hands as if indicating that he had fully unburdened himself of the truth.

'Did you see Mr Kingsley when you got here?' Simon asked.

'No, I wasn't even aware he was here, or anyone else for that matter. I thought the clinic was empty. Anyway, it was only a matter of moments before I was outside again.'

It was a perfectly plausible explanation. And Kingsley might even have been already dead when Hadden arrived, estimation of time of death being, as he had remarked, an inexact science.

'And did you buy your take-away as planned, Mr Hadden?' Longman asked, sounding as if he doubted it.

'Yes, I did. I went to the Lotus take-away in the West Gate and bought a not particularly enjoyable chicken chow mein and a vegetable dish. But that's what happens when you don't organize your life properly.' Hadden smiled self-deprecatingly.

The combined piano and wind sounds were having their desired effect on Simon, who was beginning to feel happily relaxed and ready to accept, at least until any evidence should suggest otherwise, that Hadden had spent an innocent evening and night.

'I don't suppose you have a receipt for the meal, do you?' Longman said roughly.

'I shouldn't think so,' Hadden said regretfully. 'I don't usually keep such things.'

'So we only have your word for it that you left the clinic before half-past ten?'

Hadden, his eyes on Longman with sudden fearfulness, bit his lip and gave a slight nod.

'Unless the young woman who served me can remember. But it's not likely, and she probably wouldn't recall what time it was. It was quite busy at that hour with the pubs getting near to closing time.'

'You didn't pay by card by any chance?' Simon asked, rousing himself a little.

'Yes, I did!' Hadden brightened. 'I remember now that I had very little cash in my wallet and I used my debit card. And I keep the slips in the back section of my wallet so that I keep track of them.'

He moved quickly across the room to his desk, reached inside the central drawer and produced a brown-leather wallet, holding it up for them to see. He returned to his seat and began sifting through.

'Here it is!' He held up a small piece of yellow paper and handed it to Simon.

It was a Visa receipt from the Lotus Take-away for a purchase total of £9.39, the time 10.38 p.m., the date the correct one. That meant an approximately twenty-three-minute gap between the time Hadden had been observed by the housemaster from the Cathedral School and the time he paid for his meal. The Lotus, Simon estimated, was less than a five-minute walk from the clinic, leaving around fifteen minutes unaccounted for, except by the likely explanation that, as Hadden had said, the place was busy at that time of night and it might well have taken that long to be served. Even so, there would not have been remotely enough time for Hadden to have killed Kingsley *and* spent at least half an hour wiping his flat clean of fingerprints. He handed the receipt to Longman who examined it closely then passed it back to Hadden.

'Thank you,' Hadden said, now sounding wounded. 'Are you satisfied with that?'

'For the time being, Mr Hadden,' Longman said formally.

'And you are certain you saw and heard nothing at all, that night at the clinic?' Simon added.

'Quite sure.' Hadden glanced at his watch, his mind probably on his next client.

'We won't keep you much longer,' Simon

said. 'But I wanted to ask you some more about Sebastian Kingsley's private life, since you seem to have known him longer than anyone else. You were presumably aware that he was gay?'

'Was he?' Despite the question, Hadden didn't sound surprised.

'You must have known, surely?'

'I wasn't certain. I mean, I knew he had been bisexual but I had the impression that he had decided to fix his interest on women. He was never 'out' as far as the homosexual side of his nature was concerned and I suppose I imagined he had put that side of his life behind him. Though I did wonder about all the weekends he spent in London.'

'You were his friend, he must have talked to you about his private life?' Simon was finding this puzzling. Hadden and Kingsley had known each other from their schooldays. Was the gay side of his nature something that had been evident at that time, but that Hadden really assumed had somehow become latent?

'I think I told you that Seb was discreet about his private life. We didn't talk about our relationships, anyway. I suppose we were like most blokes, not discussing the emotional side of life. Seb and I talked about work and the clinic.' He paused. 'You're quite sure, are you, about this?'

'Quite sure,' Simon said. 'Medical evidence.'

Hadden pulled a pained expression.

'I see. Are you thinking, then, that his being gay had something to do with his death? I don't see why it should.'

'There's no particular reason for thinking so,' Simon said. 'It's just another facet of his life — and one that he obviously was keeping quiet about.'

'Poor Seb,' Hadden said quietly. 'I suppose he thought it wasn't good for the image of the clinic. As you know, he was very image-conscious. But I can't imagine why it should be an issue in this day and age.'

'The law moves faster than some people's prejudices,' Simon remarked, reiterating the sentiment of what Hermione had said to him.

'I suppose so.' Hadden looked thoughtful.

'Are you in any relationship yourself, Mr Hadden?' Longman said abruptly. Hadden looked resentful.

'Is it really any of your business, Sergeant?'

Longman gave a heavy sigh.

'I'm afraid almost everything is our business at the moment, sir.'

Hadden looked to Simon as if expecting support, but Simon merely raised his eyebrows, waiting for his answer. Hadden shrugged.

'It's not that I've anything to hide — more that it's a painful subject really. There was someone but my spare time is given to my son, Marcus.' Seeing their expressions he went on reluctantly, 'My ex-wife and I were completely incompatible but she's never forgiven me for leaving her. This means that she makes things as difficult for me as she can. If she ever found out I was seeing someone some evening she would ring up and insist that I came to babysit Marcus, or had him to stay — anything, really, to disrupt my personal life. You find that people don't want a relationship with you if you are always putting someone else first, even if it is your son.'

'Very difficult for you, sir,' Longman said sympathetically, his current sensibilities touched by Hadden's plight.

Simon, inwardly amused at Longman's *volte face* stood up, conscious that Hadden's next client would be waiting.

He was about to make some remark about the encouraging signs of clients returning to the clinic and it reminded him of Frances.

'Did you know,' he asked, turning to Hadden, who was about to open the door for them, 'that Frances Fulton is the daughter of the doctor who made threats to Mr Kingsley after his wife died?'

Hadden stood still.

'I had no idea,' he said. 'She's never mentioned it, though that is possibly for understandable reasons.'

He looked thoughtful all the same.

21

Simon paused at the top of the clinic steps, Longman beside him. Before them, as the sun began to break through, the frost seemed to hang in the air several feet above the ground so that people crossing the cathedral green appeared to float without legs, gliding through the mist. Looking further, towards Precinct Row, Simon watched the dean emerge from this strange illusion into the clearer air near his gate, open it and enter his house. Simon was reminded of Munro's admonishments when he had spoken to her the day before; now was as convenient a time as any, he thought.

'Are you happy enough with Hadden's alibi?' Longman said, as they crossed the green.

'I suppose so. We've no reason to suspect him, anyway, and he couldn't have had time to go upstairs to Kingsley's flat, give it a clean and still get to the Chinese take-away.'

'He could have gone back afterwards. But you don't think that's likely, do you?' Longman's argumentative tone was back again and Simon repressed his irritation.

'I think whoever did it would be taking double the risk of being seen. Hadden's story is perfectly plausible but if you can come up with any motive for him killing Kingsley please let me know.'

Longman didn't reply, sinking into what felt like a huffy silence.

Relenting, Simon asked: 'Have you heard anything from Julie? Is she going to be home soon?' He profoundly hoped so.

'Not yet, by the look of things. Noel came round again yesterday and they had a big row on the doorstep. Sue's told him to see a solicitor and communicate that way. But it doesn't always work out like that though, does it? Women can go on stalling over access to children for some time and the law doesn't seem to make a lot of difference.'

'Just let's focus on the job, shall we?' Simon interupted, realizing he was not after all prepared to listen to the details of Longman's discontent. He opened the dean's gate and pushed hard on the doorbell.

'He should have valued what he had before he jeopardized it,' Longman muttered as they waited. 'But all the same, the woman doesn't usually get punished in the same way if she's the one that plays around.'

With some relief Simon saw the door open and Mrs Chambers standing there wiping her hands on a pristine apron. She stood back as they entered the hall.

'The dean has just come in. He's in his study. Would you gentlemen both like to go through?'

The dean was sitting as before, staring vacantly out of the window. He courteously rose to his feet as they entered the room and thanked them for calling. Not until he had settled them in their chairs did he ask if there had been any developments in the case.

'We've found out a few more things,' Simon said. He would have expected the dean to pay attention at that but instead the man gave an odd duck of his head and returned his focus to the garden. It was a combination of irritation at Longman's problems and impatience at the dean's reticence on the subject of his nephew along with a sudden leap of intuition that made Simon choose the words he used next.

'Why is it, Dean, that you didn't tell us about your nephew's sexual proclivities?'

A look of real pain passed over the older man's features and he seemed to sink further into his chair.

'I'm sorry,' he said, head bowed. 'I was hoping it wouldn't need to come out.'

Simon glanced at Longman who was frowning in fierce concentration.

'Perhaps you'd better tell us the whole story,' Simon said, in a tone that indicated prevarication would not be acceptable. His words had obviously hit a sensitive spot. He could not believe that the dean was merely reacting to the idea that they had discovered Sebastian Kingsley's homosexuality. It was no longer illegal, and even if the church had ambivalent feelings about it, it couldn't explain the man's reaction to his words.

The dean turned to Simon, his mouth working, as if he were trying to form the necessary words.

'I must apologize,' he said at last. 'I just could not believe that it had anything to do with Sebastian's death, or I would have told you about it.'

Simon forbore to point out that he was not the judge of what might or might not be relevant to the murder of his nephew, waiting for the dean to come out with whatever he so evidently did not want to say.

'It was four years ago now. There's been no trouble since. I'm sure there hasn't and I did keep an eye on Sebastian, but he promised me that it was a moment's aberration and it wouldn't happen again.' The man's voice was noticeably weaker than in their last interview, even though he had been in shock.

'You must tell me exactly what happened,'

Simon said firmly.

Dean Kingsley was looking down at his hands, picking at his nails.

'It was hushed up. So bad for the choir and the cathedral. The bishop was involved: we considered making Sebastian resign from the choir but Bishop Chessman agreed to give him another chance.' He gave Simon a quick glance. 'There was never any doubt about Sebastian's love of church music. It would have broken his heart to have to leave the choir.'

'Tell me what happened exactly,' Simon repeated, suppressing his impatience.

The dean lowered his head again.

'It was one of the boys in the choir, Justin Groves. He complained that Sebastian had . . . touched him. In a way that he shouldn't.' He looked up. 'It was only the boy's word against Sebastian's and Sebastian swore at the time that he had done nothing improper. But the boy told his parents and the bishop got involved and Sebastian had to be interviewed. There was no evidence of wrongdoing that would be strong enough to make a case against my nephew, and Sebastian continued to insist that the boy had misinterpreted an affectionate gesture.'

'But you obviously thought otherwise,' Simon suggested.

'I was deeply concerned about it,' Dean Kingsley said. 'Justin was an honest little boy, with a wonderful pure voice. His parents took him away from the choir, of course, and he was a great loss.' He pressed his lips together and swallowed. 'I questioned Sebastian very closely about it afterwards, however, and he eventually admitted that he did have what he called 'special' feelings for the boy. He swore he had never done anything of the kind before and that he would never give in to such feelings again.'

The dean raised his eyebrows with a look that suggested he was now doubting that promise. 'But you have no reason to suppose that that incident has any connection, surely, with Sebastian's death? I knew he was bisexual, but that he kept his homosexual activities mostly confined to his contacts in London. And paedophile tendencies,' he grimaced at the emotive word, 'are no more likely in homosexuals than in heterosexuals.' He looked appealingly to Simon to agree with him.

Simon had no idea of the statistics involved and felt he should have. Young flesh was irresistibly appealing to sexual predators of either sexual proclivity, whether heterosexual or homosexual, he was at least sure of that. And Sebastian Kingsley seemed to have been sexually predatory.

'It hasn't, has it,' the dean said again, 'anything to do with Sebastian's death? I mean, my not telling you hasn't hampered your investigation in any way?'

Simon was on the point of reassuring him, distressed as the man obviously was, when the thought occurred that Sebastian Kingsley's attraction to young boys might well be linked to his death. However much he might have reassured his uncle, however much he may have meant what he said at the time, such appetites are not so easily repressed.

'It's a pity you took Sebastian's word that he would change his ways,' he said to the dean. 'You should have insisted that he sought treatment for his aberrant behaviour. I can only hope,' he added, 'that should such behaviour ever confront you again, you will be a little more exigent in your efforts to avoid them happening once more.'

The dean could hardly have looked more chastened. Simon decided to leave it at that for now. He had more urgent questions to ask elsewhere.

They crossed the cathedral green again.

'Are you wondering what I'm wondering?' Longman asked.

'And what are you wondering?'

'I'm wondering about the boy who ran

272

away for a year and has just come home.'

'It would answer my usual question, wouldn't it, of 'Why now? — What has happened very recently that might have some bearing on why the murder occurred when it did'?'

'You haven't asked the question until now,' Longman reminded Simon.

'Perhaps I should have,' Simon said shortly. He was annoyed with himself for not having raised his favourite issue of the timing of the murder. He had completely ignored the coincidence of the arrival of Jock's son Kevin on the very day that Sebastian Kingsley had been killed.

At the rear of the clinic Jock was repairing a wooden tub which had contained a clipped shrub, now lying on its side on a pile of compost, the paving protected by a sheet of tarpaulin. He straightened up, a forced smile on his face.

'What can I do for you gentlemen?'

Simon thought it likely that Jock's formality of address would have changed to something less polite before the afternoon.

'We'd like to speak to you and your family, Jock. May we step inside for a while?'

Jock silently wrapped the tarpaulin around the roots of the shrub, weighting it with stones, and gathered up his tools before leading them into the basement flat. As they stood in the entrance hall, Simon asked if Kevin were at home.

'Yes, he's here.'

'Would you fetch him, please?'

Jock gestured for them to enter the living-room and moved on along the passageway.

Valerie Patterson was seated in her wheelchair watching a television programme emitting antipodean accents. She looked up at them, her hand immediately moving to clutch her crucifix.

'Is something the matter, Detective Chief Inspector?' she asked.

There were few moments of true satisfaction in his job, and they were greatly outweighed by moments of distress. Looking down into Valerie Patterson's face, so lined by pain and experience, Simon felt a sinking of the heart at what further anguish he might be bringing into her life.

'We'd just like to clarify a few things with you all, Mrs Patterson,' he prevaricated.

Jock appeared, Kevin at his elbow. It was the first clear look at the boy Simon had had. He was wearing baggy jeans with a black sweatshirt, a thin, zipped fleece with a hood and thick-soled trainers that looked too big at the end of his thin legs. The boy looked young for his age, slight in build, pinch-faced, his brown hair straight and long, adding to his girlish appearance. But his eyes looked old as he watched Simon: old and wary.

'Please,' Simon said, 'Can we all sit down?'

Jock ushered the boy forward and they sat together on the sofa, Simon and Longman on two hardbacked chairs by the table at the back of the room. Since they had last been here the room had been hung with Christmas decorations, the brave effort at cheer only increasing Simon's distaste for what he had to ask them.

'We haven't thought of anything else that might help you,' Valerie Patterson began defensively. 'Have we, Jock?'

Jock shook his head, his eyes as fixed on the two policemen as were his son's.

'What do you want with us?' he asked.

These were going to be difficult questions to frame. The anxiety of the parents, the fear in the boy, were palpable and Simon wanted to be careful not to frighten any of them into silence.

'Tell me, Kevin,' he said gently. 'Why did you run away from home?'

The boy's eyes shuttered.

'It seemed like something I wanted to do at the time,' he said. His voice had scarcely finished breaking.

'But why did you want to? You have a good home with parents who obviously care about you a great deal, you had a place at an excellent school.'

'It was bullying, bullying at school,' the boy said defiantly, his voice cracking, undermining his effort to assert himself and making him seem what he probably was — a boy who was frightened of what he might be persuaded to admit.

'So your parents will have spoken to the head teacher about this, no doubt?' Simon looked from Jock to Valerie.

'We didn't know,' Valerie said hastily. 'We didn't know until he came home and told us.'

Jock kept his eyes fixed on Simon, his expression rigid.

'Why didn't you tell your parents before you ran away, Kevin, so that they could take steps to put the situation right?'

The boy folded his arms and looked at Simon with an effort at contempt.

'That never does any good,' he said.

'But I understand you were doing well at school. You were a member of the cathedral choir, weren't you?'

Kevin didn't answer. He looked away, shifting his small body a little closer to his father's.

'You knew Mr Kingsley quite well then,

both as your father's employer and as a fellow choir-member.'

Kevin blinked, but again made no reply.

'Tell me, Kevin,' Simon said quietly, 'did Mr Kingsley ever try to make you do anything improper, or did he ever touch you in a way that he shouldn't?'

There was no real warning; Valerie and Jock seemed frozen, Kevin's eyes seemed to flicker a little more rapidly, and then he made a sudden bolt for the door. He was through and away before Simon or Longman had fully got to their feet. They ran, Jock close behind them, out of the building, only to see Kevin's small figure racing up the narrow path beside the back garden that led to the North Gate, his jacket flying out behind him. They had no chance of overtaking him.

Jock turned on them, eyes blazing.

'You stupid buggers. Now look what you've done!'

Stupid Simon certainly felt. He should never have sat in that room in a way that left the door unguarded. It was this awareness that made him react to Jock's attack with a degree of courtesy.

'I'm very sorry that happened, Mr Patterson, but we'll get him picked up.'

'Like you did last time, you mean!' Jock shouted.

'You reported him missing when he left last year?' Longman asked.

'Of course we did. But your lot never found him. He ended up in London like a lot of other young kids.' Jock was almost in tears now. 'And you might imagine what happened to him there.'

Shock and pity mixed in Simon's voice.

'I'm very sorry.'

Longman was less contrite.

'If you'd been more open with us about what had happened to your son, we might not be in this situation,' he said.

Valerie had wheeled herself to the back door.

'Has he gone?' she asked, the tears unchecked on her face.

22

The extra manpower required to find Kevin Patterson and bring him in needed the involvement of Detective Superintendent Munro. She accepted the urgency of the matter and set things in motion even before Simon was asked to give a full account of its necessity.

'Tell!' she demanded finally, pouring him a filter coffee and joining him at the table in her room, sinking opposite him into one of the low chairs and showing an attractive length of leg. She was wearing a cream woollen suit today that made her warm brown skin glow. The cut of its top, though, made every concession to modern fashion and none whatever to the current state of the weather.

Despite the vision before him Simon was still feeling distracted with remorse at how badly he had handled the interview with the Pattersons and especially the boy — a child who, if he were a victim of Kingsley in the way he suspected, Simon should have treated far more sensitively and cautiously. He hesitated over how to begin to recount his catalogue of failures, not least of which was his remissness in not surmising much earlier in the case that the return of Kevin Patterson and the death of Sebastian Kingsley on the same day were connected.

'You think this boy was involved in Kingsley's murder,' Munro prompted.

'I should have thought of it earlier,' Simon said, and went on to point out the coincidence of the two events. 'It's something I always ask — why now? And I failed to do so this time.'

Munro sighed and put down her cup.

'Perhaps when you have finished with self-flagellation you might get to the nub of the matter. I'm feeling a little lost and I have just demanded a large police presence in the city and its environs. I'd like to be assured that it's not going to be an embarrassing waste of time.'

'The autopsy report showed that Kingsley was a practising homosexual, or rather bisexual,' Simon said hurriedly, 'but I hadn't yet spoken to the dean about it. When I did, it came out a bit sharply. I think,' he said slowly, 'that I picked up on his unease when Longman and I went to see him this morning to report progress, as you asked. It made me phrase my question rather differently from the way I might have done and he looked very troubled. He came out with a story about

280

how Sebastian Kingsley had been accused four years ago of molesting a young boy in the cathedral choir.'

'And nothing was done about it, I suppose,' Munro said drily. 'It was hushed up?'

'Basically, yes. Kingsley promised his uncle not to be a naughty boy again and he was allowed, amazingly, back into the choir, while the young boy, a talented member of the choir apparently, was withdrawn by his parents.'

'And your thoughts turned immediately to young Kevin Patterson who had been in the choir before running away a year ago.'

'Exactly. As I said, he arrived home the very day Kingsley died. It struck me that, if Kingsley had been abusing him in some way the boy would have found himself in a truly invidious position — quite apart from the horrors of the abuse itself. He would have needed little reminding from Kingsley that his father's job, his parents' home, were at risk if the boy kicked up any fuss. Kingsley would have had the perfect victim. The boy would have had little option but to make a run for it as the only way he could avoid Kingsley's perverted attentions and hope to protect his parents at the same time.'

'And you think he came home intent on killing Kingsley? Did the boy strike you as capable of that?'

Simon hesitated. 'I can't say that he looked capable of killing anyone to be honest. He's a slightly built kid, physically young for his age.'

Munro grimaced. 'Only apparently, perhaps. It doesn't take much imagination to suppose what happened to him when he was wandering the streets of London. He'd be old in experience, anyway.'

'It's true, though, that I'm not convinced he had the physical strength to have killed Kingsley in that way.'

'So why did he come back? Did he suppose Kingsley would have lost interest in him by now?'

'Possibly. His voice has broken so he may have hoped that. But it may not be the boy who actually attacked Kingsley. His parents would have questioned him about why he left, what had happened to him since. Kevin told me that he ran away because he was being bullied in school — a plausible enough excuse with him being such a little lad and a story they may have thought up between them. But if he told his parents everything it's pretty obvious how they would have reacted, Jock especially. And he would have lost his job and home if he had merely confronted Kingsley. With an invalid wife and a damaged child Jock couldn't afford to risk simple confrontation, even if it were followed up by a prosecution. By the time it came to that they might be homeless with Jock out of a job. Killing Kingsley must have seemed the only solution.'

'How does this theory of yours — and remember it is only theory at this stage — fit with the evidence you have?' Munro looked at him over the rim of her coffee-cup.

Simon had not taken time to question this. It had been something he just felt he 'knew', and knew it fitted with what little they had so far.

'The Pattersons had easier access to Kingsley than anyone. Jock just had to use the internal staircase from the basement and let himself into the main building. He may have planned to go to Kingsley's flat to confront him and then found him in his consulting-room. I'm pretty sure that this would have been an act of impulse. I can only imagine the rage that Jock must have been feeling when his son told his story. I think he confronted Kingsley in his room, hit him over the head with the nearest heavy object to hand. And the fact that Kingsley's flat was wiped clean would fit very well with its being Jock.'

'Why?'

'He would have wanted to make sure there was no evidence of Kevin's presence there. He might have taken away photographs as well. Anyone who watches crime documentaries or dramas these days knows that fingerprints can remain for a long period of time. He wiped clean any places where he thought his son might have been, perhaps taking Kevin with him to be sure of being thorough. Then he locked up, put Kingsley's keys back in his pocket and returned to the basement. In the morning he did his rounds as usual, 'discovered' the body and rang the police as any good citizen would. End of story.'

'It certainly fits.' Munro leaned forward and placed her empty cup on the table. Simon's remained, cooling with a slight film on its surface. He picked it up and took a large swallow.

'And it makes plenty of sense,' she added.

Simon felt relieved and vindicated. He did not, though, feel any sense of satisfaction. If his theory were correct, Jock Patterson had acted out of a thoroughly human rage and urge to avenge his damaged child. Simon's own thoughts as to Jock protecting his job and home at the same time were mere addenda and in all likelihood had not even entered Jock's mind when he rushed to challenge Kingsley. Any parent, any compassionate human being, would find it difficult to condemn Jock's actions. But the law would have to take its course regardless, and chaos would take over the lives of Valerie and her son. A disturbing thought occurred to him.

'It may be difficult to get a clear confession of guilt in this case,' he said.

'Why's that?' Munro said sharply.

'Suppose they both admit separately to having murdered Kingsley? After all, we can't be sure which of them did it. We know, though, that it was one person because the man died from a single blow. If they both claim guilt we're in trouble.'

'Cross that one if it comes to it,' Munro said, straightening her skirt as she stood up. 'Don't look for trouble before it happens.'

He would make an effort not to, he thought as he made his way back to the incident room, but at the moment he felt he had little useful to do but worry. He had avoided bringing Patterson in for questioning, waiting until his son was found. Simon had simply set a discreet watch on the back and front entrances to the clinic and asked Jock to be sure to stay in until they had news of Kevin. He had questioned the obviously distressed parents no further at the time: he needed some admission of abuse from Kevin before any motive could be established.

News of the latest developments involving the Pattersons had already been conveyed to those members of the team who were present in the incident room, and was currently being passed on to those who were returning from carrying out their own investigations. Their reactions were all of them mixed: a combination of quickened interest that the Pattersons seemed likely to provide the solution to all their questions, and a weary resignation and tossing of their own reports on to desks as being no longer of any value.

He repeated for the benefit of the new arrivals what precisely had taken place and there was a muttering of discussion.

'Nevertheless, I think we need to hear what the team have found out, sir,' DI Rebecca Stone said, pedantically, Simon thought sourly. 'After all,' she added loudly, 'the case isn't solved just yet, is it?'

She was right, though he didn't like her any the more for saying so.

'Let's hear it then,' he said, resting a hip on one of the tables. 'What have you turned up, DI Stone?'

'I managed to get confirmation that Jonathan Hadden's finances are as healthy as claimed,' she said briefly. 'And in addition to his converted warehouse apartment he has a cottage in remote west Wales.'

'Well done,' Simon said blandly. 'Anyone else? Rogers, Tremaine, what did you find in London?'

'The cards were for gay clubs, as expected,' Rogers, the more dominant of the two, said. 'A bartender in one of the clubs, the Jolly Roger, recognized our photograph of Kingsley.' He paused while a chuckle went round the room. 'He said Kingsley was in quite regularly at weekends but rarely with the same partner.' He shrugged. 'There's nothing else that we found out. In the other club they were less helpful, obviously didn't like the police, and said he might or might not have been in.'

'I'm sorry it wasn't more productive for you,' Simon said. 'What about you, Rhiannon? Have you been to question Anne Stillings yet?'

'I'm going later on today,' Rhiannon said. 'But there is one other bit of news. Anil Patel was home earlier than he claimed on the night of the murder. A neighbour saw him park his car just outside his garage at just after ten.'

'And he claimed he left Aisha and Frances at nearer eleven, didn't he? So I wonder why he lied,' Simon said. He felt the question was merely academic, his thoughts focused on the Pattersons.

'We'll have to ask him, won't we, sir,' DI Stone pointed out.

'We shall do that if it proves necessary,' Simon asserted firmly. 'You've done a good job in keeping all the reports up to date, DI Stone. Perhaps you could assemble these latest ones.'

'I just thought that, as DC Jones is going to question Anne Stillings about her whereabouts when she left the Corn Exchange that night, you might want another loose end tied up,' she said blandly. 'Have you read the report from SOCO that's on your desk, sir?' she asked.

'I haven't. Is it something I should read urgently?'

'That's for you to judge, sir,' she said primly. At Simon's level gaze she added: 'but I think you'll find that it's mainly Grantham's report on the computer they removed from Kingsley's flat. Kingsley had obviously visited several gay web sites and downloaded some stuff consistent with his interests.'

'So there's nothing to add to what we already know of him. Was there any evidence he'd been looking at paedophile sites as well?'

'Yes, sir.'

They had found neither computer disks

nor photographs in Kingsley's flat. If they had contained illegal images it was possible that the person who had so assidiously cleaned the flat might have removed them.

'Anything else to report?' he asked the room in general.

DC Bryn Williams spoke up. 'We've been checking on the evening-class groups. There's a total of thirty-one persons all together and so far they all seem to have alibis for the night in question. We've still got sixteen to speak to and then there's the checking-up to do as well, to see if they're telling the truth.'

He sounded wounded about the whole process, or perhaps that was the effect of his Welsh accent, one which often seemed to Simon to carry within it a certain protest at life and its vicissitudes. Williams had moved to the force recently from South Wales but Simon had noted no particular bonding between him and his compatriot Rhiannon Jones. Williams was typically dark with the build of a scrum forward, which he was. Rhiannon, from more ancient Celtic stock, had an untameable mane of red hair, a due warning of her rare but impressive temper.

Those with no pressing engagement elsewhere were allotted to help Williams and Savage with checking on the evening-class members. It was looking like a futile exercise in the present circumstances, and they all seemed acutely aware of it. But he couldn't neglect any angle in an inquiry, however much he might believe that the case was already solved. The case continued to be properly investigated until it really was officially wrapped up.

'You'll let us know as soon as you make an arrest, won't you, sir?' Williams suggested as they filed out.

'I'll do that,' Simon promised.

He turned away to stand by the huge plate-glass window with its view of the illuminated cathedral, already glowing in the early dusk. Seeming immutable, it soared serenely over the dwarfed buildings surrounding it, a proper symbol of the eternity of the hereafter and the littleness of the lives lived under its shadow. He gave an involuntary shiver. It was already bitterly cold out there and young Kevin had worn only thin clothing. Simon hoped they would find him very soon.

23

Kevin Patterson was found within a few hours, huddled and blue with cold in a bus shelter on the main road beyond Walmcot. The road joined the motorway a mile or so further on and he had probably been trying to hitch back to London. He didn't say so, though; he said nothing as they brought him in.

Simon took one glance at his pinched features — he looked more like a wizened old man than a boy — and arranged for him to have a hot meal and cup of tea in a warm room. Then he contacted Anderley and Broath, who had been keeping watch on Jock's flat, and instructed them to bring him in.

Jock was showing relief that his son had been found rather than anxiety about being questioned. Simon showed him to the room Kevin was in and left them together for a while. He was feeling no elation at the idea of wrapping up the case in the circumstances. Simon's only comfort was the belief that any jury would treat them with the sympathy they deserved and that the trial would result in a minor sentence.

The role of a police officer, he reflected not for the first time, was a strange one. Though the police had the job of enabling the law of the land, they didn't make the laws, and it sometimes happened that they could be in disagreement with those that they were required to uphold. It occurred to him that a police officer of a hundred years ago would have been completely lost in the police force of today. What society had then defined as crimes of a serious nature — homosexual acts for example, even the poaching of a rabbit — were punished severely and now were either no longer illegal or no longer taken to court, whereas crimes which were now felt to be serious ones, such as incest and rape, in those days were ignored — and that was a part of society's indifference at that time to women's and children's rights.

He asked Rhiannon, as the least threatening available presence, to sit with him in the interview with Jock and Kevin. Jock had already declined assistance from the on-duty solicitor or any other. It occurred to Simon that something would have to be done to offer support and help to Valerie Patterson. He was not sure just how disabled she was when it came to simple survival in the home. But first he wanted to get over the initial interview with her husband and son; he might then have some more certain idea of how long-term her needs were likely to be.

The two had been brought to the grim interview room to await him, PC Broath standing guard at the door. They both looked diminished by their environment, their faces drained of colour under the strip lighting, Jock's upright military bearing bent under the weight of circumstance, his arm around the shoulder of his son; Kevin staring blankly into space. Jock straightened up though when he saw Simon and folded his arms across his chest.

Simon sat, switched on the tape-recorder, spoke the formalities and turned to Jock.

'Mr Patterson, you are here with your son to answer questions about the death of Sebastian Kingsley,' he began.

'Are we under arrest?' Jock asked, his chin jutting.

'No, you are what is known as 'helping the police with their inquiries'.'

'So we could go if we want?'

For the first time Kevin showed a reaction and looked up with interest at his father's words.

'You could, but then I would have to formally arrest you and bring you back again. I think you'll find this the better option for the time being,' Simon said, conveying sympathy.

Jock settled back a little and again put his arm around his son.

'I did not kill Mr Kingsley and neither did my son.'

'But you had the motive and opportunity, and the means were to hand, Mr Patterson, so I have to question you.'

'Y'seem to have made up y'r mind,' Jock said, the thickness of his accent almost a jibe.

'I can't find out what happened either way unless you help me, Jock. Tell me Kevin,' Simon turned to the son, 'what was your relationship with Mr Kingsley?'

Kevin's eyes widened and darted round the room as if seeking another escape.

'Sebastian Kingsley behaved with you in a way that he shouldn't, didn't he, Kevin?' Simon asked, more cautiously than the last time he had spoken to the boy on the subject.

Kevin's eyes seemed to grow larger as they came back to Simon.

'It was not in any way your fault, Kevin,' Rhiannon said quietly. 'You must understand that. What he did to you was a crime.'

'You don't *know* what he did, though, do you?' the boy's voice cracked on a high note.

'Are you saying that he had nothing to do with the fact that you ran away from home?'

Rhiannon kept her voice gentle, non-confrontational.

Kevin stared back at her. Jock shifted slightly, as if about to speak, and then seemed to change his mind.

'Because if Mr Kingsley had nothing to do with you running away, why did you run away when DCI Simon here asked you about him?'

Rhiannon leaned towards to the boy, as if to exclude anyone else in the room. 'Let me explain a little bit, Kevin. If your father or you were involved in Mr Kingsley's death we *will* be able to find proof of it. You probably know about forensic evidence and how the smallest hair or fibre can link a person to a crime scene, don't you?'

The boy nodded, his dark eyes still fixed on her face.

'So, with that evidence we can make a case against your father or both of you. But if you tell us all about what happened, volunteer the information, before we have to arrest you, it will go easier with you when it comes to court. Any jury, after all, is going to sympathize with you both after what Mr Kingsley did to you.'

'Don't try to bamboozle the lad, missy,' Jock said sharply. 'If you had any real evidence against us you'd already have arrested us.' He turned to Kevin. 'Don't take any notice, laddie, you don't have to say a word.'

'But you could go to court, couldn't you, Dad? If they find evidence you were there?' Kevin's small face was puckered with anxiety.

'Of course I was there, lad! I found the body, didn't I? Just keep your wee mouth shut.' Despite his words, Jock spoke kindly, giving the boy's shoulder a shake.

'But evidence of your presence in Mr Kingsley's flat is another matter, Jock, isn't it?' Simon said quietly. 'We have fibres from that which we have still to identify. You were there, and perpetrators of crimes always leave something of themselves behind, or take something with them, such as blood.'

'You see, Dad! We're only making things worse.' Kevin put his head in his hands and started to cry.

Simon spoke a few words into the recorder and switched it off. He turned to Jock.

'Believe me, Mr Patterson — Jock — I am not enjoying this situation one little bit. If you are, as you say, really not involved in Sebastian Kingsley's death then it is much wiser to tell us what you do know that has the remotest bearing on it.'

Kevin lifted his head.

'We've got to, Dad. We didn't do anything really, did we?'

His father showed no response, staring stubbornly at Simon. Simon switched on the recorder again.

'He did!' Kevin blurted out. 'Mr Kingsley did do bad things to me and made me do things . . . ' He buried his face in his arms and began crying again.

'Kevin, lad!' Jock leaned over to enfold his son in his arms.

'Tell them what happened, Dad,' Kevin pleaded, his voice muffled. He looked up at his father. 'Please!'

'We've done nothing wrong, son,' Jock said stubbornly, folding his arms again.

Kevin looked wildly from his father to Rhiannon and Simon.

'When Dad found him he was already dead!'

'Be quiet, son!' Jock said sharply.

'Were you with your father at the time, Kevin?' Rhiannon asked. The boy looked startled.

'No. But he told us. He came back down the stairs and he said; 'The bastard's dead already. Someone else got to him and they've hit him over the head and killed him'.'

Jock looked down, defeat on his face.

'What happened then, Kevin?' Simon asked.

Kevin looked anxiously at his father.

'It's better that we tell them, Dad. How can they find out what really happened if we don't tell them what we know?'

'Laddie, laddie,' Jock said pityingly. 'They won't want to be looking any further now you've said what you said. Why should they? They've got us neatly tied up now and they can close their case.'

There was silence in the room for a few moments, each of them contemplating the truth or otherwise of Jock's words. Simon, though, could not leave them unchallenged.

'You're mistaken, Mr Patterson. I have no interest in arresting the wrong person for this murder. If, as you say, you did not kill Kingsley, then now that your son has told us what he has it would be best for both of you if you explain just what did happen that night.'

Simon had no real expectation that Jock could explain away his involvement in Kingsley's death. The boy had made it clear that his father had gone looking for him and he had only his father's word that he was not the one who had murdered the man. It would have suited Jock best if, overcome with anger at Kingsley, he had hit out in rage and killed him and brought back to his family the news that the man who had molested Kevin was now dead, but that he himself had not done the deed. It would have been a situation ideal for them all — if it were true.

Jock gave his eyebrows a cynical lift.

'Aye, well no doubt now that Kevin here has opened his wee mouth when he shouldn't, there's no point in me keeping quiet myself. Not, of course,' he looked wryly from Simon to Rhiannon, 'that I believe it will make you change your mind about me being the guilty person.'

'Try us, Mr Patterson,' Rhiannon said earnestly. 'DCI Simon here is not known for making wrongful arrests. He's always interested only in getting at the truth.'

'Oh, aye?' Jock smiled at Simon. 'I see you have an admirer in your ranks, Chief Inspector.'

Rhiannon coloured up and bit her lip. Simon, always uncomfortable with Rhiannon's open admiration of him, refused all the same to let her be treated as an object of amusement.

'DC Jones is a person of great discrimination and integrity, Mr Patterson,' he said, smiling back and sensing Rhiannon relax a little.

Jock nodded. 'A regular mutual admiration society, then,' he remarked. But his words were friendlier and Simon hoped that, at last, they might be making some progress in getting Jock to talk.

'You say you found Kingsley already dead, Jock. What time was this?'

Jock eyed Simon for a moment, his son watching him closely.

'Hold on just a minute, Chief Inspector. I'll tell my story in my own way and in my own time and you can make what you want of it.'

Simon and Rhiannon sat back and waited.

'My boy here,' Jock began, putting his arm again around his son's shoulders, 'ran away from home a year ago, just before Christmas. I hope you can imagine how we felt. Valerie had a turn for the worse worrying about him and I didna feel so good myself. We had no idea why he had gone, we searched our minds for what we might have said or done to cause him to leave. Neither of us even dreamt of the real reason that our wee Kevin felt he had no option but to run. We reported him missing to the police of course but we were told that kids go missing every day and it's usually their own choice and had he got himself involved in drugs.' A look of contempt and distaste crossed Jock's face.

'He had been doing well at school, he was doing well in the choir. But when we thought about it we realized that the lad had been getting more and more withdrawn. We put it down to his age — he'd just become a teenager and we're all told that teenagers are moody and difficult, but he'd always been such a sunny lad and anyway we realized that this had all begun some time before.' Jock broke off and scrabbled in his pocket for a handkerchief. He blew his nose noisily.

'Do you think we could have a cup of tea sent in?' he asked.

Simon and Rhiannon drank their tea in the corridor outside, mainly to give the father and son a little time alone again. It was probably not clever police practice but Simon sensed that the more relaxed the two were, the more likely he was to get the full story, at least now that Jock had agreed to talk.

'You did well focusing on the boy as you did,' he said to Rhiannon.

'Thank you sir,' she said. 'But it seemed the obvious thing to do.' She was clearly pleased with his accolade though.

'However, it doesn't mean that Jock is necessarily going to tell us the truth. Kevin knows only what Jock told him and his mother and it looks as if Jock is going to stick to his story that he wasn't responsible for Kingsley's death.'

'Well, he might not be,' Rhiannon said cautiously, always careful in her manner if she had occasion to disagree with Simon. 'He might be telling the truth. It *could* be that someone else did it.'

301

Simon made a gesture of impatience and placed his cup and saucer on a trolley nearby.

'There's just no one else with the kind of motive that Jock had.'

'That we know of so far, sir,' Rhiannon reminded him. 'As far as I'm concerned, I'll be delighted if it turns out that Jock Patterson didn't do it. He's honest enough that he went to find him with murder on his mind, and he had very good reason for it. But I'm not sure he'd really have done it if he'd had the chance. Look at the way he is with his son: he's a gentle sort, affectionate and kind. That sort of person doesn't easily kill someone, whatever the provocation.'

Simon looked at her with some dismay. He had been so sure that Patterson was his man and now she was casting real doubts in his mind. But Rhiannon's instincts were good and he respected them.

'Sorry sir,' she said. Conscious of his gaze still on her, she broke the moment by moving to put down her own cup.

'We'd better get in there and see what else Jock has to say. I promise to keep an open mind though, Rhiannon.'

'You always do, sir,' Rhiannon said shyly, only adding to his feeling that he probably did nothing of the sort.

Jock and Kevin were sitting composed and

silent waiting for them. Simon switched on the recorder, spoke into it and turned to Jock.

'I'll carry on, shall I?' Jock said.

He seemed much calmer, as did Kevin. It even looked as if Kevin had combed his long hair, drawing it back from his face more, encouraging body language, Simon hoped. He nodded to Jock.

'Please do,' he said.

'So Kevin had run away, and we agonized over why he'd gone, what had happened to him. We thought he might have been murdered and we listened to the local news, watched the television, to see if the body of a boy had been found. It was a terrible time.'

Jock paused as if looking back through a dark tunnel. 'Then we wondered if he *had* got mixed up in drugs, whether he might still be somewhere here in the city. I used to wander the streets at night and by day trying to catch a glimpse of him somewhere. I took copies of his photograph with me and showed them everywhere — .' Kevin's hand stole into his and he looked down, giving it a squeeze.

'Anyway, I found out nothing.' He heaved a sigh. 'After about six months of this we became almost resigned that we might never see our lad again. Valerie had got more ill and that took time, seeing specialists. She even

303

tried the people in the clinic.' He frowned, his eyes dark beneath his brows. 'But that was set up by Kingsley, of course. I didn't realize at the time but it must have been his conscience that made him arrange it. The foul bastard had known all along why Kevin had run away and there he was pretending to be all concern and sympathy.'

It was probably the reason, too, that Kingsley had left the Pattersons money in his will, Simon thought. It was unlikely they would wish to accept it. Kingsley's little attempts at kindness and helpfulness could only smell bad in the knowledge of his behaviour.

'But Kevin eventually came home,' Simon said, anxious, despite his sympathy with Jock's needs to tell his story, to get closer to the nub of the matter.

'Don't prompt me,' Jock said, with the manner of the NCO he had once been.

Simon sat back.

'Remembering how he had behaved, how he'd appeared to be a friend, only added to the rage I felt when Kevin told us what had happened, that Kingsley had been doing those terrible things to him,' Jock resumed. He fell silent for a moment, lost in recollection.

'What *did* Kevin tell you, Mr Patterson?'

Rhiannon asked softly, 'after he came home at last.'

Jock stared into the distance as if hypnotized.

'First he told us where he had been. He'd been living on the streets of London, begging. My boy, begging.' Jock swallowed hard and turned his eyes to Rhiannon. 'He told us what had happened to him there, how he'd almost been raped.' He put his face in his hands. His voice muffled, he said: 'It took a wee while to get the whole story out of him. It came in bits and pieces. We were all so upset, y'see.' He looked up, wiping his face with his hands, as if emerging from the depths.

'He said that the rape attempt wasn't so very bad after what he'd already been through whilst he was here in Westwich, that he was lucky worse didn't happen to him. And then he told us how Kingsley had got him up to his flat one evening after choir practice . . . ' Jock's hands were over his eyes again as he broke off.

'Would you rather tell your side of the story yourself, Kevin?' Simon asked quietly.

They both looked at Kevin's father, obviously struggling to compose himself.

'Well,' Kevin said, his eyes still on Jock. 'I don't want to go into any detail, if you don't mind.'

'Whatever you think we ought to know, Kevin,' Rhiannon encouraged. Simon noticed that her own eyes were moist.

'He gave me something to drink,' the boy said. 'He told me it was orange juice but it must have had vodka in it or something. Then he started getting sort of affectionate. I was just embarrassed at first and then I don't remember anything much of what happened next exactly. But I realized afterwards what had happened to me.' He gulped, examining his small hands clasped on the table in front of him. Jock reached out and squeezed them.

'Are you sure you want to do this, my lad?'

'It's all right, Dad. I'm OK.'

Throughout their interview, Simon had noticed, it had seemed to be Kevin who was the stronger one, the one who could deal best with the situation and all the recollections required. But Simon imagined that any child of Kevin's age who could survive the total of what he had experienced as well as apparently he had must be resilient indeed.

'I cried,' Kevin said simply. 'I was frightened. Mr Kingsley told me not to be so silly, that all boys had this sort of thing done to them by a proper grown-up. But then he said that I wasn't to tell my parents because some people didn't understand these things.'

The boy bit his lip. 'He said that if I told

my dad he'd give him the sack and chuck us out of our flat so we'd have nowhere to live and that it wouldn't be a nice thing to do to my mother in the circumstances with her being ill. That I'd make her more ill than ever.' His voice cracked on a high note as he broke off. He squeezed his father's hand again. 'Then he made me do things to him.'

Kevin looked at them, white-faced, his pupils dark. 'I can't tell you any more. Except he kept making me do these things whenever he could get me. He used to threaten me if I wasn't there when he told me to be. So I had to run away, you see. It was the only way I could make sure that Mum and Dad didn't get thrown out. And I ran off because I couldn't stand it, you see,' he said with immense dignity. 'I felt so dirty. I still do.'

There was silence while they all digested what the boy had said. It was no less shocking for being what they had expected to hear.

'You're not dirty, Kevin,' Rhiannon said at last. 'You never were. That man was a criminal to do what he did to you. None of it was your fault and you've been very brave.'

'That's what Mum and Dad say,' Kevin said solemnly. 'I'm glad I came back.'

'What made you decide to come home?' Simon asked. After all, the problem had not been solved: Kingsley was still *in situ*. Unless

Kevin had decided on his own solution to the problem of Kingsley.

'I was lonely. I was so cold, too. I'd got in with some people at a squat who were kind to me and looked after me a bit but they didn't have any money either and I was hungry all the time. I told them in the end what had happened to me and they said I should come back home and get Mr Kingsley prosecuted for what he did to me. That then he wouldn't be able to do it any more. He wouldn't be able to do it to any other kid.'

'So he told us all about it,' Jock said. 'He told his mother a bit of it first, while I was still doing my rounds in the clinic that evening. It took him a while to tell us all of it, though.' The boy's father suddenly seemed stronger, as if the pair of them unburdening themselves had relieved him of some of the responsibility he so evidently and painfully felt.

'Then you went looking for Kingsley?' Simon askd. Jock nodded.

'I wasn't sure we'd get any prosecution after so long. But I admit that even if I'd thought we could, I had to confront the man. And I did have murder in my heart.' He nodded again.

'And you say you found him already dead?'

'I say it and it's the truth.' Jock jutted his

308

chin again and set his mouth in a firm line.

'And did you alter anything in the room. Did you leave it as we found it?'

'I did nothing but check his neck for a pulse. But he was obviously dead, though still warm.'

'What time was this?'

'About eleven o'clock. Though I can't be precise, you'll understand. I wasn't looking at clocks that night.'

'Why didn't you telephone for the police when you found him?'

Jock shrugged. 'I should have, of course. But I was still too near in my heart to killing him myself. I thought you would be more likely to question me in detail if I'd found him when his body was still warm and I didn't want all this coming out about him and Kevin. You see, even if I'd thought we could get a prosecution I didn't want the publicity it might cause. Kevin had suffered enough. I didn't want him being shouted at by some clever defence lawyer, making out my boy had been responsible in some way for what had happened to him, like it happens to women in these rape cases. No, I'd gladly have killed the bastard there and then the way I was feeling that night. I just didn't get there in time.' He reached out to Kevin again.

'I'm glad that it didn't come to that, you

having to go to court. It would have meant all the publicity I didn't want.

'If I had killed him,' he said to Simon, 'I wouldn't have given his treatment of Kevin as my motive but it might have been found out. I wasna thinking straight.'

'But you thought straight enough to go up to his flat and wipe it clear of any of Kevin's fingerprints?' Simon said.

'I did.' Jock nodded again. 'But that was later, after we'd talked some more. I realized that his fingerprints might still be there somewhere, so I went back to the body and got his keys out of his pocket. I put them back afterwards. If you'd found fingerprint evidence that Kevin had been there — the boy has small hands and I thought it might be obvious it was a child — you'd be bound to think of him, and of me.' He sat back for a moment and looked at Simon defiantly.

'I also took all the photographs I could find, and his computer discs and I checked the digital camera — not that I thought there'd really be anything of Kevin still there after all this time.'

There might have been evidence of Kingsley and some other young boy, Simon thought.

'Did you examine the photographs, Jock?' he asked.

'I burned the lot without looking at them.' He leaned forward over the table. 'Well that's my story and you can believe me or not, as you wish, but for God's sake let the wee lad go home. He's nothing but a victim in all this.'

They were unlikely to know, then, whether Kingsley had abused any other boys, Simon thought, Jock probably having destroyed all likely evidence. He wondered if Jock and his wife had been worried about any health implications for their son as a result of abuse from Kingsley. The post mortem report from Evelyn Starkey had stated that the body was free of disease, but he felt that now, in front of Kevin, was not the time to raise this subject. He would send a confidential letter to the Pattersons, setting their minds at rest. He fleetingly thought of Hannah Crossley, questioning whether she might have discovered that her lover was bisexual. She might have reacted with real anger and fear.

'Well?' Jock said gruffly. 'Are you going to accept what I'm telling you?'

It was hard to disbelieve all that Patterson had told them. Everything he said was plausible and rang true. And yet he admitted that he had gone looking for Kingsley with every intention of murdering the man. There was nothing to say that he had not actually

311

done so. Kevin obviously believed his father, but had not been with him when he had gone upstairs to find Kingsley. Simon wondered whether Jock had been more open with, or had had a different story to tell, his wife.

24

'Why are we going to see Valerie Patterson?' Rhiannon Jones asked. She and Simon were crossing the West Gate on their way to the clinic.

'To see if she has anything to add to what Kevin and Jock have to say.'

They passed from the brightly lit pedestrianized street into the Cathedral Approach, contrastingly crepuscular, its few lights casting only a ghostly glow.

'We're not trying any tricks on her, are we, sir?' Rhiannon sounded uneasy.

She had read him well, Simon thought with as much misgiving as Rhiannon was expressing. He had indeed considered implying to Valerie Patterson that her husband had confessed to Kingsley's murder, in the hope that they could get a clearer idea of what really had happened that night. Rhiannon's words had reminded him that it was a shabby thing to do. Not only that; should Jock prove to have told the truth, Valerie and the rest of her family could only in the future hold both him and the police force in contempt.

He used his key to open the pedestrian gate

into the cathedral precinct and held it open for Rhiannon to pass through. None of the media was present, a government scandal having removed the murder of Kingsley to the inner depths of newspapers with a consequent falling away of the numbers gathered at the gates.

'No,' he said. 'I won't do that, Rhiannon, but I shall feel justified in withholding what information I think we need to.'

They turned right and skirted the carpark, facing an icy wind that blew fiercely around the high walls of the cathedral.

Rhiannon wrapped her long scarf more securely around her neck and pulled up her coat collar.

'You'll try not telling her the truth about what Jock and Kevin have told us, you mean? That will be close to lying.'

'Spare me your Welsh Methodist chapel morality, Rhiannon! I'm trying to catch a murderer here, not find out who's been fingering the chapel funds.'

It was a sure sign of his stress over the issue of Kevin Patterson and his father that Simon was provoked to being uncharacteristically rude to Rhiannon. He immediately regretted his words and his manner of delivering them.

Rhiannon's silence made it clear that she was wounded.

'Sorry,' he said and put a hand on her shoulder.

'It's all right. I didn't mean to nag.' She blinked up at him and he was not sure whether it was the wind that had made her eyes water or his unnecessary sharpness.

They were entering the lane that ran by the clinic, their view of the dimly lit building obscured by the tree on the edge of the shrubbery. Suddenly a piercing scream shattered the air, followed by a muffled thump.

Simon and Rhiannon moved fast. Within seconds the scene impressed on Simon's retina was of the curtain being drawn aside in Jonathan Hadden's room, a sash window being raised and Jonathan Hadden himself, backlit by the light in his room, peering out at the dark form that was wrapped over the railings in front of the building. As Simon and Rhiannon came within a few yards of the clinic Hadden raced down the steps and bent over the body.

He straightened up as Simon reached him and shook his head, his face pale in the light that shone from his room.

'Who is it?' Simon asked, though as soon as the words were out of his mouth he could see from the mass of tumbled hair and the dark velvet cloak that spread out over the railings that it must be Anne Stillings.

He bent to feel for a pulse in her neck but there was none. Her eyes were staring and sightless and a thin trickle of blood had run from the corner of her mouth.

Rhiannon, on the other side of the body, said, her voice pitched higher than normal:

'Did she jump? Or was she pushed?'

'Run upstairs,' said Simon. 'Make sure there's no one up there. She probably fell from the top floor.' Rhiannon was already flying up the steps and into the building as he finished speaking. He turned to Hadden, standing beside him looking shocked and disbelieving.

'Is anyone else in the clinic, do you know?'

'I don't think so. I didn't even know Anne was here. I was in my room going through the accounts and sorting out what needs to be done now that . . . ' He characteristically ran a hand through his hair. 'My God, this is terrible. Poor Anne.' He gazed at the grotesque image impaled on the *fleur de lis* railings, his eyes wide.

Simon immediately made the necessary phone calls with a special request for Elaine Starkey to attend if possible. In the middle of one report Rhiannon's voice came from above.

'She must have fallen from here, sir. The

window's still open.' He could dimly discern her outline leaning over the low parapet on the top floor.

'Come on down,' he called back, suddenly conscious that there might be a killer still lurking within the building — unless Anne Stillings had jumped of her own volition. The scream they had heard was no proof that she had gone unwillingly to her death. The body had its own survival instincts and suicides were known to struggle in their death throes, the body trying to defeat oblivion even while the mind had determined on it.

He became aware that Hadden was shivering, probably as much from shock as from the fact that he was standing there in his shirt-sleeves.

'Go on in,' he said to him. 'I'll join you when we get some back-up.'

Hadden stumbled up the steps as Rhiannon came down them again.

'I couldn't see any sign of anyone, but I haven't looked in all the rooms,' she panted, her breath coming in white puffs.

'No suicide note?'

'Nothing in the room with the open window. It was their meditation room. Do you want me to check some others?'

'Better wait until we get some support here.' They couldn't leave Anne Stillings's body unattended while they searched the clinic.

'Do you think it was suicide, then?' Rhiannon asked.

'I've no more idea than you have at the moment. Maybe she killed Kingsley and decided to jump out of remorse.'

'Oh God, do you think she heard about my visit to her flat this evening and thought we'd got some evidence against her?'

'For all we know at the moment, she could have been killed by the person who killed Kingsley. They would have just about had time to get down the stairs and out the back way in the time it took her to fall and for us to reach her. So we might as well stop speculating until we have a bit more evidence one way or the other.'

'Well, it lets one person off the hook,' Rhiannon said. 'Hadden couldn't have pushed her. He was in his office when she fell.'

They heard the sound of footsteps on the cobbles of the lane and turned to see a man approaching them. Rhiannon went forward to intercept him and advise him to take a different route. It was obvious he was not taking kindly to such advice. Simon watched as Rhiannon took out a small torch from her pocket and shone it on her ID. He grudgingly turned and walked away, peering over his shoulder as he went.

While they waited Simon felt in a state of suspended animation, suspended thought. He could do nothing at the moment, not until the body had been properly examined and taken away for a post mortem. It was a shock, the death of Anne Stillings, an entirely unexpected event, and he doubted if he could think too straight about it yet, even if he did have the information he needed.

Evelyn Starkey was not available at the moment but she would be able to do the post mortem the following day. The on-call MO, Nibley, who did arrive to do the preliminary examination of the body looked as if he had been brought away from nothing more demanding than a slouch in front of the television, but he was scratchy and monosyllabic nevertheless. Since the man was being paid considerably more than he was himself Simon took a slightly malicious pleasure in holding him to as much detail and investigation as possible. But it had small effect.

Despite the fact that the screening tent had been set up by now, with bright arc-lights within, the doctor insisted that there wasn't much he could do except confirm that the woman was dead.

'Time of death you are perfectly well aware

319

of since I understand you witnessed it, so you won't be bugging me on that one.'

'Perish the thought, Doctor,' Simon murmured.

The man looked up at him morosely. He was young to be so world-weary, Simon thought. So far he had done nothing except check for a pulse and take a rectal temperature. This indignity perpetrated on corpses always made Simon wince and did so particularly tonight as Anne Stillings's petticoats were raised and the wind stole in to the tent and blew around her plump thighs.

'In this weather the corpse is cooling rapidly of course,' Nibley said.

'Perhaps we could lift the body from its present position now?' Simon suggested. The photographers had done their job and there was no reason to delay. It bothered him to see her dangling there like some grotesque rag-doll.

As Anne Stillings was lifted off, Rhiannon came into the tent. She had been to tell Valerie Patterson what had happened and the reason for all the commotion at the front of the building.

'Mrs Patterson asked if Kevin and Jock would be coming home now. She seemed to think that Anne must have jumped because she was guilty of Kingsley's death.'

Simon had completely forgotten the two still waiting at headquarters. Mrs Patterson might be right in her assumption but, whether Anne Stillings had jumped or was pushed, her death had not had anything to do with her husband or son and he couldn't feel justified in keeping them incarcerated.

'Arrange for them to come home, would you, Rhiannon?' he said. 'But tell them not to go too far away in the near future. Tell Jock I'm holding him responsible.'

Rhiannon nodded and slipped away.

Simon turned back to the doctor, who had made the effort of getting on to his knees beside the now recumbent body. Two wounds were evenly spaced just below her breasts, the blood still seeping.

'She barked her shins as she fell,' Nibley said, pointing to the scraped skin on the lower part of the legs. 'She's unlikely to have done that if she jumped willingly, she'd have stepped on to the balustrade first.'

'Perhaps we should go and look at the room we think she fell from.'

The doctor followed him into the building. In the meditation room the window was open as Rhiannon had found it, the freezing wind swirling in. Nothing appeared to have been disturbed, there was no sign of any struggle.

They both stepped in to the high dormer,

its windows floor to ceiling, and on to the narrow parapet. Nibley bent to examine the stonework. 'I can't see anything in this light but I imagine you'll find some traces of the woman's blood and skin here.'

The damage to Anne Stillings's shins was evidence enough on its own that she had not willingly gone to her death. Someone must have pushed her with some force.

'There's no other place she might have fallen from?' Nibley asked.

'The rest of this floor is a private apartment,' Simon said, 'accessed by a separate staircase.'

'Sebastian Kingsley's, I suppose,' the doctor said. 'The clinic isn't going to take much more of this sort of publicity.'

He sounded satisfied rather than sympathetic, Simon thought. Like many other doctors, Woolbridge included, he probably either felt threatened by alternative health options or dismissed them as worthless.

'We'll check the next floor down,' Simon said to the increasingly impatient Nibley.

But the consulting-rooms on the floor below were locked, their windows closed and nothing appeared out of place.

'Whoever pushed her wouldn't have had time to stop and close the window,' Nibley remarked. 'And the room we first looked at is

322

the only one likely to have produced the damage to her shins.'

'Thank you Doctor,' Simon said.

'Perhaps I could go home now?' Nibley suggested as they approached the front door.

'Of course, if you're satisfied you've done all you should.' Simon sounded surprised that the doctor should need to ask.

The body could now be taken away, to await the attentions of Evelyn Starkey on the morrow. Simon supposed he had better arrange for an official identification as soon as possible which meant a visit to Anne Stillings's partner. While he waited for Rhiannon to return he decided to speak to Jonathan Hadden.

As he reached the top of the steps he heard a restrained altercation coming from near the end of the lane where two policemen had been posted to deter passers-by. He peered into the gloom, his vision impaired by the dazzle of the brightly lit tent close by. One of the voices rose in intensity against the gruff utterances of the policemen and he thought he recognized the sound and shape of the dean.

He joined them and ushered the dean through the police tape. Rhiannon arrived at that moment with another police officer and Jock and Kevin Patterson. The Pattersons passed by without pausing, their eyes focused firmly on their destination.

'I told them what had happened, sir,' Rhiannon said. 'They had to know.'

'Just what *has* happened?' Dean Kingsley asked querulously. 'What on earth is going on?'

Simon drew him to one side.

'There has been another death at the clinic, sir,' he said.

'That boy,' the dean pointed after the figures of Kevin and Jock, stepping on to the narrow path that led to their flat. 'He *is* the boy who used to be in the choir, young Patterson, isn't he?'

'That's right.'

'Oh, thank God! I have been so tortured with remorse, imagining all sorts.' Kingsley looked up at Simon. 'He's not involved in all this terrible business, is he?'

'It seems unlikely,' Simon said. He put a hand on the dean's shoulder. 'I think you should go home now. We can't have people wandering about here.'

Kingsley began to move away then turned back.

'But someone else is dead? Who is it?'

Had the man been anyone else, Simon realized, he would by now have got one of the officers to escort him home. But he was the dean of the cathedral and Simon had been told to keep him informed.

'Mrs Stillings. She fell from the top floor of the building it seems,' he said with as much economy as he could master.

'Anne Stillings! Oh, poor woman. Such a pleasant sort, I thought, though Sebastian disagreed with me.'

Simon nodded and waited.

'Chief Inspector, I know you must think I am a nuisance but I was so disturbed after you spoke to me. I felt in some way responsible. You see it occurred to me that Sebastian might have done it again,' his voice lowered, 'that he might have hurt that young boy Patterson.'

'Did you come to that understanding before or after I spoke to you, Dean?' Simon said expressionlessly. He was cold, his feet were aching and he had things to do.

'I was pondering what I should say about it when you arrived at my door.'

They lived in different worlds, Simon thought sardonically. He wanted to push the dean to admit that he had knowledge that could have influenced the case at a much earlier stage. With this latest development, though, it appeared that the Dean's reticence on the subject of Kingsley and young boys might actually have done no harm since the

Pattersons now seemed to have been exonerated. If he'd spoken up at first, however, they might not have been misled into thinking that the person who had cleaned up Kingsley's flat was also the killer.

Anne Stillings's death seemed to have elicited surprisingly little curiosity on the part of the dean — his concerns were entirely wrapped up in whether or not he had sinned in omitting to tell of his nephew's earlier transgressions. Worry about the fate of his own soul seemed to have won out in the circumstances.

Simon made another movement to encourage the dean to move on but the cleric turned back again, partly modifying Simon's assessment of his mere self-interest.

'Just how did Mrs Stillings come to fall? Did she jump? Oh, I do hope not. But if she did, was it because she was filled with remorse? Because she had killed Sebastian?' he whispered. 'Did she kill him because he was going to fire her?'

'I'm sure you understand, dean, that I can't discuss anything of what has happened until investigations are more complete.' Simon's annoyance with the dean was beginning to break free of constraint.

'In that case you must be considering whether she was pushed!' The dean seemed to be getting more, rather than less, agitated through his continued questioning.

It was with some relief that Simon saw, over the man's shoulder, Detective Superintendent Munro approaching. She seemed to have quickly assessed what was happening.

'Dean Kingsley!' she exclaimed, as if they had just met at a garden fête. 'How very good to see you, though in such sad circumstances.' She grasped his hand and shook it. 'Why don't I walk with you to your home and I'll do what I can to fill you in on anything you need to know?'

He meekly went with her.

'I'll be back,' she said *sotto voce* to Simon as they moved away.

Did that mean he had to delay the removal of the body? He assumed so and returned to the shelter of the tent to inform those waiting there. The scene of crime officers arrived behind him and he sent Rhiannon to show them the room from which Anne Stillings had apparently fallen, with particular instructions to carry out tests on the stone parapet.

Conscious that Jonathan Hadden was still waiting in his room, Simon told Rhiannon to inform Superintendent Munro of his whereabouts on her return and went back into the clinic.

Hadden was sitting at his desk, his hair in

some disorder, apparently poring over some accountancy figures. He slammed the book shut as Simon came into the room.

'I don't know why I'm even trying to concentrate on this lot. I can't see the clinic surviving after yet another mysterious death.'

He stood up and came around the desk, going to sit in one of the easy-chairs by the window.

'That sounds awful. Poor Anne, it's her I should be thinking about. I hadn't noticed she was troubled about anything.'

Simon sat opposite him.

'Do you think she killed herself then; jumped to her death?'

'That was my first thought.' Hadden made an effort to smooth down his hair. 'I assumed that she must have killed Sebastian and couldn't face the prospect of prosecution and prison. But,' he rubbed his jaw, the bristles rasping against his palm, 'I just don't know really. I can't imagine Anne killing Sebastian any more than I can imagine her committing suicide. She was so full of life. Well, you know, you met her.'

'Yes,' Simon said quietly.

'Do you have any idea,' Hadden said fearfully, 'what did happen? Did she jump, do you think?'

'We can't know for sure, yet,' Simon said.

In the presence of one of the people he knew for certain could not have pushed Anne Stillings, he was prepared to say more than he would otherwise have done. 'It's looking more likely that she was pushed.'

Hadden focused on him intently.

'How can you tell?'

'Her shins hit the parapet it seems, before she fell. That wouldn't happen in a suicide.'

'But that means . . . ' Hadden stared, 'there was someone else in the clinic tonight.'

'You didn't see or hear anyone?'

'I didn't leave my room after my last client today — she left at just before six o'clock. I got out my paperwork and started work on that. I made myself a cup of coffee in an effort to keep awake at some point but I didn't hear or see anything that was going on outside this room. I assumed everyone had gone home and that Jock would be in at some point when he did his rounds.' He frowned. 'Come to think of it, Jock hasn't appeared at all.'

He had been so absorbed, then, that he had not noticed Jock being accompanied from his flat by two policemen.

'Jock was in for questioning with his son Kevin this evening. They've just come home,' Simon told him.

'You suspect Jock of something? And

Kevin?' Hadden looked dismayed.

'They were just clearing up a few points with us,' Simon said, concerned that he had said more than he should have. He didn't want Hadden believing that the Pattersons were in any way suspect. It would be ironical if they should again be put under threat of their home and Jock's job because the new head of the clinic thought they were guilty of some kind of misdemeanour. 'They've done nothing wrong at all.'

Hadden was still looking troubled. 'I hope not. I don't know how we'd manage without Jock. Why were you questioning them?'

'You'll understand that I can't answer that,' Simon said. 'But they've satisfied us that they are completely innocent of any wrong.' A bit overdone, he thought. Jock had, after all, admitted to tampering with evidence when he cleaned Kingsley's flat of fingerprints. But it was appropriate enough for Hadden's ears at the moment.

'When did you last see Mrs Stillings?' he asked.

Hadden seemed to have difficulty thinking.

'I believe it was when I went up to the restroom this afternoon. Morale is pretty low at the moment with the number of cancellations we've had from existing clients and I thought I'd go and see if anyone needed a bit of bucking up.'

Hadden's public-school background was showing through, Simon thought.

'And Anne was there?'

'Yes, we had a few words.' Hadden rubbed his hands together and hunched his shoulders. 'She seemed to have been less affected in terms of cancellations than some of us.' He smiled sadly, 'I suppose no one could imagine that a motherly soul like Anne would commit murder.'

'And, of course, she had a very good reputation as well,' Simon said, finding himself defending Anne Stillings against being patronized even now she was dead.

'She did,' Hadden agreed.

'When did Jock normally begin his rounds?'

'Usually around seven. If anyone was working late with a client he'd come back to their room after they had finished.'

But that night, Simon thought, there had been no Jock there to carry out his usual duties. He wondered whether someone had been aware of that fact and it had made it easier for them to push Anne Stillings from the top-floor window.

'Can you tell me when the last client's appointment was tonight?' he asked.

Hadden stood up. 'We can go and look at

Franny's computer.'

Simon followed him into the main hall where he booted up the computer and pressed a few keys.

'It looks as if Ruth Maguire had a half-past five appointment.' He tapped the keys again. 'No one else was working that late except me.'

'And Mrs Maguire would have finished at around half-past six.'

'Probably earlier. It depends on the nature of the appointment.'

'What time did Mrs Stillings's last client arrive?'

Hadden checked. 'She had a Mr Roach arrive at five according to Franny's records.'

'And he would have left at six or before?'

'Right.'

'Frances Fulton would have already gone home?'

'I expect so. She usually left after the last appointment had arrived, or six o'clock, depending on which came later.'

Simon would have to speak to the receptionist to ask what she could recall of people's comings and goings that day. But even if the supposed killer of Anne Stillings — if he or she was a member of staff — had left early, they could have come back again. Had she seen who had murdered Sebastian

Kingsley and made it known to them? She might even have had some sympathy with the killer, given her first-hand experience of Kingsley's insensitive behaviour. Or she might have threatened whoever it was, asking for money in return for silence She had been in need of money for her house purchase, and the girlfriend, Rhiannon had said, looked high-maintenance.

There was a quick knock on the door and Rhiannon held it open for Detective Superintendent Munro to enter.

'Couldn't wait in that freezing tent,' she said, rubbing her hands.

Simon turned to Hadden and told him he could go home now.

'Please use my room, if you need to talk,' Hadden said to Munro.

She gave him a dazzling smile. 'Thank you,' she said.

25

Munro had departed with considerate celerity. Her main concern had been whether the death of Anne Stillings was something that might have been prevented or foreseen. Satisfied that it had not been something that any of them could have predicted, and with a request for his report to be completed before he went home that night, she left content that she would be sufficiently well-briefed for her dealings with the media on the morrow.

Simon was not looking forward to confronting Jenny Knowles with news of her partner's death.

'What's she like, this Jenny Knowles? How do you think she'll take it?' he asked Rhiannon as they approached Prior's Court.

'Hard to tell, really. I got the impression that Mrs Stillings was the nurturing partner in the relationship, so it could work either way. She's unlikely to be as devastated as Anne would have been if the circumstances were reversed, but on the other hand she's going to be pretty upset at having her supportive partner taken away from her.'

'Hysterics?' Simon asked, reading between the lines.

'Possibly. She struck me as pretty self-centred. She's completely unlike Anne; rather calculating I thought. Looks as if she takes great care of herself.'

They had left the ice-cold, limb-numbing staircase and were almost at the door of the flat when it opened and Jenny Knowles appeared, dressed in a coat and in the process of wrapping a scarf around her neck. She stopped, startled, her eyes focusing on Simon who was the bigger and more dominant figure of the two. No concern showed in her eyes. Simon, as usual less than impeccable, was not obviously a policeman. But when her eyes shifted to Rhiannon they widened in alarm.

'I was just going to look for Anne,' she said. 'She hasn't come home. I thought I'd see if she was still at the clinic or at our usual supermarket. I can't imagine why she's not here, she usually phones me if she's going to be this late.'

It was pathetically obvious that Jenny Knowles's chatter was a desperate attempt to ward off any dreaded news the two police officers might have brought with them.

'Can we come in, Ms Knowles?' Rhiannon asked softly.

Jenny Knowles tied her scarf more firmly around her neck.

'No, you can't. I've got to go and find Anne.' She made to move past them.

Rhiannon held out her hand to bar her.

'We've found Anne,' she said.

'Where is she?' Jenny again moved forward. 'I've got to see her. She's all right, isn't she?' she appealed to Rhiannon.

'I'm very sorry. We have bad news for you.' Rhiannon put her arm around the smaller woman's shoulders.

She shook it off. 'No! Anne's just gone shopping that's all. It often makes her late. She meets her clients sometimes and she stands there handing out free advice on the supermarket floor. Can you imagine!' She gave a wild laugh, but she made no further attempt to push past them. Then she put her hands over her face. 'Is Anne dead?' she asked in a small voice.

'I'm very sorry to tell you that she is,' Simon said, deciding to take charge. It was almost as cold in the upper hallway as it had been on the staircase and he was convinced that his sensitivities on this grim occasion might be improved by the warming of his extremities.

Jenny backed blindly into the flat, Rhiannon holding her arm. Rhiannon led her through to the living-room and Simon left them sitting beside each other on the pink sofa while he went to make some hot sweet tea.

When he came back Jenny had produced a desperately inadequate lace handkerchief and was dabbing at her eyes and nose.

'Somebody pushed her,' she was saying. 'Anne would never have killed herself. She would never have left me willingly.'

Simon handed her the tea and she took it from him without acknowledgement, gulping it down as if it might somehow numb her pain.

'When did it happen?' she asked Simon over the rim of the cup rattling in its saucer.

He told her, watching her thoughts flicker sadly across her face.

'After you'd gone,' she said to Rhiannon, 'I watched television. I was getting annoyed with Anne for not being home. She always cooked the evening meal. How terrible, that while Anne was dying, being killed,' she looked fiercely at Simon, 'I was sitting here selfishly wanting her to cook my meal.' She dissolved into tears again and Rhiannon got up to fetch a box of tissues from a nearby unit, the pretty handkerchief having been rendered uselessly sodden.

'Did she suffer. Did she feel pain?' she

looked fearfully to Rhiannon for the answer.

'It was very quick,' was all Rhiannon thought she could say with truth. 'We shall know more after the post mortem.'

The thought of a post mortem brought on more floods of tears.

'Cutting up my lovely Anne,' she sobbed. 'I can't bear it!'

Simon sat down opposite them in a voluptuous chair and wondered aloud whether they should send for a doctor.

'I haven't got one,' Jenny gulped. 'I always used the clinic for any health problems — not that I ever have many.'

'Whatever your opinions, there are times when doctors can be helpful,' Simon said mildly.

'If you mean do I need to be sedated then the answer is that I would ask Ruth Maguire to treat me. But I don't need anyone. I need to think.' Jenny Knowles scrubbed at her eyes, her carefully applied make-up smearing grotesquely. 'Who pushed her? She *was* pushed wasn't she?'

'We can't be absolutely sure just yet,' Simon said cautiously. The sight of this apparently self-indulgent and pampered woman's messy face made him warm to her more: her grief must be genuine enough if it had overcome a habitual concern with her appearance. 'But it is looking likely, yes.'

'But you obviously have no idea who might have pushed her?' She was tense, waiting for his answer.

'Not yet. We were hoping that you might be able to help us find out. Are you sure you feel up to it?'

She brushed the question aside.

'This is linked to Kingsley's death, isn't it?'

'It seems very likely.'

Her cup of tea lay forgotten on the low table between them after her first few frenzied mouthfuls. She looked at him thoughtfully.

'I don't know,' she said. 'I don't know who did this.'

'Do you think that Anne knew who had killed Sebastian Kingsley?' Rhiannon asked.

Jenny turned as if she had forgotten she was there.

'I don't know,' she said again. She seemed suddenly afraid rather than distraught, wary of them.

Simon immediately wondered whether she did indeed know, whether Anne had confided to her something she knew about Kingsley's murderer and that she was now afraid that he, or she, might come after her in turn. Because, if Anne Stillings had indeed been pushed by someone from that building tonight, it seemed most likely that it was because she knew who had murdered Sebastian Kingsley and that the murderer knew that she knew. She might have made an arrangement to speak to the killer.

But if Simon let Jenny Knowles realize that he thought she had some knowledge of what her partner might have been up to that evening at the clinic she was more likely to close up even further. Jenny might be more ready to speak if she thought the police believed Anne to be entirely innocent of anything.

'We believe that when Anne left the film-show the night Kingsley died, she went to the clinic and may have seen who killed him,' he said. 'Did she show no sign of having witnessed something that night? How did she behave afterwards?'

Jenny Knowles gave a little shrug.

'I didn't notice anything different about her.'

'And she said nothing at all to you about it?'

'No,' she said, her eyes fixed on Simon like an animal's in headlights.

'Had Anne's behaviour changed in any way lately, since Kingsley's death?'

'I don't think so,' she said, looking down at the tissue in her hands and twisting it until it fell apart and she reached for a new one.

Simon decided that discretion was getting him nowhere.

'Ms Knowles, I think you are afraid that whoever may have killed Anne will assume that you have the same knowledge that she had and may attack you as well.'

She looked up at him quickly with frightened eyes. They were pale blue and the pupils had darkened perceptibly.

'But if that *is* the case, you have nothing whatever to gain by keeping what you know from the police. He or she may assume your knowledge but your only danger is in not having entrusted it to us, and making us free to act on it.'

'That's just it!' she burst out. 'She *didn't* tell me. But whoever it is must think I would know.'

'Anne would have told the person that you didn't know anything about it,' Rhiannon reassured her. 'You can be sure of that.'

'I know.' Jenny choked on her words. 'But he, or she, wouldn't necessarily believe her, would they?'

'It doesn't alter the fact that you are safer in confiding in us anything that you do know,' Simon said. 'Anything that helps us to catch the killer makes you safer.' He briefly wondered whether he was in any position to offer her police protection, but staffing was short and he would have to put up a very good case.

'Can you stay with someone for a while, so that you are not alone?' he asked. 'You shouldn't anyway have to be on your own at this time.'

She considered the idea.

'I can get compassionate leave from the college,' she said slowly. 'I could go to my parents in Swindon. It's not ideal, but I can't stay here.' He eyes watered again. 'We were buying a house, Anne and I. We were going to have a dog.' She wept again, pulling handfuls of tissues from their box.

They waited while she wept fresh tears, scrubbing at her face again until most of the smeared make-up had disappeared.

When she had composed herself again she said: 'I *did* know something was up with Anne.' She drew a shuddering breath. 'She was sort of nervous these past few days. But she really didn't say why. When we left the Corn Exchange that night she was very quiet and I asked her what was up. She said that it wasn't anything I needed to know about. Of course I questioned her all the more but she just shrugged me off. And when I heard the news about Kingsley's death from her the next day she didn't seem as shocked as I'd have expected her to be. I mean, I know she didn't like him much, but she didn't seem as surprised about it as I would have thought she'd be.'

She turned to Rhiannon. 'She didn't say anything to me about Kingsley planning to sack her, but I think she must have known because she said something like I shouldn't worry about the house, that she was sure we'd manage to buy it all right.'

But it might not just have been the ending of the threat that she was going to lose her job that caused her to say that. It might also mean that Anne Stillings had demanded money from the killer, and had paid instead with her life. It surprised Simon that the pleasant woman he had interviewed might have stooped to grubby blackmail. But having met her high-maintenance partner Simon found it more understandable. Anne had probably not felt any distress in discovering that Kingsley had been violently attacked: she had had no more affection for him than had most people of his aquaintance, and if she *had* known of his plans to dismiss her she would have felt even less.

If his killer was someone well-known to her, someone familiar and for whom she felt no fear, she might have thought it reasonable to request that she should be helped out financially at a time when she needed it and

343

when she was afraid of letting down her partner. She might even have felt some sympathy with the killer's motive, had she known of it. Familiarity might have bred, if not contempt, then a lack of caution.

Jenny Knowles was waiting for him to give some kind of response.

'There's nothing else you can think of that Anne said that might give us any lead? Was there anyone at work, for instance, whom she mentioned more often than usual?'

She shook her head. 'I'm sorry, I can't think of anything else. Anne didn't like to worry me about anything, you see.' Tears came again but she wiped them away quickly. 'How am I going to get to Swindon tonight?'

Simon thought quickly.

'I'll get a squad car to take you. But first, Ms Knowles, do you think you are up to doing the official identification of Anne's body?'

Her face crumpled into defiant despair.

'I don't think I can,' she wailed.

'Is there anyone else,' he asked, 'who could do it? Her ex-husband perhaps?'

'No,' she moaned, 'she wouldn't want that.'

'I'll come with you,' Rhiannon reassured her. 'You will want to see her once again and she would want you to do this for her.'

After a pause Jenny nodded.

'Yes,' she said, straightening up. 'I need to say goodbye to her.' She looked fearfully at Rhiannon. 'Is she, is her face very . . . messed up?'

'Her face isn't marked,' Rhiannon assured her. 'She looks quite peaceful.'

Which was true, Simon thought. Her eyes closed, there was a look of supreme indifference on the dead woman's face.

★   ★   ★

It was very late by the time Simon drove westwards again to Oxton. He had considered staying in his flat in town where he had kept the central heating on in this very cold spell of weather, but he preferred the inconvenience of the drive so long as Jessie was at the end of it. He wondered whether it might be time to sell the flat now that he and Jessie were heading for a permanent footing in their relationship, but that seemed like tempting fate.

He was weary, the thrumming of the tyres on the road creating a rhythm that made his eyes heavy. He opened the window a crack and the icy blast numbed his face and shocked him awake. His exhaustion owed much to the emotions of the day — the anxiety over Kevin Patterson's disappearance,

345

the distressing interview with him followed by the shock of the death of Anne Stillings and the ordeal of interviewing her partner Jenny Knowles.

Now they would have to begin all over again, questioning suspects who, until now, had been only at the periphery of his mind. Anne's death had removed her from the list, Jonathan Hadden made a second and Jock and Kevin could no longer be considered implicated. It had also helped to define the time of Kingsley's death. If Anne had witnessed the murder then it was between the time she left the Corn Exchange and the time she arrived back. With ten minutes maximum to walk the distance either way that confirmed Kingsley's death at very close to the 10.30 p.m. time they had expected it to be.

He was too tired to think, the freezing air blasting through the car now numbing his brain as well as the rest of his body. He felt as if he had not thawed out properly for hours and looked forward to the fire in Jessie's cottage, with time to relax, time to talk to her and warm his soul along with his bones.

But when he reached the cottage it was in total darkness. He had telephoned her earlier and suggested that she need not stay up for him but he was dismayed all the same. He had got used to her waiting for him on such occasions, a book on her knees, a — usually — warm smile of greeting.

He crept through the house to the living-room in the hope that she had fallen asleep there in the dark, but the embers of the fire were almost dead and when he switched on the light to be sure she'd retired to bed only Jessie's cat lay there, opening one eye for a moment before returning to her dreams.

In the kitchen there was a savoury smell and a note from Jessie telling him that there was a casserole in the stove and that he should make sure he ate some. He tried, but he seemed to have gone past hunger so he cleared things away, had a quick hot shower which did little to thaw him out and crept into their room. He sidled quietly into bed and lay there for a moment listening for her breathing, keeping himself separate in case his cold limbs should disturb her sleep. But a warm hand crept across to caress his chest.

'Bad day?' she asked in a voice that had no trace of sleep in it.

'I'll tell you about it in the morning,' he whispered.

She switched on the bedside light and sat up, folding her arms.

'I'm awake. What's been happening?' she asked.

347

He obeyed, omitting the Pattersons and telling her only of Anne Stillings's death.

'Anne's dead!' Jessie exclaimed in dismay, pulling herself more upright. 'That's terrible! I am so, so sorry. I was very fond of Anne. How awful!' She looked at him closely. 'She was pushed, wasn't she? She'd never have killed herself.'

Simon explained the evidence pointing to murder.

'No, she wouldn't have killed herself,' Jessie said sombrely. Then she said more briskly: 'And neither would she have killed Sebastian. She just didn't have it in her to hit out in violence, whatever the provocation. Anne always looked at both points of view in any confrontation. She put up with years of bad treatment by her husband and was still capable of forgiving him, never blaming.

'So do you think she was killed by the person who murdered Sebastian?' Jessie asked. 'Because Anne must have seen who it was that night with Sebastian?'

'It seems she might have been blackmailing him, or her.'

'She wouldn't,' Jessie said, shaking her head from side to side.

Simon could smell the scent of Jessie's body, the scent of her hair. He wanted nothing more than to curl closely into her and let her warm him, mind, body and spirit.

He sighed. 'She was worried about money, taking on a new mortgage. She told her partner Jenny after Kingsley died that she needn't worry about money now.'

'She must have meant that her job would no longer be on the line, that's all. She would certainly have been concerned about losing her job when she was planning to move house. But if Anne saw whoever it was who killed Sebastian she was more likely to be in some sympathy with them. She might have overheard what was said and thought the killer was provoked. If she did speak to whoever it was, she's more likely to have told them in all innocence that they had nothing to worry about from her.'

'And the killer might still take that as a veiled threat. Whatever,' he yawned, 'however it happened, the killer must have got Anne up to the meditation room on some pretext this evening and killed her, believing she was a danger to him, or her.' He nudged a little closer to Jessie, hoping she would take the hint and let him go peacefully into her arms or to sleep.

But Jessie didn't give up a subject so easily and ignored his body language.

'I got to know Anne well. She used to talk to me a lot, when she was first getting involved with Jenny. She was very disturbed by her feelings, confused about her sexuality. She had never had lesbian leanings before.'

'And what did you advise her?' Simon asked sleepily.

'I said I thought that love should be honoured wherever it is found, not circumscribed by convention.

'It's a danger for the homosexual male, though,' she went on. 'Because of the male sex-drive there are none of the restraints men have in the relationship with women, and you can get unbridled sexual promiscuity, particularly among young men. But some of them grow out of the phase and either go on to have quite normal relations with women, or they settle into stable homosexual partnerships.'

'I always thought sexual identity was a more fixed thing.'

'No, it can be quite fluid. People fall in love with other people and their gender can be quite incidental. But, you know, the breakdown in social mores — '

'Jessie,' he groaned, sliding deeper under the bedclothes, 'dearest love, please shut up.'

She wrapped her arms around him. There was peace, their breathing falling into the same rhythm.

'How amazing that you should have been

there and witnessed poor Anne's death,' Jessie murmured into his shoulder. 'Why were you going to the clinic this evening?'

Wearily, he said: 'We'd been questioning Jock and Kevin Patterson. I was going to speak to Valerie.'

'Jock wouldn't have killed Kingsley. What an idea!'

'He was a soldier, he might have killed lots of people in his time,' Simon pointed out, resentment of her scorn raising enough energy for him to respond. 'Kingsley had been abusing young Kevin.'

'Oh God,' she groaned, 'what a world we live in.'

26

Simon had already spent time with the pathologist Elaine Starkey that morning: he had taken her to the clinic and shown her the room from which Anne Stillings had fallen and the parapet, where she took measurements.

Now, garbed in green scrubs and cap, protective eye-shields perched for the moment high on her head, she looked sombrely at the naked body of the dead woman.

'The position of the injuries to her legs is, as we thought, consistent with her legs catching on the stone parapet as she fell. Point one to the theory that she was pushed and did not commit suicide.'

Simon and Longman nodded, coping so far with this least onerous aspect of their duty of attendance here.

'Point two,' she indicated the mouth area where speckled bruising showed, 'she had had her mouth taped shut. We've found traces of adhesive. Also,' she gently lifted the left arm, 'point three, there is bruising around the wrists which indicates she had been bound and restrained.'

So she had not been suddenly pushed from that height by her attacker, the lethal railings positioned directly below, she had first been held captive for a while. Simon watched Elaine Starkey carefully replace the arm beside the body, registering, as he always did with her, the respect with which she handled every stage of the autopsy procedure.

'I've found fibres under her nails,' she said, lifting the right hand, 'so she may have grabbed at whoever was holding her. They look like woollen fibres.'

They would be very helpful as proof when they found the killer, Simon thought. They might even have to pre-empt that event and take samples from suspects' clothing rather sooner if something more useful didn't turn up in the next few days.

'You know when she died,' Mrs Starkey observed, 'and you know how she died. I doubt that there is much I shall be able to add to what I've said already but this has to be got through all the same.' She smiled sympathetically at the two men, acknowledging their distaste at the procedures she was about to begin.

They did get through it, of course: Longman as usual pushing vapour rub up his nostrils, Simon urgently recalling some of the highlights of an international rugby match he'd been to recently, but it was as unpleasant as ever, more so than in many murder cases, because Simon had met this woman when she was live flesh and blood and very human. It was always a little easier if the victim was unknown.

Elaine Starkey summed up: 'She had not eaten anything of substance since around midday, she was healthy and in good condition for her age. If I find anything of interest I'll telephone you, and my report will be with you as soon as possible.'

The two men thanked her and escaped gratefully into the sharp air outside.

'We need to find out who saw her last,' Longman said, taking a deep breath and blowing his nose. 'Or rather, whoever admits to seeing her last.'

'She died at just after half-past seven,' Simon said. 'Jonathan Hadden was still in his room and Ruth Maguire had the last appointment of the day. Frances Fulton would probably have gone home around six as she usually did. So I think we need to speak to Mrs Maguire first.'

The clinic was once again closed because of recent events so they headed for Ruth Maguire's home, Simon driving.

'There's one thing about it,' Longman said,

echoing Simon's assessment, 'Anne Stillings's death has reduced the number of suspects by two, Hadden and Jock, and probably even three if we're including Anne herself. That's if she was killed by whoever killed Kingsley, as seems likely. Hadden and Jock have impeccable alibis anyway.'

'Now we have to start rechecking alibis and looking at the ones they claim for Anne's murder,' Simon said. He felt unhappy with this method of procedure though. It always seemed to him like painting by numbers. Means, motive and opportunity had all to be shown before they could make an arrest, and of these he least liked focusing on opportunity because of its potential malleability and the ease with which it could be lied about. He was happier to begin with motive, with understanding the people involved in the case, their personalities, their relationship with the victim and so on. Admittedly, this latter was less important in the case of Anne's death: she must have died because she knew who Kingsley's killer was. But even then, he thought, remembering Jessie's assessment of last night, the nature of the woman herself must have influenced how she came to die — whether she had threatened the killer, or whether she had simply made some sympathetic or understanding comment that told the killer that she knew what he or she had done.

The woman they were going to see now was still a potential suspect for both deaths. Ruth Maguire had denied that Kingsley was talking blackmail with her, but Simon had telephoned Hannah Crossley that morning to ask her to confirm that he was sure about what she had heard being said between Kingsley and Ruth Maguire. What had troubled him was that Hannah had apparently not stayed listening long enough to discover what the blackmail was about, if someone was interested enough to listen at another person's door, surely they didn't just walk away when things started to get interesting.

But Hannah had answered that question satisfactorily enough. She said that Jock had come up the stairs so that she was too embarrassed to linger. She was quite open and frank about it all, her ease of manner with Simon probably a result of their friendly meeting at the art exhibition at the weekend. Despite her shock over the news of Anne's death she had sounded relaxed, making him more inclined to believe what she had to say.

'I am quite sure of what I heard,' she assured him. 'But I only heard a minute or so of the conversation. It was only because she raised her voice that I paused by the door. Then they were quiet and Sebastian said something about her bringing her daughter to the open day that was planned. That was when I heard Jock coming and I moved on.'

She added: 'I feel very uncomfortable about having told you any of this. I don't think for a moment that Ruth killed Sebastian. And now that poor Anne is dead, if it was Sebastian's killer who also killed Anne I find it even less possible to believe in Ruth's involvement. She and Anne got on well, there was a lot of trust between them.'

Enough trust, Simon wondered, to get Anne Stillings on some pretext to the top of the building, restrain her and then push her to her death? Anne had not been a big woman, but neither was Ruth. Simon wondered if it was really possible for her to have overcome the other woman sufficiently to have tied her wrists and forcibly gagged her.

He stopped the car in front of Ruth Maguire's house, Longman having relapsed into silence. Simon considered asking him about the latest developments with his wife and in-laws, but decided that he did not want to go there, not just now.

When Ruth answered the door she was not her customary well-groomed self. Still in her dressing-gown, her hair uncombed and with no make-up on, she appeared older and tired.

She looked at them coldly and held open the door, leading them into the room they had been in before. Simon caught sight of a pair of jeans-clad legs disappearing around the bend in the staircase as they crossed the hall.

There was a tray with the remains of toast and coffee on the low table by her chair but this time she made no effort to offer them anything.

'Could Anne's death have been foreseen, or prevented?' she asked as soon as they were seated.

'We had absolutely no idea that she might be in any danger,' Simon assured her. It was clear that she was upset and that she held the police in some way responsible. She looked at him, her expression sceptical.

'Why though?' she asked. 'Why was she killed? Was it because she knew who killed Sebastian, do you think?'

'It seems the most likely explanation,' Simon said. 'We are trying to find out who was the last to see Anne. You had the latest appointment last night. Did you see Anne yesterday evening?'

'No, I didn't. I left at about half-past six. Franny had left the desk light on in the entrance hall and I could see a light under Jonathan's door, but I didn't see Anne. The last time I saw her was when we were both in the staff restroom about mid-afternoon. We had a hot drink together and a short chat.' Her eyes watered and she produced a tissue, wiping them vigorously.

'Did she seem any different from usual, as if she had anything on her mind?'

Ruth chewed at her lip, thinking.

'I can't really say I noticed anything. We were talking about a client of mine and whether she might benefit from seeing Anne, the woman's weight being an issue with her health. But she seemed quite normal, I thought.'

'Can you tell us where you were exactly, Mrs Maguire, between seven and eight last night?' Simon asked.

As expected, she reacted with anger.

'You really are clutching at straws if you have to ask me that! Why would I kill Anne? I was very fond of her. And why would I kill Sebastian either? I didn't like the man, but he hardly aroused my passions that much!'

'You must realize, Mrs Maguire,' Simon said, 'we are not, as police officers, allowed to tell our senior officers that people have been eliminated from inquiries because we like the look of their faces or because they are kind to animals. We are expected to back up everything we do with as much solid evidence as we can muster. This *is* as much for the purpose of elimination as anything else, though, so that it allows us to focus our attentions where they are most needed. So, for the record, would you mind answering my question, please?'

'I'm sorry,' she said. 'It's just that it's like adding insult to injury to explain where I was when Anne died.' She paused as if gathering breath. 'I came home from the clinic, getting back at about a quarter to seven. Cass, my daughter, was preparing the evening meal. She's home from university for Christmas. I sat in the kitchen with her, having a glass of wine and chatting. I suppose we ate at about half-past seven and cleared away the meal around eight.'

As alibis went, it wasn't much of one. Alibis from close family members never amounted to a great deal in a police officer's mind. It was quite possibly true, it was equally possibly not true.

'I have something else I have to ask you, again,' he said.

'For the purposes of your paperwork?' she asked caustically.

'Exactly. I should like a truthful answer to the question of why Sebastian Kingsley was threatening you with blackmail.'

She sighed. 'Not that again.'

'I warn you it would be wise to answer truthfully. If you have nothing to hide you have no reason to lie to us.'

'If I had nothing to hide, as you suggest, then Sebastian would hardly have been blackmailing me, would he?' She raised her eyebrows and smiled patronizingly.

'So he was?'

'Yes, or he thought he was,' she said wearily. 'I may as well tell you and you can give as much weight to it as you will. Sebastian had found out about a relationship between myself and someone else, which we would prefer to remain secret, at least for the time being. He saw us together at a restaurant in London.'

'James Flamborough?'

'The same,' she nodded with a wry smile. 'With the by-election coming up he really can do without any whiff of scandal or adverse publicity.' She added defensively: 'His marriage was more or less over when we met, but his wife agreed to keeping up the charade until after he's elected. Sebastian, of course, was perfectly well aware of the implications and our need to keep things quiet, so he used it to try to persuade me to vote with him to get Anne dismissed from the clinic.'

'And would you have?' Simon asked, interested.

'I don't think so,' she said. She bit her lip. 'I hope not. But it's all irrelevant now, isn't it? Sebastian, and Anne, are both dead.'

'That was certainly putting you in a very unenviable situation, Mrs Maguire,' said Simon. After a moment's thought he added: 'Kingsley also mentioned your daughter at the time he was suggesting blackmail. Why would he do that?'

She looked as if a bad smell had emerged in the room.

'You do have a mucky job, don't you, Chief Inspector? You cuddle up to some unpleasant people if all this is anything to go by. Just *who* was it who told you this tale? And why, I wonder.'

She was right of course — police officer or not, there was something distasteful about inquiring into people's private affairs. It hadn't seemed so underhand when Hannah Crossley had been so ready to tell her story at the exhibition, and it was, after all, a necessary part of his job to collect such information.

'You're right that we do have some unenviable tasks in our work, Mrs Maguire. I'll leave it to you to decide whether such people are worse than murderers, but I'm

362

afraid in law they are not and I listen because it's my job to remove from society those who kill by the sword rather than those cowards who kill by the word. Meanwhile I'd be grateful if you would answer my question.'

'Sorry,' she said, surprising him. 'That's another cheap shot I've made at you.' She leaned forward and poured a little more coffee into her cup. 'Sebastian's remark about Cass was just designed to annoy me, that was all. He had some influence over my daughter at one time and I suppose he wanted to remind me of the fact, perhaps suggesting he might manipulate her again should he choose to.'

'And would he still be able to have influence? Did it trouble you?'

She gave a brief laugh. 'Cass has moved on. She has a new life with far more interesting people in it than Sebastian Kingsley. No, I had no fears in that direction, it was just Sebastian being obnoxious.'

Simon considered asking to speak to her daughter, requesting her own story of how she had spent the evening before. But he decided it might be unnecessarily confrontational at this point. If the need arose he could do it another time.

As he and Longman, still silent apart from the sound of the pages of his notebook turning, got up to leave, Ruth Maguire got to her feet as well.

'Have you no idea at all who might have killed Anne?' she asked hesitantly. 'I was shocked, of course, by Sebastian's death, but not personally upset. Anne is something else. I should not like to think of her killer getting away with it.'

'Nor I, Mrs Maguire,' Simon agreed.

27

They drove to Anil Patel's through roads congested with traffic. Christmas was looming closer at an alarming pace. Simon had had no time to give much thought to Jessie's Christmas present and, though he knew she would shrug it off, she would be disappointed if he gave her nothing at all.

'What am I going to get Jess for Christmas, Geoff?' he asked. Given Longman's preoccupation, he should have realized that the sergeant was not in any mood to sympathize with trivialities.

'You'll be having a Christmas then?' Longman sniffed. 'I'm not sure that I shall.'

It was a cue to show proper concern, one that Simon felt he could no longer ignore.

'What's been happening? No chance that Julie will be coming home soon?'

'Doesn't look like it,' Longman said gloomily. 'Noel's around at the house every day, with Sue refusing to open the door. Julie says he should be allowed in to talk but Sue won't listen. Julie's afraid he's going to break down the door and the kids are frightened and upset.'

'You should go over there and see them. Maybe you could take Noel out for a drink, be a go-between or something.'

'With another murder complicating everything? Not likely Munro would agree to that!'

'I can make it all right with Munro. Let's get the next couple of interviews out of the way. We should manage that today and then I think you should go.'

Simon thought Longman would stubbornly refuse: he had a sometimes annoying stoicism, but instead, surprising him, he cocked his head on one side.

'You sure?'

'Sure,' Simon said firmly. Munro would say they were too short-staffed, but Longman in his present distracted state bordered on a hindrance rather than a help.

'What does Jessie generally buy people for Christmas?' Longman asked, visibly cheered. 'I usually find that people give the kind of presents they themselves would like to receive. For instance, people who like a good bottle of wine tend to give the same. I've got an uncle who insists on giving me packets of seeds every Christmas. It may be because they're a cheap present but it's more likely because he's a keen gardener.'

Simon told him about the tigers and

whales. 'But I can't give her the same.'

'No, you can't.' Longman considered for a moment. 'I think you should buy Jessie a rainforest.'

Simon laughed. 'If only! She'd love that.'

'No, you can. At least, you can buy a bit of rainforest. I've been reading about it. You'd find plenty of information on the internet. It doesn't cost much per acre. You could probably manage to buy quite a few if you're feeling generous.'

Simon thought it an inspired idea and said so.

At peace with each other they left the car and approached Patel's mews flat just as the man himself appeared around a corner carrying a bag of groceries. He stopped at the door, fumbling for his key.

'Didn't expect to be at home today and I was out of food,' he observed to them as they waited.

Anne's death in this case appeared to be more of an inconvenience than cause for sorrow, then, Simon thought. But there was always something a little inscrutable about this young man, so you could never be sure what his real feelings were.

Dumping his groceries inside the kitchen, Patel offered them a coffee and they accepted.

Longman said, as Patel arrived with the tray of mugs:

'I'm surprised so many of you healthy-living types still drink ordinary coffee and tea.'

'Not ordinary,' Patel said. 'I drink excellent quality coffee and tea and in great moderation. Moderation in all things is the key. I also drink healthy herbal teas and lots of spring water. People don't drink enough water.'

Patel settled himself back in his chair after handing their mugs to them.

'I'm very sorry about what's happened to Anne,' he said, almost as if she were their colleague rather than his own. 'Jonathan rang us all to let us know what had happened. He left a message on my phone. She was definitely pushed, was she? I rang Jonathan back this morning and I gather that he virtually saw it happen. As did you. Amazing really. It must have been quite a shock.'

'There is no doubt that Anne was murdered,' Simon said.

'But why do you wish to speak to me? I know nothing about it.'

'A couple of things, Mr Patel. When did you last see Anne? We're trying to establish everyone's movements at the clinic yesterday afternoon and evening.'

'I've been thinking about that. You do when

someone dies, don't you? The last I saw of Anne was in passing in the afternoon. She had just come down from the staffroom upstairs. She said she had an appointment due with a particularly stubborn woman who told her lies about what she ate. She laughed about it. She was quite cheerful, I thought, not troubled at all.'

'And what time did you leave the clinic yesterday evening, sir?' Longman asked.

'My last appointment ended at just after four and I left soon after. My clients have fallen off rather since Sebastian died, as have my colleagues'. But I think my needles are more threatening in the circumstances.' Patel's eyes gleamed with amusement. He certainly seemed less bothered than before by the bad publicity the clinic had received and its consequent implications for his job.

He added, confirming the impression:

'I suppose Anne's death is going to make things worse. Poor Jonathan. He has more invested in the clinic than the rest of us. I can get work easily enough as a well-qualified acupuncturist.'

'Not something Mrs Stillings will have to worry about too much any more either,' Longman observed coolly.

'No, indeed,' Patel agreed. 'She has gone to that great mystery we will all enter one day.

She'll be all right, though, she was a good woman.'

'Sudden shocking death is not the best way to go, though, is it sir?' Longman said. 'I'd prefer to meet my maker with a little more preparation.'

'Yes, you're quite right, Sergeant,' Patel said more sombrely. 'I would prefer to have the Book of the Dead read to me as I lie dying than be catapulted into the beyond in such a way. I'm sorry, I didn't mean to appear flippant. I shall say my prayers for Anne.'

Simon coughed. Given half the chance, Longman would now launch into an extended discussion of esoteric imponderables.

'Would you tell us where you were last night around seven thirty, please, Mr Patel?'

The look of amusement returned to Anil Patel's face.

'Well, I wasn't pushing Anne Stillings out of a top-floor window. I was leaving here, as a matter of fact, to go for a meal with a friend.'

'Name of friend, and restaurant?' Longman asked, pen poised.

'Aisha Markandya and the Bengal Tiger,' Patel said, his voice clipped.

'Miss Markandya again,' Longman nodded as he scribbled. 'What time was your table booked for?' The Bengal Tiger was a very upmarket Indian restaurant where booking was always required.

'Seven forty-five. Aisha came here and we walked there since it is only a short distance and we both enjoy good wine.'

The time would be easy to check with the restaurant and, if it proved accurate, would almost certainly put Anil Patel out of the frame. He could not have driven from the clinic and been home to meet Aisha in time, certainly not without speeding and being greatly out of breath. And given the distance of the clinic from his flat and the fact that he would have had to park some way from the clinic now that the gates were firmly locked against vehicles in the evening, it would have to be impossible.

'Miss Markandya was also your alibi for Mr Kingsley's death,' Simon remarked. 'And in that case we've found it to be faulty.'

'Have you?' Patel seemed less confident. 'In what way?'

'You came home at nearer ten, rather than leaving Aisha Markandya at around eleven as you claimed.'

Patel made a deprecating gesture. 'Does it matter exactly what time it was? I have no idea what time Sebastian was killed, so why should I deliberately lie?'

'It happens, Mr Patel,' Longman said with

371

evident patience, 'that you now have no alibi for the time Mr Kingsley was killed. If you really had been with the two young women as you claim, you would have been unable to be at the clinic at that time bludgeoning him to death. As it is, you could have done so without difficulty.'

'But I had no reason to,' Patel said uneasily. 'I have no motive for wanting Sebastian dead. Nor Anne, either. And I wouldn't kill even if I did. I am far too conscious of my karma to risk such behaviour.'

'Motive is something we may have still to uncover,' Simon said. 'But what interests me is why you should lie about where you were at the significant time if it wasn't because you knew exactly what that significant time was.'

Anil Patel looked down at his mug, fiddling with its handle.

'I suppose I shall have to tell you,' he said after a long pause. 'Franny asked me to tell you that time.' He looked up. 'I wouldn't have agreed if I had thought for a moment that she had anything to do with Sebastian's death. But she had gone out for a walk, and she said it might look suspicious for her.'

'She *persuaded* you to lie?' Simon suggested.

He nodded. 'Yes, I suppose so.'

372

'Because she might otherwise make things difficult for you where your fiancée is concerned.'

'Yes.' Patel squirmed uncomfortably on his seat.

'Do you know at what time Frances actually did return that night?'

'No, obviously not. I had already gone home by then. I was expecting a call from India early next morning and I was tired.'

'But I suppose Miss Markandya must have told you afterwards,' Simon remarked.

'We didn't talk about it,' Patel said shortly.

Simon frowned. 'So when did Mrs Fulton *persuade* you to tell this lie?' There had been little time to fix their story between the two of them, though plenty for Frances and Aisha to have done so. Had Frances felt impelled to ring Patel after she had got back from her walk that night? And if so, was it because she had seen, or done, something at the clinic?

'You gave us all plenty of time to speak to each other before you arrived on the scene the next morning, *Detective* Chief Inspector.' Patel said giving one of his small secret smiles.

28

Frances Fulton was not at home so Simon and Longman drove back to headquarters.

'Write up your reports and then get going to see Julie,' Simon said as they got out of the car.

Longman was away ahead of him by the time Simon entered the building.

It was already beginning to get dark, the dull, cold day seemed hardly to have properly woken since dawn and lights were on all over the building. Simon collected Rhiannon Jones and they walked to the Cathedral Approach where the media crowd, gathered in even greater numbers than before, brought them to a halt. They retreated to the West Gate and took the longer route to the clinic via the Martyr's Arch entrance, free of any avid observers, the gates being solid ancient wood.

Frances Fulton seemed shaken and upset, even pleased to see them both.

'Jonathan asked me to come in and contact all the appointments for today,' she said. 'I'm to stay here until I've got hold of them all and I'm not having much success.'

'I imagine they will have heard the news by

now,' Simon said. He had listened to the radio on the way into work that morning and Anne's death had been a lead story — though it had not made the morning papers. 'And the gate attendant will explain to them if not.'

'I expect so,' she said dully. 'It's awful what happened to Anne. I can't concentrate.' She looked up at him, her dark eyes showing circles almost as dark beneath them. 'Jonathan rang me with the news last night and I couldn't sleep.'

'It's been a terrible shock,' Rhiannon said sympathetically.

'We're going to see the scene of crime officers upstairs,' Simon said. 'But we'd like to speak to you afterwards. Perhaps not here in the reception area,' he suggested.

She seemed untroubled at the prospect.

'We can go in there,' she pointed with her pen at the room used for evening classes. 'Then I can listen for the telephone.'

It began to ring as she finished speaking so they went on their way to see Richards and company. Apparently all the practitioners used the meditation room from time to time, some more regularly than others, so fibres from clothes found there were unlikely to prove helpful. The same was true of fingerprints and somehow Simon doubted that the killer of Anne Stillings would have helpfully left his or her fingerprints, around the dormer window from which Anne had been pushed.

Richards shook his head as the two of them entered the room.

'We've taken samples from the parapet where we found the traces of blood you expected, but we've found no other evidence. We've vacuumed the carpet in case of samples that may be of use, but there is no other sign of blood.

'Nothing around the window-frame or on the doors neither,' Richards added. 'Whoever it was must have worn gloves, or, more likely, they wiped the surfaces clean because there are no prints anywhere there.'

As Simon and Rhiannon walked down the staircase through the silent, almost deserted building it seemed to take on a haunted quality. It made him think of Hermione and her store of useful psychics. This building seemed full of what Hermione would call 'vibrations', emanations of the dead of ages in a building of such venerability. He gave a brief laugh. If it came to it and the case looked insoluble, he just might be desperate enough to take up Hermione's standing offer.

'Something funny sir?' Rhiannon asked, looking surprised.

'Not really, Rhiannon. Just a whimsical thought.'

Frances put down the telephone as they approached and led them into the adjacent room, leaving the door open.

'Is Mr Hadden here today?' Simon asked.

'He was, but he left about an hour ago.' She drew a set of hard chairs into a small circle. 'Anne was pushed out of that window, wasn't she? Jonathan told me only that she had fallen, but I think she must have been killed by the person who killed Sebastian Kingsley.'

'Yes, she was pushed. There is no doubt about it from the evidence we have,' Simon said.

'I hope you've got some idea who did it,' Frances said. 'I mean, apart from feeling very upset about her death, I'm beginning to feel just a bit nervous about working here.'

'I understand that,' Simon said sympathetically. 'But I don't think our killer is some random homicidal maniac. We think he must have killed Anne because she knew something about Sebastian Kingsley's death. So, unless you do too, you should be safe enough.'

'I don't know who killed Sebastian, or Anne either,' she said, folding her arms across her chest.

'Then you shouldn't have anything to

worry about, Mrs Fulton.' Simon studied her for a moment. She seemed defiant but not in obvious possession of guilty knowledge.

'But we have some questions to ask you all the same,' he added. 'When did you last see Mrs Stillings?'

'Just as I was leaving, around six. She came down from her room and asked me if I had seen what had been going on with Jock. I didn't know what she meant. She said it looked as if he had been arrested, she had heard raised voices below her window and looked out to see him being taken off by a couple of uniformed policemen.' She looked accusing. '*Did* you arrest Jock? I haven't seen him today.'

'No, we didn't' Simon said. 'He came home last night.'

'You'd have to release him, wouldn't you? I mean he obviously didn't push Anne out of the window if he was with you.'

'We have taken that into account, Mrs Fulton,' Simon said wryly. 'Perhaps you could tell us if Anne said anything else?'

'She said she was going to see if Valerie was all right. She didn't know if Kevin was there with her or whether she was alone. She was going to make her a cup of tea or something.' Frances blinked. 'That was typical of Anne, to think immediately of someone who might be in need of help.'

'And did she go downstairs straight away?' Simon asked.

'She went round by the outside of the building to their back door.'

'And you didn't see her come back?'

'No, I went home soon after she left and I never saw her again.' Frances blinked again and produced a tissue. 'I shall miss her — if this place manages to stay open after all that's happened. She was very kind to me when I came to work here. She took a lot of trouble to explain things and what the therapists were all doing so that I'd find it easier to talk to the clients.'

'Was anyone else in the building when you left?' he asked.

'Just Mr Hadden and Mrs Maguire. She was still seeing a client. Everyone else went home before I did.'

Went, and returned, Simon thought, unless Ruth Maguire had lied to them, or Frances herself was lying.

'Mrs Fulton,' he said, 'where were you on the night of Sebastian Kingsley's death?'

She went very still. 'I told you. I was at home,' she faltered, 'with Aisha and Anil.'

'You may well have been, for a while, but not for the length of time claimed. Mr Patel was seen returning home at around ten. He's admitted that you went out and were not back when he left Aisha that night. So you told us an untruth about where you were for the whole of that time. Where did you go?' He looked at her enquiringly.

Either she was not thinking quickly or the shock of Anne's death had prompted her to be more open with them.

'I just went for a walk. It's a pain being in the flat with Aisha and Anil when they get together, so I decided to go out for a while.'

'Did you come to the clinic?'

'No,' she said, her lips set in a line.

'Mrs Fulton,' Simon said, pulling his coat more closely around him: it was cold in the large room, 'We understand that your mother was treated here at the clinic.'

She would know that they knew this, she would have spoken to her father.

'Yes,' she said. 'She died.'

'And I'm very sorry for your loss. But did her death leave you with the kind of anger your father showed — in particular to Sebastian Kingsley? Enough perhaps to give you a motive for killing him?'

'No, I didn't.' Her voice was tight. 'I didn't kill him and I didn't kill Anne.'

'But you did come here that night? Perhaps to cause a little more mayhem in your role as the clinic gremlin?'

Rhiannon was watching Frances with quickened interest.

The young woman was kneading the hem of her skirt. It was a quite short skirt and she was unheedingly revealing a large slice of slender thigh. She suddenly stopped the movement and smoothed out the fabric.

'You're right that I'm the one they took to calling the gremlin,' she said unsteadily. 'I got the job here because I wanted to find some way of punishing them, Kingsley in particular, for keeping my mother from proper treatment. I didn't start causing any trouble until quite a while after I started work, otherwise they would have guessed who it was.'

'Your father said that you supported the treatment your mother had decided on,' Simon said. 'He was obviously trying to deflect suspicion from you.'

'Poor Dad,' she said sadly. 'I think that at first he was afraid I *had* killed Kingsley.' She took a breath. 'So, yes I *was* on my way here that night. I was planning to break some of Kingsley's things and make a real mess of his room.'

She gave a wry smile. 'Funny to think that if I had done what I planned I might have saved Kingsley's life, being there around that time.'

'Or you might have been in danger yourself,' Rhiannon pointed out.

'Just as well I didn't come here then,' Frances said drily.

The telephone trilled in the hallway and she went out to answer it. They heard her murmur a few words, then she returned and sat down.

'Someone else cancelling an appointment,' she said, 'and not wanting to make another one. Not surprising I suppose.'

'So tell us what you *did* do that night,' Simon said.

'I walked down the West Gate and I stood in the Cathedral Approach at the gates, looking through at the cathedral lit up against the sky. I had never really *looked* at the cathedral before, I'd always been in a hurry to leave work and when I'd come here at night before I was too busy thinking about what I was planning to do.'

She glanced at Simon. 'And as I stood there I just felt silly, foolish. I felt small. I imagined what my mother would think of what I was doing and I realized it wasn't what she would have wanted. She had made her own choice about what treatment she wanted for her illness and I should respect that.

'Besides, it's a lottery in a way, whatever treatment you choose. Some people have all the conventional treatment and still die, while others try the alternative approach and live. Or it works the other way round. There are never any guarantees. I've learned a bit about that since I've been working here. Maybe when your time is up, it's up and there's nothing much you can do about it.'

She shrugged. 'So I decided to stop it there and then. I went for a walk around the outside of the cathedral instead. Then I sat on one of the old benches looking up at all the wonderful statues and carvings. I felt safe and sort of peaceful there. And I realized it was really my own feelings of guilt that made me blame Kingsley and the clinic for my mother's death. I felt so bad that I wasn't there for her.'

Frances put a hand to her eyes. 'It was the first time I had let myself cry for her.' She blew her nose.

'I'm sure she doesn't want you to feel any guilt, Frances,' Rhiannon said quietly. 'She would just want you to get on with your life as fully as possible.'

'I suppose so.' Frances looked unsure.

Simon showed lamentably less sensitivity and circumspection.

'And did you see anyone going in to the clinic, or coming out?' he said.

Frances shook her head.

'I'm sorry, no. I didn't go near the clinic itself. I doubt whether I even *could* have seen anything from where I was. It's very bright under the floodlights and all you can see is that wonderful building.'

Simon studied her for a moment longer before beginning to unfold himself from his stiff position on the merciless chair.

'I'm sorry,' Frances said again. 'I'm really sorry if anything I've done has made it more difficult for you.' She looked up at him, her eyes large and dark.

She had certainly changed, Simon thought. Or was that merely what she wished them to believe? Her transformation had not taken place in any obvious way after the night of Kingsley's death as she was suggesting. It was only now, since Anne's murder, that Frances was showing any evidence of a change of heart. It could be that it was remorse over Anne rather than acceptance of her mother's death that had brought about this softer, more contrite image. She could have waited for Anne's return from visiting Valerie Patterson and lured her to the top floor on some pretext.

'Miss Fulton, where were you last night around half-past seven?' he asked.

'I was on the bus on the way to visit my father,' she said sullenly with a return to her

384

more usual manner.

'Where and when did you catch the bus?'

'At the bottom of the West Gate at twenty past seven.'

'I don't suppose you kept the ticket?' he asked.

'I'll look in my purse.' She got up with a flounce and went out to her desk, returning with her shoulder-bag. After delving in its depths she produced a small black purse and looked inside, extracting a few pieces of paper that looked more like receipts than bus tickets. 'No, it's not there' she said. 'I must have thrown it away. But the bus-driver may remember me, I suppose.'

'Let's hope so,' Simon said.

He and Rhiannon followed Anne Stillings's route to the Patterson's flat, Simon uncomfortable at the prospect of seeing them all again.

Jock answered the door promptly. He didn't exactly beam a smile of welcome, but he was civil enough.

'Come in,' he said quietly to Simon. 'And we'd both of us like to thank you for the letter you sent us, about the fact we need have no concerns that Kevin has been affected healthwise. It put our minds more at rest.'

He ushered them to the living-room, saying: 'A sad business about poor Mrs

385

Stillings. She was a very nice woman.'

The accolades that had followed Anne Stillings's death were rather different from Kingsley's obituaries, Simon had noticed.

Valerie Patterson was fixing a Christmas card to a column of them hanging on the wall. It was the first time Simon had seen her on her feet and he realized that she was quite tall, only a couple of inches shorter than her husband. There was no sign of Kevin, though sounds of rap music were emanating from his room.

Valerie Patterson clutched her crucifix again as soon as she was settled into her high chair. Simon's letter had obviously not had any softening effect on Jock's wife: he had the impression she viewed him as a demonic presence the way her hand always seemed to fly to her silver cross whenever she encountered him.

'What can we do for you now, Chief Inspector?' she asked, allowing her expression to soften a little as she looked at Rhiannon.

'We are really sorry to bother you again, Mrs Patterson,' Simon began, making no move to sit down when so obviously uninvited. 'But, as you must realize, we're now investigating the murder of Mrs Stillings.'

'Well, I hope you're convinced enough that

my husband and son didn't kill her. I hope that being at the police station is alibi enough for you.'

'Yes, of course. I wanted to ask you about Mrs Stillings's visit to you yesterday evening.'

'What do you want to know? She was kind enough,' Valerie Patterson said with some emphasis, 'to come and see if I was going to be all right after your policemen had dragged Jock off to the police station.'

'Yes, we gathered that that was why she came here, Mrs Patterson,' Rhiannon said with all her considerable charm, 'it was indeed very thoughtful of her. But we are trying to establish what Mrs Stillings was doing before she died in the hope that it may help us establish who killed her. Was she here very long?'

'No, not long. Maybe half an hour I suppose. She made me a cup of tea and sympathized that the Chief Inspector here should have been thinking Jock and Kevin had anything to do with Mr Kingsley's death. She said not to worry and that they were certain to be home soon because she was quite sure they would never have hurt that man.' She looked reproachfully at Simon.

'Mrs Patterson, we think she may have known who killed Mr Kingsley and that the same person may have killed her too,' he said.

'Did she make any mention of her own belief about how and why Kingsley died?'

'No she didn't. Pity that she didn't if what you say is true. Not that I wasn't sympathizing with Kingsley's murderer until this happened. But this is different, isn't it. Mrs Stillings was a lovely woman. She tried very hard to help me with my arthritis, but I'm afraid I let her down. I kept eating all the wrong things — comfort-eating she called it.'

Jock had been standing silently beside them while this conversation took place. He said, rather to Rhiannon than to Simon:

'Would you want to sit down?'

'Thank you, no,' Simon replied for her. 'We won't bother you any further. Except to ask whether you heard anyone leave the building last night, Mrs Patterson, around half past seven?'

'Is that when Anne died?

'So you heard nothing at all?' Simon repeated.

'Nothing,' she said. 'But I was consoling myself with one of my soaps. Since Jock got me set up with satellite I can watch them more or less whenever I want. And, as Jock says, they're a noisy lot with all the rows and fights that go on, so I didn't hear anything at all last night coming from the clinic.'

29

The next day was something of a hiatus for Simon. There seemed nothing to go on but the chance of breaking someone's alibi and he had no option in the circumstances but to send the team on their way to find out the truth or otherwise of the alibis for Anne's death. None of the current investigations had thrown up any leads and, short of demanding that suspects handed over all their clothing that contained any woollen fibres, there was no forensic evidence pointing to any others.

He lurked despondently at headquarters for a while, missing Longman. The sergeant hadn't phoned but Simon hoped he would soon return restored to his usual self, his family of in-laws pacified. After a few hours of reading through reports and DI Stone's immaculate summaries he decided to go back to his flat and see if he could arrange Jessie's Christmas present.

He turned up the central heating, made himself a mug of coffee and set himself to exploring the possibilities the internet had to offer. After an hour he was feeling pleased with himself: he had managed to purchase several acres of rainforest in Brazil for Jessie along with the promise of a map showing the location of the acres and a jolly Christmas card to go with it to arrive before the day itself.

As he returned to the incident room members of the team were filtering back. Rhiannon was first with her report: Hannah Crossley claimed to have gone shopping the evening before and had the till receipts to prove it. She was processing her shopping at 7.20 using her debit card. Since Waitrose was on the outskirts of the city, at least a fifteen-minute drive from the clinic, she was in the clear.

DI Stone and Savage had had difficulties running into Cass Maguire and her mother.

'For what it's worth,' the DI said, 'bearing in mind that the daughter would be likely to back up her mother, they're still saying they were having a meal together as claimed.'

'Shouldn't we look into the Maguires a little more closely, sir?' DI Stone added. 'There's not just the matter of Mrs Maguire wanting her relationship with the prospective candidate kept quiet. The business of Kingsley's relationship with the daughter might be an even more important issue. After all we have to remember that it's the motive for *Kingsley's* death that counts. It's unlikely that Anne Stillings was killed for any other reason than that she knew who had murdered him.'

Simon hoped they were right in that assumption.

'How do you suggest going about looking into Cass Maguire's relationship with Kingsley?' he asked.

'We haven't really closely questioned people about it. We might find there was more going on there than Mrs Maguire admits to.'

'Fine, go ahead,' he said. But he was uneasy about it. It just didn't feel right to him; pursuing the idea risked distressing a young woman just getting her life on course. 'But be careful how you go about it,' he said.

'You mean you don't want me speaking to the girl herself?' Rebecca Stone's disapproval was obvious.

'Not unless you can bring me very good reasons why you should.'

She raised her eyebrows at that.

'There's another possibility as well that we don't seem to have considered,' she said.

Simon didn't know whether to feel cheered that someone had some ideas at this apparent point of impasse in the case. He was more inclined to increased despondency at the burgeoning paperwork and administration involved in pursuing lines of inquiry that he had no heart for.

'Yes?' he said.

'We haven't really considered Jenny Knowles.'

'Jenny Knowles?' She had genuinely startled him.

DI Stone was immediately defensive.

'She had a motive equal to Anne's when it came to killing Kingsley, if Anne had told her he was going to dismiss her from the clinic. She seems to have been very keen on their new house and that wouldn't have been possible for them if Anne lost her job. Suppose she left the film just after Anne and went to the clinic? Anne might have seen her and Jenny might have been afraid Anne would tell the police.'

Simon remembered that Jenny Knowles had had her coat on, claiming to be going to look for her partner, when he and Rhiannon had called on her after Anne's death. It may have been that he had misinterpreted her action and that she had in fact been coming home — though that had been well over an hour after Anne had fallen to her death. Rebecca Stone however had not seen Jenny's grief and fear and to Simon it had seemed real enough. He wasn't impressed with Stone's idea.

'If you find you have the time, by all means follow up on that if you wish. But, again, be careful of intruding on the woman herself without checking with me first. As far as we know at the moment she is grieving her partner's loss and she can do without unnecessary harassment from the police.'

The content and manner of Simon's response clearly didn't please her.

'Thank you,' Stone said stiffly.

DC Williams was anxious to give his own report. Anil Patel had indeed been at the Bengal Tiger the night before, 'with a very pretty young lady'. They had arrived at the time booked, 7.45, and his credit-card payment was timed at 9.15. 'So, unless he nipped out on the off chance of finding Anne Stilling poised at the dormer window,' Williams said, 'he seems to be in the clear, too.'

Simon nodded. Suspects seemed to be vanishing into a black hole.

Adding to the cumulative effect, Williams added:

'And I checked with the bus company and managed to speak to the bus driver on the route that Frances Fulton said she took. He'd just come on shift fortunately, see.' Williams extended the moment with a true Welsh instinct for drama. 'He says she was there.

She regularly goes on that bus each week, he says, and he remembers her quite clearly. Even told me where she got off the bus in Walmcot.'

'Convincing enough, then. Well done, Bryn,' Simon said with as much enthusiasm as he could muster.

It was already dark, the floodlit cathedral casting its own glow over this part of the city, an admonitory presence reminding him of unfulfilled duty. He left the rest of them to their report-writing and went back to his office.

Within the hour Longman appeared, looking happier and considerably more relaxed. Simon was so focused on the chance to talk over the case with him that he failed to ask how his trip had gone and whether there had been any outcome. He made them both a cup of coffee — the canteen version having become even more undrinkable of late.

Longman listened intently to Simon's summary of events since his departure, not saying anything until Simon fell silent.

'It's not looking terribly hopeful, is it?' he said at last. 'If I were harder-hearted I'd say it was a pity Valerie Patterson is so immobilized, otherwise she'd make a perfect suspect. As for Frances Fulton, the bus driver could be mistaken, especially if she travelled regularly by that route. She might even have made the journey the day before in order to confuse things. As for the Maguires — '

But Simon had stopped listening. 'Sorry,' he said. 'There's something I want to check. See you tomorrow morning.'

The clinic was entirely deserted this evening. Simon went up the stairs to Anne Stillings's room. Her filing-cabinet was locked and Simon didn't hesitate in producing a Swiss army knife from one of his capacious overcoat pockets and easily breaking in. He flicked rapidly through the folders before he found the one he was looking for and left the building in as great a hurry as he had entered it.

Monk Lane Medical Practice was in the area between the North and West Gates, an old part of the city still made up of narrow streets where parking was limited. Simon went there on foot anyway, it being the quickest option.

The waiting room was crowded.

'Is Dr Spinner on duty tonight?' he asked the receptionist.

She gave him a pitying look and pointed at the board on the wall with two doctors' names slotted into it. One of them was Dr Spinner.

'Can you ask her to see me immediately after her present patient?' he asked, forgetting in his eagerness to show his ID.

'You'd be from the planet Zog, would you?' the woman asked, to the amusement of nearby patients. Simon produced the ID.

'It's very urgent,' he said. Her expression remained defiant so he added: 'It's urgent police business.'

She pursed her mouth and turned to the intercom, speaking so that he could not hear her words. Then she nodded him in the direction of a spare seat.

The scope for distraction was limited. Simon wondered what wag had in the past decided that a suitable name for anyone under the advice of a medical doctor should be called a patient. Had he or she foreseen the vast increase in their numbers, and their future need to be in possession of this virtue? He reached into one of his weighed-down pockets and pulled out a dog-eared copy of an etymological dictionary, a resource for rare idle moments. He found that the root of the word patient in the medical sense came from Middle English via Old French from the Latin *pati* meaning suffer.

A sprightly-looking eighty-year-old came through one of the doors off the waiting-room and the receptionist beckoned Simon impatiently.

Dr Spinner looked as if she could have

taken a few tips from her last patient. She was writing some notes and looked up at him wearily.

'I can't give you long,' she said. 'I'd be rather grateful to get home tonight sometime. I've been called out once during this session to a neurotic male who turned out to have an ingrowing toenail and the natives out there are getting restless.'

'Why did you go, if it was such a minor matter?' Simon asked.

'He said he thought he was bleeding to death. I didn't believe it but I didn't want an ambulance being wasted on him, perhaps causing loss of life to someone who really was at death's door. Another time I'll be glad to take his toe off for him.' She threw down her pen and grinned maliciously.

'I gather you consider yourself another emergency,' she said. 'Make it quick then, but take a seat all the same.'

'Valerie Patterson,' Simon said. 'You're her doctor, I believe. I need to know just how immobilized by arthritis she is. I am in the middle of a murder investigation.'

She sat back with an admiring smile.

'Well, that was precise enough. I wish some of my patients could be as much to the point. And it's a pleasant change from the symptoms I usually listen to. So you're

397

suffering from high levels of impatience fostered by equally dangerous levels of ignorance. Certainly the latter if you in your wildest imagination suppose that poor old Valerie Patterson with her crippled knees and degenerate hip-joints is sprightly enough to have overcome Sebastian Kingsley with a fatal blow to the head and followed it up by racing to the top of the clinic to toss the luckless Anne Stillings from a top floor window.'

She looked pityingly at his surprise. 'I may be a lowly GP, Chief Inspector, but I can read, you know, I even watch television from time to time. I'm hardly likely not to have noticed the goings on at the Cathedral Clinic, am I?'

'So Mrs Patterson really is badly disabled by her arthritis?' Simon said lamely, feeling more foolish by the minute.

'I could probably show you the X rays if I could get up the enthusiasm. Let's just say she might manage one flight of steps on her bum if an emergency called for it.'

'I'm sorry to have taken up your time,' Simon said getting to his feet.

'Hey, a little drama in the tedious round does no harm,' she said, giving him a sly smile. 'Besides, the thought of Valerie Patterson in the role of homicidal maniac will keep me amused for hours.'

30

Driving to headquarters next morning Simon thought about his actions on the evening before, still uncomfortable at the memory of the doctor's reaction when he had spoken to her about Valerie Patterson. It had been Longman's remark about her as a perfect suspect gelling with his memory of seeing her on her feet for the first time that had set Simon off. She was after all, the last person known to have spoken to Anne, and the family's motive for wanting Kingsley's death remained valid. Anne, when she went to commiserate with Valerie, might have indicated that she knew about the Patterson's involvement in Kingsley's death, and if Valerie had been sufficiently able-bodied, his suspicions would have made perfect sense.

Simon had been taciturn and unresponsive when he arrived home the night before — until Jessie had bracingly persuaded him to explain himself.

'You're just not looking closely enough at the matter of motive, at the psychology involved. And don't say that I *would* say that,' she held up a hand as he began to protest at her unfairness, 'because it's true.'

She had put another log on the fire and picked up her wine-glass again. 'Where is the passion in all this? Sebastian was killed with a single blow to the head in what appears to have been an unpremeditated murder, one motivated by sudden rage. What had Sebastian been threatening that was so important to the person with him that night that he, or she, lashed out in such desperation?'

Simon could think of no one but the Pattersons at the moment and stayed silent.

Jessie continued: 'But the killing of Anne was a different matter. It was planned, premeditated. She was gagged and tied.' She stopped speaking for a moment. 'But Anne might not have known anything really. She might have gone to the clinic, in the hope of speaking with Sebastian perhaps, and maybe the killer saw her but she didn't see him or her, maybe the killer looked out of the window and saw her leaving.'

Simon shook his head.

'It's possible I suppose, but it doesn't fit with what Jenny Knowles said. But, either way, Jess, apart from exonerating Anne from any suspicion of blackmail, it doesn't actually help us any further in the case, does it.'

'Perhaps not,' Jessie subsided. 'But even so

I think you should be concentrating on the motivation for killing Sebastian and do the refinements afterwards.'

'That's what I tried to do with the Pattersons,' Simon said.

'Who else had a motive? It must have been something visceral if it was someone from that group at the clinic. They are hardly prime homicidal material.'

But Simon, driving and attempting to think as Jessie had advised, remained as bereft of ideas as before.

A lengthy meeting that morning with Detective Superintendent Munro failed to concentrate his mind either. She, dealing with the media, was frustrated that he had nothing to offer her.

Afterwards he went for a meal in the canteen with Longman and remembered on this occasion to ask how his visit to his sister-in-law and wife had gone.

'Chaos at first,' Longman said, carefully examining the sausage on his plate. 'The kids were home for the Christmas holidays, of course, and were running wild. They kept asking their mother when they could see their dad and she'd shout at them and start crying again. The back door had been kicked so hard by Noel after Sue bolted the doors that we had to get someone in to repair it.'

'How was Julie coping?'

'Run ragged I think. She seemed very pleased to see me, anyway.' He smiled and began eating the sausage.

Longman finished his meal, with apparent enjoyment, and pushed his plate aside.

'Noel was in a state — pretty desperate really. He'd always seemed such a together sort of bloke but all this has really undermined him. I told him Sue wouldn't let him see the children as long as he was living with his new girlfriend.'

'And I suppose it will take a while for him to get it sorted with the courts,' Simon said.

'Like I said before, mothers can make a lot of difficulties — say the kids are ill, or have a dental appointment or something when dad turns up to take them out for the day.'

There had been a few cases recently where fathers had been given fairer treatment by the courts, Simon had noticed. But that was still a rare event in the thousands of such battles taking place across the country.

'Anyway,' Longman finished his cup of tea. 'Noel agreed that he would move out of the girlfriend's flat. He just couldn't cope with the thought of effectively losing the children. Sue says he has to get himself an acceptable place of his own so that the children have somewhere to visit. You can see her point of view,' Longman said, glancing out of the window at the grey skies threatening icy rain or snow. 'He can't drag them around outdoors in these sorts of temperatures. Now he's decided that he wants to come home, that it's all been a big mistake.'

'So all ended happily?'

'Not exactly. Sue says he still has to get somewhere to live anyway and then she'll see how things go. She's much too angry to let him come home just like that, and she's naturally feeling hurt.'

'Is Julie likely to be coming home now?'

'At the weekend, now that it seems sorted.' Longman patted his stomach. 'What are we looking at next?' he asked as they walked together back to the incident room.

'I was hoping you might have some suggestions. Jessie has demanded that for the moment I concentrate on thought before action.' Simon had not mentioned his trip to see Dr Spinner yet, and wasn't sure that he would unless the necessity arose. Longman had not thought to enquire where he had rushed off to the evening before.

DI Stone had just arrived and was on the look-out for Simon.

'It looks as if the Maguires *may* be in the clear,' she said, a look of dissatisfaction on her face. 'A neighbour from next door says she went round there on the night of Anne Stilling's death. She wanted some milk for her cat and Mrs Maguire went to fetch some for her. She didn't go further than the hall but she didn't see the daughter, though.'

'And what time was this?' Simon asked.

'About twenty past seven. She said it was just before *Coronation Street*, which she always watches.' Rebecca Stone looked disapproving. 'She's a bit of a vague old biddy, though, so it's not any kind of perfect alibi.'

'Always beware of the perfect alibi, DI Stone,' Simon said solemnly.

'Do you mean we should check out some of those we've got so far, sir?' she asked sweetly.

'If the mood takes you, Rebecca,' Simon replied.

'I've been wondering about something else,' she said, pushing a stray lock of hair firmly into place. 'I was wondering just how bad Valerie Patterson's arthritis really is. It's occurred to me that she was perfectly placed to kill Anne Stillings . . . '

Simon listened to her complete her justification for the immediate investigation of Jock's maligned wife before finding unexpected satisfaction in admitting to his particular knowledge of the matter.

'Valerie Patterson is incapable of making

her way up one flight of stairs, let alone several,' he said.

'Really? Is that your opinion, sir, or a fact?'

'Fact. I checked with her doctor,' he said briefly.

'Well, you never recorded the matter,' DI Stone said stiffly. 'At least, not that I've seen from your reports. Does that mean that you suspected her too?'

'It means that I try to be thorough,' Simon said, blushing inwardly. He decided to go for a walk.

A bench by the river, near the huge old converted mill, was one of his favourite places for contemplation. He often came here when things were at an impasse. Not far from headquarters, it was quiet, with a view across the flood plain to the hills in the west. He sat down, hands deep in his pockets against the cold and pulled a scarf out of his pocket, wrapping it securely around his neck, his face already beginning to freeze.

He let his mind wander as it would over the people in the case, images of Kingsley's smashed skull, Hadden's white face, the dean's shaky distress. He saw Anne Stillings in her flamboyant clothes, and her poor body slumped over the railings that pierced it, and the rest of them: the Pattersons and their anguish; Jenny Knowles as it dawned on her that her partner was dead; Ruth Maguire's cool manner in the face of descending chaos; Frances Fulton's defiance; Hannah Crossley's cold sophistication and unexpected flashes of humour and Anil Patel's dark inscrutable eyes. And nothing lit up in his mind, no prompting to pursue a thought triggered by some memory, nothing at all.

As he stared into the distance big fat flakes of snow began to flutter around him. They fell more swiftly and what sounds there had been in the back of his awareness were smothered. He watched fascinated as the distant view became filled with millions of dancing bits of white, changing his focus from one to another until he felt dizzy, all that space suddenly filled with things that had not been there a moment ago, things that were as insubstantial as thoughts. The hills slowly disappeared as the fall of snow grew thicker, everything hidden by flakes like small white feathers.

And something at last shifted in his mind, something to do with the way his view had become suddenly obscured. His mind explored the thought. What he could see clearly moments before had become veiled, limited, changed until they were no longer there at all. It was some kind of philosophical conceit that the hills and meadows therefore did not exist — the only reality being the fluttering whiteness that surrounded him.

He knew that that was not the truth, but the concept had nudged his mind. Was it that he shouldn't necessarily trust what he knew, or thought he knew — shouldn't trust what he saw?

His mind wandered to Dean Kingsley. He had never considered him a suspect and yet — suppose he had discovered what his nephew had been doing to Kevin Patterson? Had he killed Sebastian out of fear of scandal for the cathedral, and his own standing there?

Then Jessie's words about the passion that must be involved came back to him. Would that motive have provoked the sudden visceral reaction that Jessie suggested? The dean would have used a different means, something more studied, more planned. Simon saw he was doing the same thing again, grasping after straws, snowflakes.

So what was it that had clicked in the back of his mind as something significant when he watched his view disappear into nothingness? What had he seen and not recognized that he had seen? And, as Jessie had asked, why had Anne Stillings had to be tied up, her mouth taped?

The realization came slowly: he had *believed* in the meaning of what he had seen. He knew now what it was he had not seen.

He knew the *how* and he could imagine the *why*. Despite Jessie's insistence on concentrating on motive, he could see it only after he had recognized the method. He could imagine the passion behind it all, the agonized fear that had meant Sebastian Kingsley's sudden death and Anne Stillings's more calculated one. 'How amazing,' a couple of people had said, how amazing that he had witnessed her murder. It was not amazing that *someone* had.

'Are you all right?' A young man was bending over him looking deeply concerned. He was shivering, a light coat thrown around his shoulders.

Simon came to, realizing that he must look quite mad sitting here covered in snow. He shook himself free of the accumulated snowflakes and stood up.

'I'm from the Mill Restaurant,' the young man said. 'We were looking out at the snow coming down and saw you here. Can we offer you a hot drink?'

They must have thought he was some poor vagrant, Simon realized.

'That's very kind of you, but I'll be on my way,' he said. 'I was a bit lost in thought.'

The troubled expression on the young man's face remained as Simon disappeared into the swirling snow.

31

Simon trudged back to headquarters, the snow settling heavily on roofs and walls, twigs and branches, his mind filled with the implications of what he had recognized and the difficulties there might be in finding proof. Snow melting on his hair, he found Longman, startled at his appearance, and asked him to go with him to the Cathedral Clinic.

Longman questioned him as they made the familiar journey on foot but fell silent as Simon continued deep in thought and seemed not to hear him. It was partly fear of being wrong again that kept Simon from enlightening his friend. But he was becoming more convinced of his interpretation of what had happened on the night Kingsley died and the night Anne Stillings had fallen to her death.

The tent had been removed along with the police barrier-tapes and the building was apparently totally deserted. Simon knocked at Jonathan Hadden's door. When there was no reply he retrieved the bunch of keys from his pocket and let themselves in.

He went immediately to the window area and examined the expensive music centre. When he opened the tape decks no tapes were in place so he began looking through the few on the shelf beside it. Most of the music was in CD form. Longman came over, offering help and asking what they were looking for but Simon shook his head and began playing each tape for a few moments and then replacing it.

'Try this one,' Longman said, handing Simon a tape with a blank cover.

Simon placed it in the machine.

'What the hell are you doing in my room?'

They turned around. Jonathan Hadden was standing in the doorway, looking more dismayed than angry. Simon pressed the *play* button.

The room was filled with a high pitched scream, followed by a heavy thud.

'You really should have destroyed that tape,' Simon said mildly.

'I know. I was just coming to do so.' Hadden sat down heavily in his desk chair and stared at them both. 'I didn't think that you'd guess. Then I thought I really should get rid of it.' He seemed dazed and unaware of what he was saying.

Simon realized they should caution him. He nodded to Longman to say the words, arresting Jonathan Hadden for the murders of Sebastian Kingsley and Anne Stillings. Meanwhile Simon requested a squad car to pick them up, and to get as close to the clinic as it could. The media hordes were still at the gates.

★ ★ ★

'Why?' Longman asked later in Simon's office while they waited for Hadden's solicitor to arrive. 'Why did he do it?'

'I don't know for sure why he killed Kingsley, but I have a pretty good idea,' Simon said, his feet resting on his desk. He had given a quick report to Detective Superintendent Munro and she had seemed pleased. She was happy enough with the evidence of the tape proving Hadden killed Anne Stillings but she had pointed out that they had yet to find proof of his murder of Kingsley.

'You'll understand the motive well enough, Geoff, after your recent experiences,' Simon said, sipping some coffee with the first real sense of ease he had felt in a while. 'I think Kingsley made some threat to Hadden over Hadden's son Marcus. We know he was not averse to using a little emotional blackmail when it came to getting his own way. He must

411

have known something about Hadden that he could use that would threaten his relationship with his son. We know Hadden's ex-wife was making things difficult for him, that she used any excuse to disrupt his access to the boy and that she was something of a bigot.' He stopped as an earlier thought developed.

'What?' Longman prompted.

'She was a bigot,' Simon repeated. 'We know she was uncomfortable with anyone who was different from herself. She didn't feel easy with Anil and she disliked Anne Stillings because she was a lesbian. How do you think she would have reacted if Kingsley had told her that her child's father was gay, too, perhaps in an active relationship with himself?'

'Is he?' Longman looked mystified. 'Did I miss something?'

'He's not in any heterosexual relationship. He made some vague claim to his ex-wife's having disrupted any relationship he had developed since their marriage ended, but we don't know of any, and he didn't actually mention a woman, did he? Both men knew each other at their public school and had been friends ever since. What if Kingsley wanted to revive some earlier sexual experiences with Hadden, and when Hadden refused he taunted him over his son and how his wife would react if she knew all about him? She would have put every difficulty in Hadden's way, wouldn't she.'

'The boy is the centre of Hadden's life,' Longman agreed sombrely. 'But this is speculation. We don't know that it's true.'

'But we do know that he's our murderer. We can only hope he'll explain his motives.'

'He's a clever devil,' Longman said. 'I could sympathize with his reaction in hitting out at Kingsley if he really was threatening his relationship with his son. But the way he killed Anne Stillings, that's something else. How did you work that out?'

'Sheer genius,' Simon grinned. He relented at Longman's pained expression. 'Actually, it was a surfeit of snow. It made me think about seeing and believing. And I was trying to think of who, out of all our suspects, was the one who cared really deeply about something, or someone. The others all had motives of one sort or another but, with the Pattersons out of the running, there was nobody, except one, who showed that they had really visceral feelings about anything. Frances was deeply upset about her mother, for sure, but a mind that can focus on the petty nuisances she created as the clinic gremlin isn't really likely to leap from that to violent murder.

'It made me think about Hadden and his

son, how obviously deeply he cared for him, how everyone remarked that the boy was the centre of his universe, or words to that effect. Talking to you about Noel and the children helped.'

Simon pulled his legs to the floor and leaned over the desk. 'When I thought of Hadden it connected to that vivid image of him at the window a moment after I heard Anne's scream, or what I thought was Anne's scream.'

'Because he recorded his own scream, didn't he.' Longman said eagerly, 'and the loud thump. And he played the tape at full blast just as you approached. But Anne was already dead — he had pushed her from that window a bit before.'

'Another thing that clicked with me was remembering how a few people had remarked on how amazing it was that I should have actually witnessed Anne's fall. It was amazing all right, because it didn't happen. If I'd thought on just how much of a coincidence it was I might have figured it all out sooner.

'Hadden had a clear view of the lane from his window, and of course from the meditation room. He would have pushed her out when the area was deserted, then gone back to his room to wait until somebody started walking along the lane. Then just as the person approaching was out of view behind that tree near the entrance to the lane, he pressed the button on the tape deck. The speaker was on the window sill, and when I saw him with the window open, his body hid the shape of the speaker as he removed it and took it inside the room. What looked like an alarmed reaction of pulling up the window to see what had happened was something else entirely.' Simon gave a disgusted laugh. 'I think even Hadden must have been amazed — and delighted — to find that his witness to his apparent innocence was none other than the investigating officer.'

'It was why Anne's mouth had to be taped, so that she couldn't scream when she *actually* fell,' Longman said.

'And why he tied her up — because he had to wait for a witness to her death. He was already standing over the body with his back to me as I arrived,' Simon said. 'He probably removed the ahesive tape then, the ties just before she fell.'

'How the hell did he make that recording? A scream like that would have wakened his neighbours.'

'I imagine he went to his isolated country cottage and had a chance to practise his high-pitched screams until he was satisfied.' Simon stood up. 'Let's go and ask him to

415

enlighten us a bit further.'

Hadden was seated beside his elegant young solicitor, looking, in his navy-blue overcoat, a little more worn than she did. Simon imagined that the light-coloured coat he had been seen wearing on the night of Kingsley's death had probably been destroyed along with any bloodstains. He was wearing the tie he had worn the day Simon had visited him as a client, the brightly patterned one he had proudly claimed his son had chosen for him. Like its owner it was beginning to look a little frayed at the edges.

Simon began the preliminaries with the tape and turned to Hadden.

'Mr Hadden, we have irrefutable evidence in the form of the tape you made that you murdered Anne Stillings, and we shall no doubt find more evidence of your guilt. We already have fibres from under her nails. I assume you are not denying her murder?'

The young solicitor nodded to Hadden.

'I admit that I killed her,' he said.

'Why did you kill her?'

'Because she murdered my friend Sebastian.' Simon caught a glint of triumph in Hadden's eyes.

It was entirely unexpected and a shock. For a moment Simon could think of nothing to say.

'Why didn't you report the fact to the police if that was the case?'

'Because the law as it stands would have given her too short a sentence and then let her out even before the time due.' Hadden looked levelly at Simon, as inscrutable as Anil Patel had ever seemed.

'How did you know that it was supposedly Anne Stillings who killed Sebastian Kingsley, Mr Hadden?' Longman asked.

'I saw her leaving the clinic just as I was approaching it that night. She knew I'd seen her. I went up to see if Sebastian was in his room and I found him dead. Anyway, she admitted it to me later.'

'Did she indeed? Tell us again, Mr Hadden, where exactly you were when you saw Anne leaving the building,' said Simon.

'I was actually in the lane, only a few yards away as she came out.' Hadden kept his eyes on Simon's face throughout, entirely focused, Simon thought, as if trying not to forget his lines.

'But you were seen at that time, Mr Hadden, quite clearly by a witness who is sure that there was no one else around at the time.'

'Perhaps they just didn't notice her,' Hadden replied, apparently untroubled.

'Did Mrs Stillings, when you spoke to her

about Kingsley's murder, tell you why she had done it?' asked Longman.

'She said he'd told her he was going to dismiss her from the clinic.' He gave a brief unpleasant smile. 'She seemed to think I would keep her on, after what she had done.'

'I don't believe any of this, Hadden,' Simon said, suddenly angry — angry that this man had not only murdered Anne Stillings but was trying to muddy her name at the same time. 'I think that *you* killed Sebastian Kingsley and that, on the contrary, it was Anne Stillings who was aware of the fact. And why should you go up to his room that night if you were there only to collect your wallet as you claimed?'

The smile on Hadden's face stiffened a little and he began to fiddle with his tie.

'I just thought I'd see if he was in. I thought she'd looked a bit shifty.'

'Mr Hadden,' Simon said, 'Would you take that off please?'

The other three looked at him mystified.

'Your tie, if you wouldn't mind,' Simon added.

Hadden looked to his solicitor but she raised her eyebrows and again nodded her agreement. He loosened it and handed it to Simon.

'I don't know what you want it for but be

careful with it because — '

'I know,' Simon said, 'your son gave it to you, didn't he?' He spoke a few words of explanation to the tape recorder and switched it off. Longman followed him from the room.

'What was that all about?' he asked, staring at the article in Simon's hand.

'I keep forgetting,' Simon said. 'It's as if it all happened in a different age. Hadden was wearing this tie the day I went to him for treatment for my back.'

'So?'

'It was the same day,' Simon said. 'It was the same day that Kingsley was killed, except it all seems to have taken place ages apart. Hadden stated that he had gone straight from work to see his son. So he would still have been wearing this tie when he killed Kingsley.'

'So it'll have Kingsley's bloodstains on it,' Longman agreed. 'What about the coat he was wearing?'

'We'll look for it but he probably got rid of it. He wouldn't have worn it into the take-away for sure. It would have had a fair bit of blood on it. But he'd avoid destroying this tie, it was too precious an association and he'd hate to disappoint his son if the boy asked where it was.'

419

Longman peered at the article in Simon's hand.

'He'll have washed it, of course, and with that pattern on it nobody would notice any stains that were left.'

'Forensics will find them,' Simon said. He called to a uniformed sergeant and instructed him to bag the item and get it sent over immediately.

Hadden and his solicitor were speaking quietly to each other when Simon and Longman went back into the interview room.

Simon switched on the tape again.

'Where's my tie?' Hadden asked, his face set.

'It's gone for forensic examination, Mr Hadden, and I'm sure you understand the implications of that,' Simon replied.

Hadden shrugged. 'If you mean you expect to find evidence of blood on it then that doesn't prove anything. I told you I found Sebastian's body and naturally I leaned over him to check if he was really dead.'

'Since you were the one who killed him you're more aware than I am that there is a great difference between a smear and splashes of blood. The forensic team is very good at distinguishing the different blood patterns that come from a lethal blow.'

'Even after I washed the *smear* away?'

Hadden looked less confident despite his words.

'Yes,' Simon said. 'The initial staining is what is retained. They have some amazing technology these days.'

Hadden shrugged again and was silent.

Simon leaned towards him.

'I want you to listen very carefully to what I have to say, Mr Hadden, while I explain a few things. Whatever you may be thinking, no jury, or judge, is going to condone in any way the manner of your murder of Anne Stillings, whatever you claim to be your motive. You will rightly serve a long jail sentence. But your motive for killing Sebastian Kingsley was different, wasn't it.'

There was a mere flicker of an eyelid from Hadden.

'He threatened you, didn't he?' Simon continued. 'He threatened your relationship with your son. What did he say? Did he blackmail you in some way? We know he wasn't averse to a little blackmail to get his way. Did he threaten to tell your ex-wife that you were gay?'

'I'm not gay!' Hadden burst out.

'That's what he threatened though, wasn't it. And you knew how your former wife would react to that because she is not the most politically correct of women, is she. She would have refused you access to your son, accused you of being a corrupting influence. We all know that the courts would support you, but it doesn't work much in practice does it? And you would lose the person you love most in your life. Possibly the *only* person you really deeply love.

'So you were goaded by Kingsley beyond a point that you could tolerate and you lashed out in a fury and you killed him. Now a jury would understand that. They would understand that a man can be pushed beyond what he can take when someone precious to him is threatened. Did he make suggestions about Marcus as well?'

Hadden flashed a look of bitter anger at Simon, his face sallow under the strip-lighting, white about the lips. Simon sat back.

'So it was only because of that that you had to kill Anne, wasn't it. Because she became a threat too when she knew what you had done. But all the time all you were doing was trying to protect the most important relationship in your life. Now a jury would understand that better than the idea that you killed her because she had killed your so-called friend.'

There was silence for a full minute before Hadden began to speak, his voice hoarse. The young woman solicitor put a hand on his arm and spoke quietly to him but he ignored her.

'You are not all-knowing, Chief Inspector,' he said. 'But you're almost there.' He put his head in his hands, as if his pretence at control were all too much of an effort. He said nothing for a few moments, then he cleared his throat and looked up at Simon, his eyes wet.

'I'll tell you. I'll tell you how it really happened. I did go back to the clinic that night for my wallet and Sebastian saw me. He asked me to have a word with him so I went up. He . . . ' Hadden hesitated, 'he wanted me to . . . ' Hadden seemed unable to complete the sentence.

'Resume your sexual relationship with him?' Simon suggested.

Haddens lips turned down at the corners.

'It wasn't quite like that. We were schoolboys together. We did have that kind of relationship, and for a while afterwards. But I wanted a straight life. I wanted a family. So I tried to put it all behind me, and I did. But lately Sebastian had started referring a lot to our past and showing interest in me again, in that way. So when he said what he did that night and I said plainly that it wasn't on, he started jeering at me, saying that I was just hiding in the closet. Then he threatened me, as you said.'

For a few moments Hadden sat and twisted his hands, his mouth working. 'I just couldn't bear to lose Marcus,' he suddenly burst out. 'Jean would have made it impossible for me. It's been hard enough already, but I couldn't bear it if . . . ' He started sobbing, his face in his hands.

Had the killing stopped with Sebastian Kingsley, Simon thought, it would be difficult not to sympathize entirely with Hadden. As it was, the fact and manner of Anne's death had revealed something darker in the soul of this man.

After a few minutes of Hadden's stifled crying he calmed down and Simon resumed questioning him.

Kingsley had indeed said he would inform Jean Hadden about her husband's past and even tell her that their homosexual relationship was still going on, unless Hadden agreed to what he wanted. Then he had made suggestive comments about Hadden's son Marcus and what a pretty young boy he was becoming. It was that that finally broke Hadden and made him lash out with such a deadly effect.

They all sat back at that point and there was silence for a while.

'So why did you kill Anne Stillings? Did she speak to you about Kingsley's death? Did she blackmail you too?' Longman asked Hadden.

'I killed Anne,' Hadden said. 'The least I can do is tell the truth about her now. She didn't say anything to me about it. But I saw her from Sebastian's window, leaving the clinic. I thought I'd heard the front door so I looked out. Next day she kept watching me in an odd way so I guessed she must have known what had happened. I didn't know what to do. I wasn't sure she'd feel able to keep quiet about it, so I spoke to her. She had heard us but she assured me that she'd say nothing, especially when I explained why I had hit out at Sebastian.'

He chewed his lip for a moment, a nerve in his cheek jumping. 'I couldn't risk her changing her mind. So I waited for an opportunity when we were both alone together in the clinic and I got her up to the meditation room by saying I'd put something there that she'd like, as a thank you present. Poor Anne,' he said. 'She was so trusting.'

Poor Anne indeed, Simon thought. She had been entirely innocent in it all, apart from being possessed of a dangerous naïvety and a far too understanding heart.

He brought the interview to a close at that point. Tomorrow they could get Hadden's full statement completed. The man looked completely exhausted, and Simon was not feeling too different himself.

Outside the room, Longman said: 'When you think about it, all these horrors stem from the kind of woman Jean Hadden is. If she weren't such a narrow, prejudiced individual Hadden could have laughed in Kingsley's face and nobody would have died.'

'It's a salutary thought,' Simon agreed, 'that our seemingly little sins can lead to such horrific consequences. The character of everyone involved played a part. Hadden's lack of awareness led him to marry such an unsuitable and incompatible woman in the first place. Kingsley's ruthlessness was the main influence in everything that followed. If Hadden hadn't killed him, Jock Patterson might have. Even with Anne, it seems that her too understanding heart and her lack of wisdom had a part to play in her demise.'

They went back to the incident room, deserted since the team had all by now been informed that the case was being wound up. Simon went over to one of the white boards and wrote the announcement that Hadden had confessed to both murders and added thanks to the team for all their hard work.

Longman was by the window.

'The snow's stopped,' he said. 'It's not very thick on the ground and the roads are clear.

You should get back to Oxton all right tonight.'

Simon joined him and looked out at the seasonal scene, the snow sparkling under the lights. It was only three days to Christmas and his thoughts were with Marcus Hadden.

'It's going to come down again soon though, quite heavily,' Longman added. 'I heard the weather forecast. You'd better make sure you don't get snowed in.'

'Or, alternatively . . . ' Simon said, a smile on his face. It looked as if the seasonal visiting question might be resolved and that it was going to be an enjoyable Christmas after all.

We do hope that you have enjoyed reading this large print book.

Did you know that all of our titles are available for purchase?

We publish a wide range of high quality large print books including:
Romances, Mysteries, Classics
General Fiction
Non Fiction and Westerns

Special interest titles available in large print are:
The Little Oxford Dictionary
Music Book
Song Book
Hymn Book
Service Book

Also available from us courtesy of Oxford University Press:
Young Readers' Dictionary
(large print edition)
Young Readers' Thesaurus
(large print edition)

For further information or a free brochure, please contact us at:
Ulverscroft Large Print Books Ltd.,
The Green, Bradgate Road, Anstey,
Leicester, LE7 7FU, England.
Tel: (00 44) 0116 236 4325
Fax: (00 44) 0116 234 0205

THE SAME CORRUPTION THERE

Joanna Trevor

Emily Sanderson, a student at the University of Westwich, is young and beautiful, with everything to live for. But at the beginning of her second term she disappears from her bedsit, bloodstains showing signs that she had put up a struggle. All of DCI Chris Simon's sympathies go out to Emily's distressed sister Charlotte, especially when she tells him that Emily is her last remaining relative. During Simon's investigation, it emerges that Emily was not quite the innocent that Charlotte has painted her. There was more than one man in her life — and more than one person who might have wanted her dead . . .

A GATHERING OF DUST

Joanna Trevor

When pensioner George Probert is robbed and beaten to death, Detective Chief Inspector Christopher Simon discovers that none of Probert's neighbours have a good word to say about him. 'Bad-tempered'; 'wicked'; even 'child-molester' is how the dead man was seen by the world — but what did he do finally to push someone's patience too far? Simon has to use all his ingenuity and intuition — combined with his girlfriend Jessie's specialist insights — to uncover the unpalatable and shocking truth.

WILL YOU STILL LOVE ME TOMORROW?

Ed Gorman

It is 21 September, 1959. The world's number-one Communist, Nikita Krushchev, has landed in Iowa during the height of the McCarthy era and in Black River Falls someone has resorted to painting the town murderously red. A high-profile writer, with Communist sympathies and a very jealous wife, turns up dead at the office of private eye and lawyer Sam McCain. Everyone — including McCain's sometime boss — believes it was the victim's politics that got him killed. But McCain isn't convinced — especially when his two suspects also turn up dead within the next twenty-four hours . . .

THE EXECUTIONER'S MASK

Dick Cady

Police Officer John Griffo died a hero in the line of duty. On national television, the entire country watched lifetime criminal J. J. Jackson shoot him in cold blood. But, facing death by lethal injection in seven days' time, Jackson insists that murder was never his intention. Attorney Sonny Ritter is trying to get his life back on track when his brilliant law school classmate Kit Lake asks him to work on J. J. Jackson's final appeal. To turn down this gorgeous blonde proves impossible and together they quickly uncover the seedy underworld of a corrupt city. Racing against the executioner's clock, Kit and Sonny must reveal the truth if Jackson is to go on breathing.